UNBRIDLED

A NOVEL

UNBRIDLED

A NOVEL

by Jude Dibia

Also by Jude Dibia

Walking With Shadows

ISBN 978-1-77009-526-7

Cover design by banana republic
Set in Adobe Garamond Pro 10/12pt
Printed and bound by CTP Book Printers, Cape Town
Job No. 000618

See a complete list of Jacana titles at www.jacana.co.za

Acknowledgments

I will always remain grateful to God for giving me the gift. Also in the journey of writing this story there are many people who have in one way or another helped me. There are the women in my life—my mother, who is quite a good storyteller herself. I spent endless hours and years listening to her talk about what it means to be a woman. There is also my best friend, Oby O. A formidable woman; your constant encouragement kept me going. I also spent a lot of time with other women who were willing to share with me the way women react to issues, think and love. The lessons I learnt were invaluable. One woman in particular was of great help—I can only identify her here as TP. TP your constant advice and badgering, even when they seemed harsh, has kept this work as authentically as possible from a woman's point of view. Thank you very much.

I would also like to thank Nancy Stohlman.

And I cannot forget my first readers, Aniete Isong, Jimi, Fela, and Onyeka—thank you for the support and encouragement. Toni Kan, thank you also for being like a big brother.

I would also like to thank my brothers who have endured with me during my writing process—I know that I'm not the best company to have around when I'm writing and I'm grateful that you all put up with my constant mood swings, even those bordering on depression. What else can I say? I'm one of those writers who become their characters throughout the duration of their writing.

Lastly, I would like to thank all my readers especially those who bought my first book and this one as well. It is because of you that I write.

Jude Dibia, Lagos, 2007.

For love... has two faces; one white, the other black; two bodies; one smooth, the other hairy. It has two hands, two feet, two tails, two, indeed, of every member and each one is the exact opposite of the other. Yet, so strictly are they joined together

Virginia Woolf

Prologue

I have finally found my voice!

I came to this sudden realization as I watched the lush, snow-coated countryside pass by as the train made its way from Leicester to King's Cross, St. Pancras Station. Past Bedford, past Flitwick, Harlington, Leagrave, Luton and Nottingham.

I recited these places in my head as the train sped past each town.

"Who would have thought...?" I said out loud before I realized I had spoken the words rather than thought them. I knew this because the people seated around me swivelled to stare at me. I stared back at no one in particular. I smiled. I turned away to look outside.

My voice had been loud and clear, which hardly surprised me, and was very much alive within me. Though I was elated, I was still very much quiet. Thoughtful and a tad bit afraid. I was afraid of all the anger and hurt that had been buried deep within me for all these years. Afraid of what damage this new-found voice of mine could cause.

"I didn't want her in my house." A female voice in front of me whispered unsuccessfully to what I imagined was the person next to it. "Oh no, but my husband wouldn't listen to me. He never listens, Marjorie... he is the reason she is with us, love."

"Are you sure she stole it?" Marjorie's voice attempted

its own unsuccessful whisper.

"Who else would…?" The voice trailed off, drowned by the noise from the railings outside but awakening in me a new sensation. An old memory.

I could hear voices again, not from the strangers seated in front of me but the voices of suppressed memories and one of the haunting voices in my head was that of Aunt Rosa. She was married to my father's brother and I had lived with them for a couple of years while growing up. Aunt Rosa used to say to me—"Your eyes are too big… always wanting what you can't have." She also used to say—"You ungrateful child, if only Kachi had listened to me before taking you in!" Kachi was my uncle, my father's younger brother who lived in the big city of Lagos. He used to call me "Ngo 'm." That abbreviation of my name still causes me untold horrors.

I stared at the elderly white man beside me. He looked sixty or maybe even seventy and there was a determined look about him. Sitting beside me wasn't a deliberate choice. He had stretched his neck to see if there was an empty seat in the coach, preferably one with a white person sitting next to it, before occupying the one beside me. But it was a Sunday and the 17:09p.m. train from Leicester to London King's Cross was always filled up by this time. He had no choice but to sit beside me. He had smiled and mumbled something polite. I ignored him.

I looked away and marvelled instead at the scenery outside my window. It was grey outside as it had been raining off and on all day and an unexpected sleet now covered the land with its harsh cold whiteness. I was drawn to the reflection of the man beside me on the glass because of the austere whiteness of his skin, almost matching the whiteness outside. He must be miserable, I thought. In spite of being layered in a wool sweater, a coat and a thick scarf round his neck, nothing could have hidden his paleness, the same sickly paleness that made him think he was superior. I noticed how he made sure he sat as far to the edge of his seat as possible, arranging his coat in a way that ensured no portion of it folded over to my side of the seat. It felt like a solid wall existed between us.

As the train made its way from one countryside to the other, the lush fold of farmland with its sprinkling of animals and vast fields fled past my eyes as if in a race for their lives. It felt soothing, this emptiness before me even though there were so many voices in my head. I was suddenly remembering many things from the past, things I had long buried within me and hoped desperately never to excavate. I knew the voice within me must speak soon—I could feel the thunder stirring.

For a moment I was roused from my thoughts. The conductor was asking for our tickets. I brought mine out from my pocket and showed it to him. The old man was fumbling in his wallet and then handed over a wad of tickets to the train manager. As it happened, his ticket was not meant for this train but for a later one and then a rather noisy argument ensued between the old man and the train official. I took some kind of pleasure watching the old man's discomfort especially as I believed he looked down on my kind. But he was the least of my problems. I had been in England long enough not to allow him to bother me.

I came to England in January of 1997. It has been four years now. It was the first and only time I had left the shores of Nigeria and I remember how excited I had been. Excited is not quite the right word, though more like—I felt triumphant, like I had accomplished something huge. Things had happened to me when I was young, some very terrible things and then I wanted something else for myself. I wanted to write my own history and not live out the history already drafted for me. So I left. I met a man and I left. I left the rot of my past behind and I was finally moving on to better things. I was so naïve. I had been so desperate for a new life and a new identity that I was ready to believe anything and anyone. Who could blame me? Life had dealt me a bad hand!

It was deathly cold this spring evening in April. The sleet from the night before had seen to this. It seemed winter was holding on desperately, refusing to let go and give way for its sibling, spring, the gateway to summer. I smiled at this thought as I realized also that no one tells you how cold it is in a foreign land. No one tells you to buy gloves and head warmers. No one tells you that you are all on your own when you leave your country and head for another man's land with your foolish dreams and hopeless hope. No one tells you to stop hoping and stop dreaming. Soon enough you find out by yourself.

"... the next stop is King's Cross, St. Pancras..." The loud speaker in the train boomed.

I picked up my duffle bag and looked at my remaining luggage in the luggage compartment. I had one more train to catch. When I got to King's Cross, I would take the Piccadilly line to London Heathrow Airport and soon I would be on my way back home. Back to Nigeria.

A certain thrill ran over me as I thought about home. I was excited and yet nervous. There were so many things I had left behind. So many lies told, so many lives destroyed. All those long years had brought me to this moment and I had to now return... knowing what I knew and knowing that my return would cause further havoc.

The train finally stopped. I got up and, after waiting for the old man to remove himself, went straight for my two suitcases. They were the same ones I brought with me four years before, two matching red Samsonite suitcases. They had been expensive then.

"Excuse me." A tall lanky man in a drab suit said as he pushed ahead of me. He had curly red hair, green eyes and very red lips. He looked like James' doppelganger. Only he was older. He was much older but they could have passed for brothers.

I found myself momentarily frozen as cold fear formed goose bumps across my arms and the back of my neck. *JAMES*, my head kept screaming. James, James, James. He had finally found me. He had come to take me back. His green eyes bore into me like red hot coal and suddenly his face transformed—James' eyes were not as far apart as the ones that stared at me, his nose was not so straight and dignified either and James' jaw line was not as square.

"I need to get off." This stranger said to me in an unfamiliar voice and I moved aside for him. He was not my James.

James was my husband. My British husband who made me a British citizen. The first time we met was when I stepped off the plane from Nigeria and he was at the airport waiting for me.

In life, we come to realize sooner or later how wrong we are about the people we think we know intimately... like the strong reliable father we discover isn't that strong or reliable at all, or like the best friend or favourite cousin to whom we divulge all our secrets only to find that they are the ones who would take pleasure in selling us out. But the most shocking revelation in our lives is discovering that we are also not who we believe we are. It is the worst deception. Far worse than dealing with the half-truths about other people we think we know.

I was lucky; the train from King's Cross to Heathrow Airport was right on schedule. I weaved my way through the traffic of people networking from one station to the other or rushing up to meet up with their train. It was as if the train had been waiting for me because the moment I stepped in with my luggage the doors slid shut behind me.

I was going home. Going back to Nigeria. I could almost feel the streets, hear the people and languages, smell the curries and spices in the open markets and experience that deep sense of community that is lacking in England. When I got back to my old neighbourhood even the little rascal by the street corner would know that a *been-to* had arrived from overseas and would ask: "Wetin you bring come for boys?" Yes, I would be returning to the place where my life began and I would have a chance to finally speak out.

Heathrow Terminal 3. I was back here again after all those years and suddenly all I could think about was James.

1

James
January 1997

"Erika?"

He looked so different from his pictures. He was much taller and more handsome than I thought. And if he hadn't called me by my name, I would never have known it was him. Erika was the name we both agreed on over the Internet before I applied for my international passport. He could not pronounce my birth name "Ngozi" and no matter how much I coached him when he called, there was no way his Caucasian tongue could roll out the name correctly. Erika was a beautiful name and it sounded like Africa. I always wanted to be known as something else other than Ngozi.

"James?" I said slowly, hoping he was indeed the one.

"Yes it's me." He said and he hugged me.

He was a tall man and I could feel my bones crush against his frame. I smelt him for the first time and wondered if the tobacco smell on him was any indication of what kind of person he was. I looked up into his green eyes when he stepped back and smiled.

"Is that all you have?" He asked pointing at my two red suitcases. I nodded. "Okay then, let's get you out of here."

He grabbed my luggage like a gentleman and I followed him through the sea of people who were reunited with loved ones. Black, Indian and white strangers leered, trying to lure you to take a ride with them for a cheaper fare than the registered black taxis. I saw strange policemen with shiny helmets, bullet-proof vests and dangerous-looking weapons. Then there were the moneychangers, telephone booths, shops and neon lights giving the lounge a surreal quality. I tried to take in everything as I hurried after him. There were just so many people of different colours and languages and they all seemed to be in a hurry. I wanted to stop for a moment to look but James was already far ahead of me. I saw him stop briefly and look back at me.

"Hurry up, love." He called out to me. "This is rush hour."

And so I hurried up to him and followed him to the Underground. He asked me if I had any money on me and I told him I did. I had £500. He took £50 from me and paid for our tickets. I watched him pocket the change, but I was so wrapped up in my surroundings and the experience that I didn't mind. I was subconsciously comparing and contrasting in my mind the difference between Nigeria and this new land, England. I had expected much more based on the stories and the perception I had from watching movies, reading books and magazines and also from the stories carried over by the more privileged girls I had known.

I remembered Tiffany Okoro who lived across the street from me when I was in my teens. She always spent the summer holidays in London. She had pictures of herself at Trafalgar Square, in front of shops in Oxford Street and sometimes in front of impressive monumental statues. It was all so beautiful in the pictures. Arriving here I had almost expected to see roads paved with silver if not gold trimmings, people dressed like the fashion models in the imported magazines at Princess's beauty shop back home; happy smiling faces all around me and of course money strewn everywhere, begging you to please pick it up and stuff it in your jackets.

But so far, I was cold. I was wearing a thin, woollen sweater over a peach-coloured cotton blouse. I had no idea! In Nigeria, cold and frosty would translate to the dry harmattan of the Jos Plateau and in the harmattan we wore woollen sweaters in the morning and took them off in the scorching hot afternoon when the sun dominated the day. So I had my woollen sweater and thankfully a scarf, which I had bought off a street urchin while I sat in a commercial bus during one of Lagos' legendary traffic standstills. I secured the scarf round my neck and followed James as he led me to the waiting train. Piccadilly line.

The train was full. There was no more room and already quite a number of commuters were standing and holding on to an overhead rail support. James pushed his way in and I followed him. A vivid image of a Lagos *molué* bus flashed through my mind—33 sitting, 50 standing—and I felt no safer in this contraption.

"Are you alright?" James asked, smiling into my face.

"Yes." I lied. What else could I say? I smiled back at him and tried to ignore the many pimples that riddled his face. He told me he was twenty-eight in the course of our electronic exchanges. He looked twenty-two or maybe younger. I told him I was eighteen. I was much older. The lies we tell ourselves when we desperately want to believe in something else. I was used to those lies. My life was built on that very foundation.

"Your skin is so beautiful." He whispered into my ears. "I really could not imagine it even with all our emails and chats and pictures we exchanged."

"Really?" I said uncomfortably. He was pressed against me with his free hand squeezing my buttocks and I was sure more than one passenger observed us. I was not used to this kind of public display and I wasn't okay with it. Regardless of how many times we had spoken to each other or emailed each other, he was essentially still a stranger to me. His hand was squeezing my buttocks and I wanted to push him away.

I was right—people were watching us, particularly an elderly black woman who stood on the other side of the carriage. Her eyes had locked with mine. They were sad eyes. African eyes. Eyes that must have witnessed many things. For a moment, I thought I saw her shake her head at me. When I looked again to confirm, she was watching the door as the train approached a stop.

"I'm so excited that you are finally here." James was saying. "I can almost not believe it."

"Me too." I said, trying hard to be excited. I was suddenly so afraid. I didn't know what had happened to the thrill I felt when I left Nigeria. At that moment I wanted to be back home.

"We have so much to talk about." James said.

I smiled without saying anything. If I had answered him, that would have encouraged him to keep talking. I buried my head in his chest with a show of feigned tiredness and he held me closer.

We changed trains once or twice, I can't really remember. But I remember the icy cold wind that hit me when we left the train station and took a double-decker bus heading for Camberwell. Those buses are the true icons of England that many Africans have imprinted in their subconscious. All the pictures I had seen of England had the double-decker buses in the background along with pictures taken beside the wax images of Madame Tussaud's. That was the London we all knew. And for some weird reason, this was motivation enough for many to want to come to London.

I was thrilled to board the bus. James took more money from me to pay for the ride, but I didn't mind, I was taking a ride in the white man's *molué*. What else could be more exhilarating than this? I almost forgot about how cold I was.

"We are almost there now." James said.

We got off at the next stop. We crossed the road, passed a BT telephone booth that had posters of naked women with phone numbers on their naked chests, passed a narrow alley and a barricaded playground and then we arrived at a block of flats.

Belham Close.

"That's us, love." James announced grandly, pointing to a window on the third floor of yet another brick building.

I quickly noticed the Indian-owned convenience store and the meat shop on the ground floor. Further down was a stationery store that doubled as a post office and another shop. I took all this in within seconds, but the thing that stood out most was the white man with filthy long dreadlocks who sat by the entrance of the building. His hair was a mix of dark brown and blonde highlights. He had a rainbow- coloured scarf wrapped round his neck and was hugging a torn and tattered black overcoat that was missing a number of buttons. The navy green khaki trousers he wore were soiled in various places and his torn boots exposed one of his big fat toes. Beside him on the wet floor was a bottle wrapped in a brown bag and several discarded cigarette stubs as well as an old but well-preserved guitar.

As I waited nervously for James to open the door with his pass, I felt a hand tug at my dress. I looked down in shock and saw the piercing blue eyes of this white Rastafarian smile up at me and at the same time noticed the hand that grabbed my dress. His fingernails were black and they shot out from a black woollen glove with the finger area cut off deliberately I imagined. I whimpered audibly.

"Spare us some change, luv!" This rancid man said to me.

I looked up at James and before I could say or do anything, he had pulled me aside and was kicking the man squarely on the face, shoulder and anywhere he could get his foot to connect with.

"Stop hitting me, man." The stranger cried. "Why you hitting an old man like me?"

"I've told you to stay away from here!" James screamed. "How dare you touch my woman? What the hell's wrong with you?"

"Okay, man! Stop kicking me. I'm sorry okay!" He cried through his bloodied lips.

When James finally stopped, he spat on the destitute man and turned round to look at me. He smiled and suddenly his demeanour transformed back to the calm man who met me at the airport. At that point, I wasn't sure whom I was terrified of the more.

"Are you okay?" He asked. "Are you alright?"

I simply nodded and the smile widened across his whole face. I felt a cold fear then. There was something in his smile that unnerved me—the upward tilt of his lips, the brilliance of his emerald eyes and the knowledge I now had that a wicked violence hid beneath it all.

He finally got the door open and we shuffled into a passageway with a flight of stairs that led up to the flats. It was a dirty hallway with graffiti-covered walls and underneath the stairs there were signs of a fire that had been put out before any real damage could occur. It smelt badly and there was also discarded garbage on the floor, crumpled wrappers of chocolate, chips, sweets and nylon bags.

We climbed up the stairs and encountered some children playing outside their flats. Most of these kids were either black or of mixed parentage. I heard loud music blaring out of some flats and smelt the acrid whiff of marijuana. Ours was the fourth flat. I could see into the kitchen of my neighbour's flat and I noticed a rather big woman staring at us as we passed by. She looked like an African woman from the typical African print dress she wore and the headgear that was wrapped round her head. She followed us with her eyes as if looking for the next story to gossip with her market-time cronies. This time it would be of the black woman with the ginger-headed *oyinbo*. I thought I had finally left Nigeria, but it seemed Africa was waiting for me right on my doorstep in Belham Close, Camberwell.

✳

James and I met five years earlier. It was the eve of my twenty-first birthday and I had just left work. I was a helper in a beauty shop, earning a moderate-enough salary that allowed me to barely survive a full month even though I shared an apartment with two other single ladies, Princess and Uloma, in Herbert Macaulay Street, Lagos. It was Princess who had saved me a year earlier and allowed me to stay with both of them and offered me work in her beauty saloon.

That night I found myself in a cybercafé after work. I had joined an Internet dating site a week before and up till that point I had had no hits on my profile. It all changed that night. As soon as I logged on with my cyber name *AfricanWomanSearching*, I noticed I had several messages from someone named *Ja_King*. The first message read:

Ja_King: *Hello lovely! Read your profile and loved it. I would love to get to know you better. I'm English and based in London. I have a thing for blacks.*

I flinched at this—I have a thing for blacks! It sounded quite derogatory. What 'thing' was he alluding to? The more I thought about this the more irritated I became. I did not respond to this message. I was not certain yet, about him.

Then the second message:

Ja_King: *Hi! No word from you yet. I want you to be sure about me. I'm looking to meet someone from Africa and marry this person. I think it may be you. I am 27 years, soon to be 28, originally from Durham, where my family owns a leather-processing factory. I'm comfortable as they come and looking to settle down with an African queen.*

I liked that bit, 'African queen'. There was a regal quality to it.

In the other two messages, he told me his real names —James Alfred King—and attached a couple of pictures of himself. I found myself smiling as I read through all the messages and I immediately saw all kinds of possibilities: marriage and life abroad. I would be able to walk away from the past, a past that still haunted me even after all those years I had stayed relatively safe with Princess and Uloma, and into a brand new one. How could I forget all those girls who had made it out of the country to places like Italy and the United States and returned with their white husbands? Here was an opportunity to finally discard that family name I was born with.

Without much ado, I replied to his messages. I told him my name was Ngozi Akachi, cut my age by three years and told him I was eighteen and was a Nigerian. I finished off by saying I, too, was searching for my king to whisk me away. As I pushed the 'send' button, I felt a wave wash over me. I was excited but at the same time apprehensive. I didn't know what to expect and didn't know what next to do.

I checked my email for any other messages and promptly deleted all messages from my brother. I was disgusted by the bad use of English and his bad spelling. But worse still was his continual begging for money or his trying to make me attend one of the hopeless family gatherings. I was having none of that. I left the cybercafé feeling quite light-headed. All I could think about was that there was a man in faraway England who was interested in me. If I was lucky, I could be with him and my life would be different.

The next night I rushed to the cybercafé again after work. As expected, James' message was waiting. He was happy I had contacted him. He had been worried that I was not interested in him. He wanted to know more about me, even though he said he could not pronounce my name—I smiled when I read that part. He wanted me to come up with an alternative name we both would be happy with. Finally he asked if I ever had been to England.

I was very happy at that moment. I replied to his message instantly, telling him all he wanted to hear. No, I hadn't been to England yet. I had a couple of names I would love to be known by like Anne, Erika, Caroline or Jasmine.

In his next reply, he stated he preferred to call me Erika

because it sounded so much like Africa. He wanted to hear my voice and see what I looked like. And it went on like this. I would rush to the cybercafé after I closed from the salon every evening and there would be a message from James waiting for me. One day he asked what perfume I wore or liked best. I replied that I hardly used perfume. Another day he wanted to know what I loved eating. I replied that I enjoyed the local delicacies best, especially mixed vegetable soup and *garri*. I was always so delighted to get his messages and it seems communicating with him was so easy and smooth. One Saturday afternoon we finally met online. It was a surprise for both of us and, for a while, communicating that day via messenger was very strained. Maybe it was the shock of finally meeting, knowing that we didn't have the luxury of crafting smart and funny responses and the thrill of waiting a day to read the other's reaction or equally smart response. It was certainly different from replying to awaiting messages. At a point we ran out of what to write to each other after exhausting the limited variations of 'It's so nice to finally meet you on-line' and 'How is London?', but then things changed when James began writing about his trauma as a child.

Ja_King: *Growing up was a bit traumatic for me. My parents were divorced when I was seven and after both remarried I felt so unloved by both. My best friend then was this kid from Ghana. I think his name was Kwami or Kwame. He taught me a lot of things then, especially how to fish. Then there were the dark days of my childhood... I hate to unload all this on you. Some terrible things happened to me when I was a kid. My father always thought that with his money all was okay...*

I could certainly relate to all he said. I had my bad memories of growing up. I had my dark days and hours but unlike him I had no Kwame to teach me how to fish nor did I have the comfort of knowing my parents had the financial wherewithal to take care of my needs. I had nothing. I could relate so well with pain.

Ja_King: What scares you the most?

AfricanWomanSearching: I don't know. I'm scared of many things.

Ja_King: Like what? Tell me...

AfricanWomanSearching: I am scared of going back to my family. I am scared of the dreams I have some nights. I am scared of wasps and bees... What about you? What are you scared of the most?

Ja_King: I am scared of being alone. Relationships have not worked for me in a long while. Why are you scared of your family?

AfricanWomanSearching: You won't understand. I left my family some years ago... I had to leave. Why do you think relationships are not working out for you?

Ja_King: I don't know. I've tried everything... being sensitive, caring and not too demanding. Women just don't get me.

AfricanWomanSearching: I think I get you.
Ja_King: I think you do too. So you live with two other ladies and not with your family...?

AfricanWomanSearching: Yes. One is called Princess and the other Uloma. We stay in this little flat. I'm sure your place is bigger. I hear things in London are bigger and better than in Nigeria is this true?

Ja_King: I don't know, I have never been to Africa or Nigeria. I live kind of well... it's very comfortable here.

AfricanWomanSearching: I can only imagine...

James' home in Belham Close was not what I expected.

I remembered all the glowing things he had previously told me about his background. At twenty-one he had claimed to have received a cheque of over £20,000 from his father as part of his trust fund. Where did all that money go? I expected to see a decent home with all the gadgets and finery. Instead a nauseous stench hit my nostrils as soon as I walked into his house. It was the stale smell of cigarette, hemp and human odour. I realized I was standing on something other than the floor and I realized my feet rested on a pile of unread mail.

James pulled me further in as he shut the door behind him. He dropped my luggage by the side of the stairs that led up to rooms and turned round to face me squarely. I tried saying something, but as my mouth opened to speak, he grabbed me and began kissing me. I was shocked. My eyes flew open and my mouth clamped shut, barring his tongue from gaining entrance. He didn't seem to mind or even notice. His tongue darted around my clenched teeth and slurped all over my mouth. My eyes were fixed to the huge pimple on his forehead. It looked like it was going to burst any minute from then and then squirt all over my face. I looked away and then I saw them. One stood at the top of the stairs peering down at us while the other stood at the end of the room in front of us, chewing on something. I screamed and pushed James away.

"Hey!" James said looking at me awkwardly. "What's the matter?"

Before I could say anything the man at the top of the stairs was jabbering in a voice I knew to be typically Nigerian.

"Man mi James," he was saying, "so she is finally here!"

He began descending the stairs in a deliberate manner. My eyes took in all of him. He was at least six feet tall and wearing a pair of loose fitting jeans that were held carelessly around his waist with a cloth belt. He was shirtless but had draped his torso with a blue and cream-patterned bed sheet, which he held in place with his scrawny black arms. As he got closer, I realized his hair was in dreadlocks.

"She's finally here, Providence." James said addressing this man.

"Yeh man." The other man who was at the end of the room said. He was now by our side. "She a real African beauty, this one."

He was light-skinned, almost as white as James. Back at home we called people like him half-caste. He had somehow got rid of what he was eating and was now sucking on a cigarette. He sounded Jamaican unlike the Nigerian-sounding one James called Providence.

"So what name we call your woman, James?" He asked, smiling at me.

James held me to himself in a proud fashion and I felt like a piece of property. There I was in this man's arm and everyone was talking around me as if I wasn't there. This hardly troubled me as much as the fact that these two men were in James' house at all. At no time had he mentioned either of them to me during our correspondences.

"This is Erika." James said, presenting me to his friends. "Erika, this is Thomas." He nodded towards the half-caste man.

"You Nigerian, nah?" Thomas asked.

I nodded.

"Wicked!" He exclaimed. "Jah man here, brother Providence comes from Nigeria too, nah!"

"Erika," Providence sampled the name like a bad taste in his mouth "wetin come be your proper naija name?" He was scratching his crotch as he spoke.

Even I didn't recognize the squeaky voice that said, "Ngozi."

"Okay," James said, "I'm taking Erika to my room and we need some privacy. Let's give her some room to rest and get to know me better."

I was glad when James led me up the stairs to his room, away from their stares and leering. As soon as I got into the tiny room, I felt my spirit drop. My room back in Herbert Macaulay was far bigger than this one. This room had just a tiny bed, one window with what later I was to learn was a heater, underneath the windowsill, a wooden wardrobe that had seen better days and a small armchair that served many purposes from what I could tell.

The moment he shut the door I said, "What is going on James?"

"What do you mean?" He asked.

"Who are these people?" I whispered. "I thought we would be alone!"

"You mean Thomas and Providence?" He asked as if he didn't know what I meant. "We share the apartment."

"Why?" I asked, still out of confusion.

"I need the extra money they pay for renting the rooms." James said. "There's nothing to worry your head about."

I wasn't satisfied with this answer. I sighed audibly as my eyes took in the details of the room. My heart was beating fast with fear and apprehension.

"Why are you living in this neighbourhood? I thought you had a trust fund?"

"Is that why you came, because of my trust fund?" He asked testily, his countenance changing again to that of the violent man that attacked the destitute downstairs. His face had suddenly gone red.

"No," I said carefully, "it's just that—"

"It's just that what?" He asked cutting me off.

"I don't feel safe here." I answered in a small voice and suddenly he burst into a loud scratchy laugh that seemed to resonate round the room.

"You don't feel safe!" He laughed. "This is Britain. I bet it is far safer here than wherever it is you came from, trust me."

No, I thought. I certainly do not trust you. How could I? He never once mentioned sharing his home with two other men or that one of them was Nigerian. I was suddenly feeling very unsure of my decision to have come all the way to England. I had left my job, sold all the little property I had managed to acquire and stuffed all that was left into two suitcases and flown to England, all for what? All for a faint hope that I was moving away from neighbourhoods with jobless youths smoking hemp, causing trouble at the slight drop of a hat, from nosy neighbours who make your business their business—and from my past. My family. My secrets. I felt I was right back to the same territory I ran away from. I wondered what Princess would say if she were here right now. She would have said in her soft but heavily accented voice; *"Don't wait for bad things to happen to you Ngozi, just walk away immediately you smell trouble—you hear me?"*

2

Saved
August 1992

It rained heavily that night.

I remember this because it seems to rain whenever something significant in my life is about to happen. I remember vividly the bright flashes of light that razored the dark skies accompanied by the loud threatening claps of thunder and rain that drenched my entire body down to my underwear, which clung to my skin.

Lagos becomes a different city when it rains. Everything looks distinct in a way that words alone can't easily convey. Busy streets once assaulted with an endless flow of people as different from one another as dogs are from cats, suddenly become deserted and almost silent. On those rainless days and nights, hard as you try, you cannot blind yourself to the conflicting fashion identity of the people as the local attire is mixed and matched with styles from America, Europe and even Asia on any given day. And so much colour, bright colours and the dreary greys and blacks worn by the corporate marionettes. Not so when it rains. Everything goes into hiding, especially when the rain comes at night.

I remember walking the empty streets of Lagos, my feet dragging me to the only place I knew to go: Madam Goodwill's pepper soup joint. It was a popular spot in those days frequented by all—the secondary school students who saved their allowance so they could afford to share a hot plate of Madam's spicy delicacy; the smartly dressed banker or corporate worker who found their way there after working hours to enjoy "happy hour", bus drivers and their conductors who wanted to knock back some bottles of cold beer and suck on the succulent chicken bone marrows, the usual over-made-up female street workers who were among the patrons of Madam Goodwill—everybody visited Madam Goodwill and it had nothing to do with class or social status.

My first encounter with Madam Goodwill was shortly after I arrived in Lagos three years earlier. Her local diner cum beer parlour was two streets away from my uncle's home and if one wanted to take the bus from Iwaya to the market or to Yaba, which was a big central point that had connecting buses to all other parts of Lagos, one would have to walk all the way to the front of Madam Goodwill's to catch a bus. Her shop was just opposite the bus stop and one could never miss it. Also, on some nights when the electricity had gone off, Aunt Rosa would instruct me to go buy some pepper soup for her from Madam Goodwill.

So, that cold raining night after my aunt kicked me out, the only place I could think of to go was to Madam Goodwill's. I was acutely aware that I was more or less a destitute but this didn't seem to faze me. Freedom once gained is so profound and so sweet that negative thoughts of the impending challenges ahead never seem to bother the beneficiary. So as I walked through the rain, I had no sense of foreboding but only a single focus sustaining me. I am free. I am free. I am free at last.

It was not until I was standing in front of the tin roof shack that I began to wonder what I would tell Madam Goodwill when she noticed me cower in some obscure corner of her shop like an intrusive rat hiding to nibble on leftovers. Madam Goodwill had made it known to all that she would not tolerate miscreants or non-paying customers hanging around her shop. She was an imposing woman with crude, mannish physical attributes. At first look one would believe she was a man in drag. She was big-boned and had well-developed and defined biceps. Her almost handsome face had bushy eyebrows as well as a moustache and on those days when she wore a low-neck blouse you could clearly see the tuft that sprouted from between her ample cleavage. If that alone didn't make you wonder, when she spoke she had a deep husky voice that seemed to be a hybrid between a squeaky female's voice and a male's baritone. There was certainly no disobeying Madam Goodwill. Men feared her wrath. Women were simply terrified of her. I had personally witnessed her beat up one of her male customers who failed to pay the correct amount for his meal and drinks. She had grabbed him by his scrawny neck and slapped him senseless after which she carried him and threw him out of her shop. She was a fear-inspiring woman, Madam Goodwill, but nonetheless everyone agreed that her pepper soup was the best this side of the equator. She was no troublemaker either. She was actually a decent woman who was fair to everyone and once you were on her good side, you enjoyed all the benefits of her warmth and charity. All her girls and the few boys who worked for her praised her to high heaven and were ready to fight anyone who as much as uttered an unflattering comment about her.

I wasn't ready to incur the wrath of Madam Goodwill, not at this point in my life. So I moved away from the entrance and hid myself at the corner of the shop, between the edge of the building and the overflowing waste bin. I had to crouch tightly by the edge so as to avoid the rainwater that flowed from the roof from landing on me. It was not a comfortable position to maintain especially as I had to periodically shoo away some rodents that were also seeking shelter. It was at that moment between enduring the cold breeze, dodging rainwater and fighting off street rats that the reality of my freedom sunk in. I was not sure anymore if I truly wanted it.

The bright lights from the headlamps of an approaching bus settled on me briefly before sweeping away. I heard the bus halt by the bus stop and the chattering voices of ladies filled the air. The rain had lessened to a light drizzle and I could make out the shape of two women underneath an umbrella, making their way towards Madam Goodwill's shop. I recognized them both. They were regulars and their air of sophistication always made me believe that they were women of the night—street workers. The dark one looked like the elder of the two; she was always dressed up nicely and wore quite a lot of make-up. Whenever she walked down the street, her large hips swaying, men always whistled after her and yelled lewd remarks. She never seemed to mind this discourtesy but always laughed it off and jiggled her hips even more as she walked away.

My eyes were fixed on the two pairs of legs as I tried to remain quiet and invincible. Just as they paused to open the door I felt wetness crawling down my upper lip and I snivelled. The legs stopped moving and I felt curious eyes on me, becoming suddenly aware of my presence.

"Princess," one of the ladies said in irritation, "A beg enter now so I fit enter or you wan make cold cash me here?"

"Enter if you wan enter." The one called Princess answered, which prompted the other young woman to sigh, push her aside and then jump into the shop.

I was staring at Princess as she stared at me. For a fleeting moment I felt something pass over her large brown eyes. I was not sure what it was but I felt a connection to her at that moment. It felt like we had known each other before, perhaps in another life.

"What are you doing here?" She asked in perfect English. There was an accent in her voice that made one know she came from the mid-west area of the country.

I wanted to speak, to respond to her, but all I could manage was to shiver and snivel again, like a child.

"Why are you in the cold?" She asked again. "Won't you go home?"

My eyes were drawn to her lips.

"You no fit talk?" She finally said.

"Nowhere to go." I mumbled.

"What?" She said moving closer to me. When she was close enough to me she bent down to be eye level with me. "I know you, don't I? I have seen you here before, haven't I?"

I nodded.

"What is your name?" She asked.

"Ngozi." I answered finding my voice.

"Yes," Princess said as if it was the most natural thing to say. "I've heard someone call you that name before. Ngozi, what are you doing in the rain?"

"I have nowhere to go." I answered.

"Why?"

"My aunt asked me to leave her house and never come back." I said.

"What did you do to her?"

"Nothing." I said. "She hates me."

"And what about your own family?"

I just shook my head vigorously at that moment. I didn't want to talk about my family. I didn't understand why this woman was interested in me. I wanted her to go away before she drew Madam Goodwill's attention to me. Instead she stretched out her right hand.

"Have you had something to eat?"

I shook my head and stared at her suspiciously. Why was she being so kind to me?

"Oya, come and let me buy you some hot pepper soup before you catch your death here." She said, pulling me up.

There was something authoritative yet sensitive about the way she dragged me into Madam Goodwill's shop. I followed her without putting up a struggle and felt somewhat safe with her next to me. As she led me to where her friend sat at the corner of the bar, I took a moment to study her closely for the first time. The rain had washed off some of her make-up and I quickly realized that she was much younger than I had earlier thought. Those days when I used to see her walking down the street all made up, I used to think she was in her late twenties or early thirties but now I realized that she was not that much older than I was. I was sixteen and looking at her now she could not be more than seven years older than I was. And her skin was quite dark. It was a beautiful hue that complemented her dark brown eyes. Her eyes spoke volumes. There was an intensity in them that caught you off guard and behind the long graceful lashes lurked the slightest hint of sadness or it might have been regret.

Her friend was already slurping on a huge bowl of soup by the time we got to her table. She gave me a rundown with her eyes before she looked at Princess.

"Who be this one you don bring come?" She asked creasing her eyebrows.

"This is Ngozi." Princess announced. "She is my new friend. And Ngozi, this one over here is Uloma."

"Good evening." I mumbled.

Uloma paid me no attention. She took a sip from her malt drink and motioned towards another steaming plate of soup on the table.

"I ordered a plate for you, Princess." She said in perfect English. I was amazed at her flawless accent. Judging by the way she spoke Pidgin English I would never have guessed that she could manage such an accent.

"Thank you." Princess said. "Ngozi, you can have it while I order another one."

She pushed the plate to me with a smile and stood up to order another from the counter. She spent a few minutes chatting with Madam Goodwill before she returned to the table with another tray of soup and some soft drinks.

There was no talking while we ate. The only sounds were the constant clanging of spoon hitting plate, of running noses snivelling and tongues slurping. The rain had started again. It beat on the tin roof, mixing with the noise of the purring generator, the television, and the other patrons in the shop. I was grateful for the noise; it allowed me to drink my soup without feeling I was being watched.

"Do you have somewhere to sleep?" Princess asked me after our plates were empty.

I shook my head. Suddenly I had to start thinking of the strange predicament I now found myself in. I noticed that Princess turned to Uloma and they began whispering in hushed tones. I couldn't make out what they were discussing but I knew it had to do with me.

"You know Aunty Goodwill will not let you loiter around her shop entrance." Princess said finally. "And it is dangerous for young ladies to walk around alone at night."

I nodded.

"I don't understand why her aunty will just throw her out of the house like that." Uloma added.

"You will stay with us tonight and we will discuss further tomorrow okay?" Princess insisted.

They must have seen the raw fear in my eyes.

"What is wrong?" Princess asked.

"I…" I stammered. "I am not a pros…prostitute."

I watched as they both looked at each other in shock and suddenly burst out in a wild laughter that drew the attention of almost everyone in the shop. I was embarrassed to say the least and didn't know whether to hide in shame.

"You think we are prostitutes!" Princess cried.

"I can't believe this!" Uloma laughed. "Why you go think that kind thing?"

Why shouldn't I? I thought. As far as I knew, they were single ladies in the city of Lagos. They went about dressed in skimpy clothes and wore a lot of make-up. Unlike the idea of decent girls that had been droned into me, they moved about in the evening on their own and seemed to mix in all sorts of company. What else was I supposed to think?

"My dear," Princess said after they had stopped laughing, "we are not prostitutes, okay?"

"But…"

"We are independent women." Princess said calmly. "I run a small beauty salon and Uloma works with me."

I had never felt so foolish!

I followed them home that night.

By the time we left Madam Goodwill's shop the rain had stopped falling but the streets were still deserted. We waited for a bus for a while before Uloma hailed a taxi.

"Na so we go take stand here till midnight." She sighed.

As the taxi stopped in front of us, she leaned into the passenger side window and said, "How much to Herbert Macaulay?"

"Hundred naira." I heard the taxi driver say without much hesitation.

"You be thief." Uloma cursed. "Na because I be woman or wetin?"

"Let's wait for another taxi." Princess said, tugging at Uloma's skirt.

"How much you wan pay?" The taxi driver asked shrewdly.

"Thirty naira." Uloma said.

"Haba, sister add something on top now." The driver said. "Make it fifty naira."

"Na thirty naira I get." Uloma insisted, already opening the door of the taxi.

"Oya, enter." The driver said resignedly.

Uloma got into the front of the car while both Princess and I entered the back. The back seat was torn and had foam sticking out from different holes. I was careful not to sit on one of the springs shooting out of the seat.

"Pius really annoyed me today." Uloma said from the front seat. "Seriously, Princess, I don tire for that man."

"Then leave him now and stop complaining." Princess sighed.

"If only it were that easy." Uloma said. "Every time I make up my mind to leave him, I realize I don't have the strength to."

"And he knows it." Princess added. "He knows you love him and that is why he keeps playing with your emotions."

"It's not like he is cheating on me-o!" She said, turning

round to look at Princess. "It's just this one that he is deeply involved in the labour union—he never has time for me anymore."

"The last time, his excuse was that his mother was very sick." Princess said. "Next month, what excuse will it be then?"

They both spoke as if I was not there or as if I had always been included in their private talks of men and relationship issues. I was very quiet, marvelling at how articulate they both sounded even when they occasionally swapped to Pidgin English.

"I love that man." Uloma said solemnly. "Even if he's as yellow as Ngozi here."

They were both now staring at me with renewed interest. I sank a little bit further into my seat and felt a faint prick in my back.

"So how old are you, Ngozi?" Uloma asked, addressing me directly for the first time that night.

"I'm sixteen." I said quietly.

"Are you sure you don't want us to take you to your home?" Uloma asked. She looked at me worriedly and placed a hand on my knee.

I shook my head.

"What about your parents?" Uloma asked. "Where are they?"

"In the village." I answered.

"What village" Princess asked.

"Ezi." I said. "Delta State."

"Why did your aunt throw you out?" Uloma asked. "Did you steal from her?"

I noticed her voice had become suspicious.

"No," I said, "I don't steal."

"What are you doing so far away from your parents?" Princess asked. "Why did you come to Lagos?"

"My father…" I started crying.

"It's okay." Princess said soothingly. "It's okay. You can stay with us…"

"For a while." Uloma added.

"In our home." Princess said.

Home was a small three-bedroom apartment in the heart of Herbert Macaulay Street. Princess stayed in the master bedroom, the one that had its own private toilet and bath. Uloma stayed in the room next to Princess and the third room had been converted into a storeroom.

There was an old 14-inch television in the living room and sparse furniture. The curtains were really dowdy-looking from what I could make out from the candlelight. There was a power outage as was common in Lagos especially when it rained.

That first night I slept on the couch in the living room, grateful that I had a roof over my head. It was a fitful sleep; I kept waking up at intervals wondering where I was. Morning came quickly and with it more questions from Princess and Uloma.

I told them I had finished secondary school but hadn't yet collected my certificate. Princess promised to help me get this from the West African Examination Council (WAEC). She knew someone who knew someone who worked with the WAEC. In the meantime, it was agreed that I would stay with them and learn a trade, help out in her salon.

These women surprised me. How often do you meet people who helped complete strangers? I eventually had to ask Princess why she was so kind to me. I followed her to the market that hot afternoon. She wanted to get some new curlers as well as hair products for her salon. She took me to a part of Yaba market I had never visited before. It was rowdy like any other part of the market but the difference was that every turn we took there were countless women seated who had one or two other women working on their hair. There were those who specialised in African plaits and weaves, working up what looked like skeletal castles on the heads of some of the women seated at their feet. In one alley, I was hit by the stench of the chemical relaxers being used on some women's hair by the hair dressers who favoured the more modern hairdos. The smell of the relaxers brought back an unpleasant memory, one that had to do with my hair and the first time it was relaxed.

"Everyone needs kindness in the beginning." Princess said in answer to my question. We had just left a shop where she had purchased a dozen packets of Jojo-Queen human hair. "When I saw you in the rain that night, you reminded me so vividly of me so many years ago."

"I did?"

"Before I settled in Lagos, I used to live in Benin with my mother." She began her story. "My father died when I was quite little and so I never knew him. We were seven children and I was the last child."

When Princess was seventeen, Ese, a cousin of hers, who was based in Italy, had come to Benin for a short visit.

"She was looking so beautiful when she breezed into our house that day wearing her expensive lace, gold chains and rings and the perfume that lingered in the air." Princess said.

I could see in her eyes and tell from her tone, as I followed her, that she was seeing Ese in her head and experiencing that moment once again.

"Customer!" A young man called out. He dashed out of his shop as Princess and I were walking past. "Customer, you no wan come my shop today? I don get that shampoo you ask for."

Princess stopped her story for a moment and smiled at the man.

"Julius," she beamed, "you no fit greet person before you begin harass me?"

"Sister Princess," he smiled, "good afternoon-o. Make you enter my shop now."

Princess looked at me and nodded towards his shop.

"Let's just see what he has for me today." She said.

I followed her inside the shop, filled with a subtle admiration of her command of English and how easy it was for her to juggle between that and the local Pidgin English. Both she and Uloma were good at this.

"Ehen," Princess said, sitting down on the couch in the shop and motioning for me to join her, "what was it we were talking about?"

"Your cousin, Ese, came to visit you in Benin." I said.

"Ah, yes," she said, "everyone was amazed by her transformation. Ese had been sponsored to Italy by a madam who wanted to help her family out of the poverty they were suffering. The madam had persuaded her family that there was plenty of work for young girls who were determined to work hard in Italy and that the rewards were well worth it. Then as if to press home her point, the Madam had offered Ese's father some money, which went a long way in helping them make up their minds."

For over a year no one heard anything from Ese, Princess went on to tell me once we had left Julius' shop and were heading back for her saloon. Soon her family began to worry, but all of a sudden, Ese appeared in Princess' living room with an offer to take Princess to Italy with her. Things were hard for Princess' family at the time and once her mother saw how rich Ese was looking, it seemed reasonable that Princess join her in Italy as well.

Princess had been extremely excited about the prospect of travelling abroad and earning huge sums of money so she could dress like Ese. The night before she left with Ese, her mother had made her promise that unlike Ese, she would remember her family back home and send them money once she was settled. Princess promised she would.

From Milan, Ese dropped Princess off in Turin under the care of another madam. As it turned out all the gold and finery that Ese wore in Benin were borrowed from this madam. Ese had no such money. To buy her freedom, she had to get another fresh girl for her madam. Princess was the price for her freedom.

When we got back to her salon that afternoon, Uloma was fixing a customer's hair while there were two other ladies having their nails done by the two shop assistants. I stored our purchase in the appropriate lockers and displayed the new hair pieces in the display shelves. As

I worked, I reflected deeply on all Princess had told me. I found it amazing that she had experienced travelling to Europe at an early age. I was curious to hear the other part of the story. I wanted to hear more about her experience in Italy. I wanted to know how she managed and what it was really like to be abroad, in a foreign country. I too had dreamt of leaving this country and making it to London where I believed my future was waiting.

"Are you daydreaming?"

I looked up and met Uloma's big eyes staring at me.

"You've been standing there for a full minute without moving." She said. "What are you thinking about?"

I smiled uncertainly. Since I moved in with Princess and Uloma, I still had a feeling that my presence was merely being tolerated by Uloma. She hardly spoke to me and her actions made me think that she was probably thinking her position as official best friend to Princess was being threatened. But I also noticed that any time I was overwhelmed with sadness, she was always very supportive. I was learning to like her and one of the ways I knew to win her trust was to be honest with her.

"I was thinking about what Princess told me this afternoon." I said.

"What did she tell you?" She asked. She dumped a handful of hair rollers into a plastic basin in the sink.

"She was telling me about how her cousin took her to Italy." I said.

"Oh God!" Uloma said, rolling her eyes. "What a dreadful story!"

"What happened to her?" Uloma asked.

I shook my head. Just then Princess walked into the backroom where we were. She looked at both of us with a questioning look in her eyes.

"So, what are you two doing here?" She asked. "We'll start locking up soon. I don't want us to be late today."

"We are not doing anything." Uloma said. "Ngozi wants to know what happened to you in Italy."

I watched Princess close her eyes and shudder slightly.

I was even more curious then.

"Why are you shaking?" Uloma sighed. "Aren't you the one who started telling her the story first? Now you must finish it, so she can know-o."

"My dear," Princess addressed me, "why do you want to know so much?"

"You told me when you saw me at the joint that I reminded you so much of you." I said.

"You did." She said. "I imagine I was hiding like you were when Catherine found me."

Nothing prepared Princess for the life she was suddenly and violently introduced into, Princess told me. Her first few days were the most harrowing; she was raped, beaten and made to partake in a fetish ritual where she, along with several other young ladies, took blood oaths not to ever betray their madam to the police or anyone else. After that the girls were handed over to pimps who fixed them up with clients and collected the money they made. They had to pay back the money that was used to bring them to Europe and all other expenses involved as well. Princess learnt that she had to make approximately $50,000 to pay off her debt to the madam!

Many nights she cried bitterly even when she had clients to service and after the clients complained about her unwillingness to perform certain sexual acts to her pimp, she would get a violent beating that left her bruised and swollen for days. Many of the girls tried consoling her, telling her that she was lucky to be just servicing clients, because the ugly girls who were brought over, and whom no one wanted sexually, always disappeared. Those girls ended up being organ donors. This had terrified Princess and so one night after she had been dropped off to meet a client, she simply made a detour and ran away. That particular arrangement had been different from all her other assignments and she feared she was being sold to a specialist because the complaints her pimp was getting about her seemed to have increased, regardless of how many times he tried to discipline her. She had even overheard the madam telling her pimp to do something productive with her because she wasn't really bringing in much money.

It was at this point in her story that she first said to me: "My dear, don't wait for bad things to happen to you, just walk away immediately you smell trouble—you hear me?"

Princess had roamed the streets of Turin for days without food, hiding from her pimp and dodging other black street workers who might recognize her and report her whereabouts to madam. It was on the third night a woman, Catherine Dubois, had found her crouching behind a waste bin, using the lid to protect herself from the rain. This woman brought her to her home, fed her and listened to her sad story. After a couple of days, Princess had allowed Catherine to take her to the police station, where she again narrated her story. Within a week the Nigerian Embassy had been contacted and arrangements were made for a one-way ticket from Milan to Lagos for Princess.

From Lagos, Princess was to make her way to Benin City, but she knew she wasn't going back there. At the airport in Malpensa, Catherine had squeezed some money into her palms and when Princess asked her why she was being so kind to her, she had simply answered, "Everyone needs kindness in the beginning!"

3

Naked

"What is the matter with you?"

I looked up at James, hoping he could see that I was not comfortable. He had two men in the house that lived with him and now I was here and I too would have to live with them. I was also worried that one of the men was Nigerian like I was. This seemed to bother me more than anything else.

"Why are you looking at me like that?" He asked.

"I would prefer it if you didn't have those men in the house." I said slowly.

"You would prefer!" He snarled. "You just got here and already you think it is your place to dictate to me what I should or should not do."

"It's just that you never told me about living with anyone." I said, a little afraid of the way he was reacting. His tone was frightening me. "And this house... this neighbourhood!"

"What is wrong with this house?" He asked. "What the hell is wrong with the neighbourhood?"

I looked around me in an attempt to avoid his eyes. It seemed everything was already going wrong. I was wondering what I should do, what would Princess have done? What would Uloma do?

"How can you criticize here when you are coming from that shit hole, Africa?" He spat. His face was squeezed up, eyebrows knotted and a thick vein protruded from the side of his neck.

Who was this man? My mind screamed. This was certainly not the sweet man who loved black people and who wanted to have an African queen to be his bride. This could certainly not be the man who courted me all these months.

He walked to the dresser and gave it a big kick. I jumped slightly in fright and stared at his back. I could hear his deep breathing from where I sat.

"You women are all the same." He said, turning round to look at me. "You always want to change things that need no changing."

"I'm sorry." I whispered.

"What?" He said.

"I'm sorry." I repeated.

I held on to his eyes for a minute and then watched them trail down to my breasts. Instinctively, I hugged my breasts closer together to make them look fuller. I noticed that this seemed to excite him.

"Please let's not fight." I said.

"Yes," he agreed, "let's not fight... God, you are beautiful."

In no time he was by my side kissing me and fiddling with my bra. I was soon naked before him. Many thoughts flashed through my head. Many questions as well. I was not given an opportunity to ask him anything at all about what I was doing here and what plans he had for me now that I was here. There were promises of marriage and citizenship while I was still in Nigeria, but nothing was said that night. The only noise he made was grunting and ejaculating expletives while he jabbed at my insides with his withering prick. Did he care that I felt no pleasure from this? Did he even notice? I didn't close my eyes once during this torrid invasion. It lasted what seemed like hours interrupted only when he offloaded his scum at intervals and then he started again after resting only for a short while. I felt wounded inside like only a woman could feel, raw and bruised from within my cave as he thrust in with so much force, imploding all my senses. As I watched his naked limbs dance on me I caught the wild look of ecstasy spreading across his face. The bed creaked and cried and shifted violently from side to side, objecting to this sudden and unexpected violation. And when he was done, he rolled over and slept, leaving me forgotten, naked and alone.

I'm sure if James had any opportunity to discuss the happenings of our first night, he would have told a very different story. He would have been the victim and I would have been the cold, unfeeling one. But whatever version is told, the bed, the wooden floor, the window and even the door would attest to one story. If only they could talk.

I lay in his bed with the covers pulled up to my chin with the stench of him still infiltrating my senses and I cried a silent sorrow. It occurred to me then that when women surrender to men, they lose all forms of their individual identity and become powerless, stripped of every vestige of their womanhood and are left feeling naked.

Naked was how I remained the next morning when he left me in his bed and dashed off. I looked out of the window and noticed it was still pitch black outside. It looked like midnight but it was morning and he was gone. I looked round the stark bedroom trying to make out all the details in the barely visible light of the half morning. Everything was as I remembered it from the night before; the ugly armchair still stared at me from the corner of the room, the wardrobe stood in all its rickety majesty with one of its doors strewn open, peeking at me. I soon dragged myself out of bed using the duvet as a cloak. I switched on the light and looked round the room for my suitcases. They were on the floor where James had left them. I noticed they had been tampered with.

Before I could get to them, I heard the bedroom door creak open and as I looked up, my eyes caught black sturdy legs, a pair of white boxer shorts that had stains close to the crotch area, an extremely lean stomach that exposed the outline of several ribs and then a flourish of black pepper-seed curls that ran from a defined chest to a quaint belly button. Providence's eyes were red; these were what captured me. He held a half-smoked cigarette between the fingers of his left hand.

My first instinct was to scream, which I did. Loudly.

"Hey, take it easy love." He said alarmingly. "It's just me, Providence. I no go bite you!"

"What do you want?" I asked as I wrapped the duvet tighter round me. My voice was shaky and my eyes were drawn to the cigarette in his hand.

"I hope you are not going to shout again?" He said. I shook my head. "Good!" He said and suddenly slumped himself on the unmade bed with such nonchalance.

"So, how is Nigeria?" He asked me as he dragged on his cigarette.

I was silent. All that passed through my mind was my nudity underneath the cover and my silent infuriation. What manner of a person would saunter into the bedroom of a couple that early in the morning, smoking a cigarette and trying to engage a stranger in conversation regarding Nigeria? Not only that, he was practically naked himself without a care in the world. I was upset with myself for not having the courage to speak up and say my mind. I hated the fact that he was in this room. I hated the fact that he had no respect for the fact that I was a woman. I hated that he felt it was okay to just walk in here this early in the morning. I hated. I hated. I hated. But I could not voice all this hate.

"Abi you no sabi English again?" He asked in Nigerian Pidgin English.

"I speak perfect English, thank you!" I said with a deliberately exaggerated British accent.

"How is Nigeria then?" He asked again, propping himself more comfortably on the bed. "You know, I haven't been home in four years."

How was I supposed to know that? I just got into the country and quite frankly I didn't really care. I wanted him to go so I could put on something.

"When James said he was getting a Nigerian woman over here, I was really intrigued." He started off again. "You know, 1 sort off encouraged him right from the beginning. I told him what fantastic women we have in Nigeria."

At that moment he realized he had finished smoking his cigarette. He looked baffled at the stub as if he had not expected that it would burn out eventually. He then looked at me and smiled vulgarly.

"You have any smokes?" He asked.

I looked on in stunned awe. He sighed helplessly. I watched him rise from the bed; drag open the drawer by the head of the bed, lift some loose paper and magazines inside and withdraw a crumpled packet of Marlboros. He smiled seeing there was still a stick left inside. He found a lighter, lit the cigarette and flopped back on the bed as if it were his room.

"This London has a way of changing a person." He said matter-of-factly. "Who would have thought that I would be this jobless after bagging a degree in Economics! Yes, I studied at U.I., Ibadan. Was the top of my class, even."

At that moment I realized that Providence had no plans of leaving the room any time soon. He wanted to talk. From the looks of things, he was dying for an audience, someone to listen to his soliloquies. I was that unfortunate someone who had the misfortune of only just arriving from Nigeria, a distant memory of a place called home for him. The look on my face softened momentarily and I moved over to the armchair and sat down.

"I didn't go to any university." I said solemnly.

"Ah!" He said with keen interest "You don't know what you missed."

I could see he had become totally relaxed now that I had shown some interest in listening to him. I quickly deduced that he didn't expect much talking from me. Rather, a mute listener would suit him perfectly, and this was fine for me. I figured that maybe if I listened without interruptions, he would finish quickly and then leave the room.

"Nigeria sweet o!" He exclaimed suddenly. "Any time I remember the tall dreams I had when I was back in school—you know, being rich, living and working abroad, shuttling in and out of Nigeria as if commuting between Dugbe and Lagos—the naiveté of the innocent!"

He looked at me then sheepishly and smiled. I noticed he had beautiful white teeth that seemed unaffected by his smoking.

"So, tell me about home." He said. "I hear things from time to time from friends by email or phone calls but nothing beats talking with a Nigerian one-to-one, especially one so fresh from home."

He was staring at me expectantly and it dawned on me after a minute that he was actually expecting me to say something. I looked away briefly as I pulled the covers more securely to my body. It was almost as if I feared he could see my nakedness underneath. I didn't trust my voice either.

"What do you want to know about Nigeria?" I finally asked. My voice was soft and unrecognizable to me.

"I don't know." Providence admitted. "Let's seew how are things generally? Are people still running away from there? I hear the price of fuel is astronomical these days, is that true?"

What did I know about these issues? I asked myself. Before I got the nerves and courage to walk away from Nigeria I was simply a Nigerian who though aware of some of the prevailing issues in the country—poor electricity that made sleeping at night unbearable, hike in fuel prices that drove the price of everything up, the occasional bus-stop commentary on the dodgy nature of our government or politicians—I really didn't bother with Nigeria or the other issues involved therein. I know there are many of my type in this generation who are vaguely involved in slapstick politics but we are all so far removed that we depend on stray comments for information. For me, Nigeria is Nigeria; good or bad, it is the only country I know. There was nothing I could think of to say.

"Fuel price did go up." I said slowly.

He sighed deeply as if this piece of stale news was going to affect his leaving the house that morning and finding his way round town. I began to wonder again when he planned to leave me alone.

"You speak well." He said as he sat up. "Which school did you go to?"

"Night school." I answered quickly, silently thanking Princess for encouraging me to finish up with my adult education classes.

"Hmmmp!" Providence sighed. "Anyway, what plans do you have now that you are here?"

I shrugged. I didn't think it was right for me to disclose any plans to him. I wondered if James had told him about our plans to get married so I could become a British citizen. It didn't seem likely, but I could never tell since James had kept so much from me already.

I didn't realize how long I remained still without answering him until he said harshly, "It was a simple question I asked, do you have a speech impediment?"

I wanted so much to ask him to leave in the foulest of ways, but I was tongue-tied as always. Those things I most desperately wanted to say—the hurtful things—never left my mouth. I had always been like that.

Finally he got up from the bed, looked at me with pity in his eyes and sighed like a typical Nigerian—a long drawn-out noise produced by sucking in air through clenched back teeth that produced a hiss.

"Woman," he said, "you need friends like me in this London-o. Don't you forget it."

I stood still. Quiet. Watching.

"I found Jesus in the streets of London." He said suddenly. "I found him because I had no real friends here. I found him when I thought I was going crazy with desperation and hunger."

He wasn't looking at me when he said all this. His eyes were focused on something else with a faraway look in them. He turned round after that and left the room as abruptly as he had entered. The stillness he left behind was very spooky. Within seconds I found myself by the door, latching it securely shut.

As I searched to find something to wear, there was a torrent of thunderous knocks on the door. In panic I cried out, believing a mad man was about to break into the room.

"It is I, Providence." His voice boomed out from the other side of the door. "Please open up."

"Why?" I asked fearfully.

"I need something from you." He said.

"What do you want?" I asked.

There was a pause before he answered: "Can I have a fiver?"

I didn't understand him and just kept quiet as I pondered his request.

"Can I have five pounds?" He said shortly, probably figuring out the reason for my silence.

Why should I give him money? I asked myself. There was an edge to his voice that didn't sound anything like when he was in the room earlier. I heard a determined surety, a certainty that he would get what he asked for. What if I didn't give him any money? Would he break the door down and assault me? How far would he go to get what he wanted? I suddenly could picture his exposed torso again and the veins that lined his temple and particularly the one that trailed down from his belly to his navel. I was reminded of a hungry hyena and my mother telling me that hyenas would charge at a lion when they are hungry and desperate.

I rushed to my suitcases. I threw one of them open and started searching for the remaining money I had stashed away, tied up in one of my handkerchiefs. I found the handkerchief but the money was gone. I searched frantically in the suitcase, emptying its contents before diving into the other one.

"Will you help me out or not?" Providence's voice

boomed, followed by fingers rapping on the door.

"Wait!" I cried out.

I was really baffled now. There was no money in any of my suitcases. I went to the wardrobe and began scanning its contents. There were empty bottles of skin and hair products, some mails, some old magazines and some videotape, but no money. I went back to the emptied suitcases and sat amidst its scattered contents. I could not have lost the money. James must have taken it. He might have kept it for me. That was a possibility, but that other voice in my head was telling me otherwise.

There was a final deliberate rap on the door: knock. Silence. Knock. Silence. Knock. Knock.

"I'm still waiting out here." Providence crooned. "Any luck for a brother?"

I stared at the door. I could imagine Providence's lean frame embracing the door from the other side with his lips pressed against the flat wood of the door, speaking to me from the outside. I had no money. How was I going to tell him I had no money? He would not believe me, he would think I was lying to him and he would surely knock the door down and begin looking for money himself, just like he had casually opened the drawer and taken the cigarette there. He would do this and I would not be able to stop him or do anything. For the second time within twenty-four hours I felt totally powerless. Helpless. Not in control.

"Woman—"

"I'm sorry," I said, cutting him off, "I can't help you. I have no money."

"Cha!" He sighed, irritated. "Why you waste my time then? Why make me hope then?"

"I thought I had some money on me," I said, "but…"

"Let me guess!" He said. "You just discovered your man take all your money without even telling you—am I right?"

He had a mocking tone in his voice and I knew his question was rhetorical to say the least if not downright patronising.

"Cha woman!" He sighed again. "How come when African women come to London, they leave behind their common sense?"

I heard him shuffle away from the other side, sighing loudly as he did so. I didn't expect this, this sudden and unexpected withdrawal of his without even a fight or a show of doubt. There was something about this man. Even though I felt quietly insulted by what he had just said, I decided to ignore it and think of what to do next while I waited for James to return from wherever it was he had run off to. To achieve this, I had to focus my mind on the following half-truths I was desperate to believe: James is keeping the money for me; James had left for work that morning and didn't want to disturb me while I slept; James respects me.

Isn't this the kind of stuff we tell ourselves when we anxiously want to believe that we are not foolish? We secretly make up excuses for the people who hurt us because we are so ashamed of other people feeling pity for us or more aptly put, we do not want to feel pity for ourselves or deal directly with what is obvious. By telling myself that all was well and that James "respected" me, was I just fooling myself once again or was I protecting James? Yes, I know what it feels like to shield or protect a tormentor. I have in my past done so many times.

Providence's last scornful remark tugged at me for the better part of the morning but I resisted the urge to ponder on its meaning. I decided instead to tidy up the bedroom. As I straightened the bed cover, cleaned out the wardrobe and swept the floor, I hoped that the phone would ring and it would be James on the line wanting to speak to me.

The sun finally peeked through the skies at a later part of the day. It was past noon and I had just finished with the bedroom. I was sure Providence and Thomas had left the flat because I had heard the front door slam shut twice that morning and I didn't hear anyone else moving around the house afterwards. Of course, I heard the constant shuffling of my neighbours above me. The ceiling was so thin that the muffled thuds could as well have been coming from my living room or kitchen. This somewhat intrigued me. For some reason, I kept comparing this England with Nigeria. I am sure many foreigners do this when they visit another country, subconsciously cataloguing the differences in surroundings, cultures and habits of the people, trying hard sometimes to discover what it is that makes the other people superior or inferior as the case may be. In my case, thin walls and ceilings were definitely on the negative count against England. In this tenement, everybody's business is your business. In the days and weeks that followed, I shared in the conversations, fights, music and heated passions of squeaky beds and satisfied grunts of my surrounding neighbours—all via the thin walls and ceilings.

I am not the confrontational type. I mostly suffer my frustrations in the seething silence of sulk with eyes crossed, mouth pouting and the complementary sighs poisoning the silence.

This was the mood I was in when James casually breezed in late that afternoon. He looked the way I remembered him from the previous night—young and irresponsible. He beamed happily at me and a million insults and questions flashed through my head but my tongue held its peace.

I was in the kitchen trying to figure out what I could possibly cook with what little I could find in the kitchen cupboards and fridge. There were some canned tomatoes, an onion that was already sprouting, a couple of potato balls, which were also sprouting, a bottle of olive oil and some spices.

"Hi, love," he said in that accent of his, "I'm so sorry I had to rush off so early this morning... I have to work."

If I were back home in Nigeria, I would have drawn out a long hissing sigh, but instead I remained quiet and unfeeling. I wanted to ask why he thought it was just okay to leave me alone in the house with his housemates, why he thought he could take my money without asking.

He walked up to me, grabbed me by the shoulders and kissed me on the cheek. With my eyes closed, all I could do was smell him. The stale sweat, faint traces of tobacco and his male scent hit me all at once and I felt like I was back in bed with him again. Did I cringe then?

"You are mad at me." He whispered in my ears. "I can tell from the way your body is responding to me."

Why was I tongue-tied? Why couldn't I just say what it was I wanted to say to him? I had spent the better part of the day rehearsing in my head the detailed argument we would have when he returned.

"You left me alone." I said instead, meekly.

"Hey," he cooed into my ears, "you have me now... you have me all to yourself now."

His words weakened my resolve. How vulnerable I was then. I just accepted without questioning the flattering comments, stolen kisses, a reassuring stroke under my chin and I locked eyes with seduction that melted all logical reasoning within me. This was a moment of absolute vulnerability. A moment of nakedness. I let my guard down. I wanted to believe. I wanted to be. *Loved.* I allowed myself to forget what was important. I simply forgot.

You have me all to yourself. My heart seemed to grab on to that and for a long time afterwards I simply forgot. There are many ways to be naked and it has nothing to do with unclothing oneself literally. As a woman, I have found I have spent almost all my life naked. I let things be. *For peace.* I let things be. *For fear.* I let things be. *For man.*

I opened my eyes and noticed he was looking at me. I saw Jesus then, just like Providence discovered Jesus in the streets of London. Out of hunger and desperation I discovered my own private Jesus. But this hunger was not the same hunger Providence spoke about. He spoke about a hunger that needed food to quench it; I hungered for something else. I hungered for control. I was desperate for it.

This Jesus with his green glacial eyes, two-day growth of beard and long tousled red hair looked down at me. If Jesus were Caucasian, he would have been standing in front of me that very minute. Suddenly I became cold again. Goose bumps covered my skin and I dragged my eyes away from his.

"Is everything all right?" He asked me.

There was much I still needed to know about James. I was still not used to his warm-one-minute-cold-the-other personality. Was this an act of his to throw me off balance? This immediately occurred to me but was quickly discarded as I replied with a big smile that I was okay.

"Good." He said. "We'll go out tonight. I want to show you a little bit of London and get you to meet some of my friends."

Friends. Not family.

I wondered why he avoided any mention of his family. I wanted to know where he came from and not who his friends were. You can tell a lot about a person by just meeting his family, my mother used to tell me. In Nigeria many parents would insist on meeting the family of their children's friends just to make sure the friends came from good, responsible stock. It was a case of "show me your family and I would tell you who you are." I wanted to know his family regardless of what trauma they may have caused him as a child. Knowing them would help me know him, I believed.

Nonetheless, I welcomed the idea of going out that evening. Being alone in that dreary house all day had been an exercise in absolute patience. I remember thinking then that this may be an opportunity to get some questions answered as well as getting to see a little bit of London.

How was I to know that after that night, the course of my life was going to change?

4

Raindrops on Roses

I was happy once, or so I believed.

Happiness cannot be an enduring phase, can it? The only enduring phase of happiness must be babyhood. Even at that, babies do grow up and traces of their innocence soon vanish abruptly along with most of their happiness. It can be likened to removing the scales from their eyes. They finally see things, as they should, without any obstacles blocking out the harsh reality of this life. It's a kind of rebirth, the transition from infancy to childhood. I remember being happy the first time I saw bits and pieces of *The Sound of Music*. I remember this now as I stand in the queue at Heathrow Airport, waiting to fly back to Nigeria.

Why am I remembering all this now? I ask myself. It was that song; that tune and the little girl with her mother humming it behind me.

The first time I was ushered into the Okoros' living room, *The Sound of Music* was playing from the television. Their daughter, Tiffany, was sitting in front of the television and singing along with Maria in her loud staccato voice. It was that song when Maria, faced with some limits from the Captain, was inspired to sing as she caressed the brocade drapes in her bedroom. "Raindrops on roses and whiskers on kittens…"

My aunt had sent me to drop off some money with

Mrs. Okoro. The Okoros were the Onye Uku of the neighbourhood—the rich and revered elite of our modest street. Mr. Okoro worked for one of the oil exploration companies in Nigeria and was well paid like most people who were fortunate enough to work in the oil industry. The Okoros owned the house they lived in, a mark of achievement in Nigeria.

Tiffany was happy. Her happiness made me very conscious of my own austere state—my worn and old dress seemed to lose more of its carefully washed and preserved lustre against the brilliance of Tiffany's chic foreign-purchased dress. The whole street knew the Okoro children spent their summer holidays in London. After one of their London sabbaticals, the neighbourhood kids would ogle for weeks at their daily changes of clothes, all purchased in London.

For a frightful moment as I stood in the check-in queue listening to the child behind me sing, I imagined I saw Tiffany Okoro. Not a grown-up version of the pompous girl I knew briefly, but the same spoilt fourteen-year old Tiffany. Unchanged. Still a child.

"Raindrops on roses and whiskers on kittens…"

I stood mesmerised as I stared at this girl who most likely was about the same age as I was. I was clutching the envelope from my aunt, my hands pressed against my lap, the length of my arm concealing my midriff area. I stole a peek at the television screen, only just briefly before I looked back at this privileged young lady. A strong feeling crossed my mind at that moment. Hate. Perhaps. Envy and shame, more appositely. I felt common standing there and for a moment it felt like all my misfortune had been caused by this girl who had no care in the world as far as I could see. I wanted to be her. I wanted not to want. To go to bed at night and not worry about tomorrow, to sit by the television and sing auspiciously tunes of raindrops, roses and favourite things.

That feeling quickly passed and was replaced by complete joy. Just like cool water running down my body in that one instant. And there was absolutely no reason for this except that it felt like I had merged bodies with this girl in front of the television. I became one with her happiness. I saw myself living in this castle, just like Tiffany. I would have a room to myself. I would have servants who cooked, did my laundry and cleaned my room. I would walk shoeless on a soft rug that covered every inch of the house from corner to corner without fear. In my mind it was a light blue rug, which was soft and lush. The walls were painted a heavenly cream shade and the high ceilings had ridged patterns.

On the walls were different pictures. A very large one of the entire family was above the mantelpiece in the living room. In it was Mr. Okoro in a dark pinstriped suit and a red necktie, his wife was seated next to him in a gold lace dress. Her plump neck was draped with endless chains of gold. You couldn't miss that, nor could you miss the fat gold rings on her fingers. The two children, Tiffany and Gerald, completed the picture of a happy and successful family. Tiffany sat at the far end of her father, beaming in her maroon velvet dress with white lace trimmings on the sleeves and collar, while Gerald sat on the other end by his mother in his dark blue suit and prescription eye glasses. Gerald's eyes intrigued me. The photograph had managed to imprison something enigmatic in them.

"Who are you?" Tiffany suddenly noticed me and was looking at me as if I was a bad smell.

"My aunt said I should give this to your mother." I said showing her the envelope in my hand.

"Don't you have a name?" She asked.

"Ngozi." I said, looking down at my feet.

"So, what's in the envelope?" She asked further.

I kept thinking how polished she sounded. Her voice had a rich quality to it, girlish and childish but distinct, not like the voice of girls who were born without privilege.

Her clear accent was not make-believe or contrived but effortless and clear.

She jumped off the sofa and rushed up to me excitedly. She was shorter than I was but fuller. Her skin was brown like black coffee mixed with a little milk and she smelt of vanilla. She grabbed some of my hair and pulled lightly.

"Your hair is too tough." She exclaimed, the contents of the envelope now totally forgotten. "Don't you relax it?"

I wanted to speak but the words wouldn't come out of my mouth. Up close and personal with her, she seemed like a real person. I had only seen her from a distance before today. She had been either entering one of her father's chauffeured cars or exiting one. I had seen her ride her bicycle on the tendered lawns of her compound or with her friends on the balcony of their huge house. She used to be real then, but in a non-intrusive way, almost like an abstract. Now she was all flesh, eyes, fingernails and hair. She was real in a very tangible way. And all I could do was gape at her.

"You don't talk much, do you?" She asked as she pranced around me, pulling at my dress at different angles as if inspecting me. "Do you want to come to my room?" She said with excitement. Her eyes were beaming mischievously as she grabbed my free hand. "Come, I will show you."

"I have to give this to your mother." I said uncomfortably. "My aunty would be very angry if I did not give it to her."

"Come on now!" She whined. "It will only take a minute...less than a minute even and we'll be done before mother comes out of her room."

She was holding my arm and pulling me towards her. She was behaving as if I were one of her friends. Her eyes were pleading with me and I could not say no to her request. She looked like an angel at that moment; so innocent and pure.

"Do you promise?" I asked as I allowed her drag me along.

"Promise!"

She led me to a stairway, skipping in an excited fashion

up the stairs, while I followed quietly behind. At the top landing I noticed five doors. All were well-crafted oak doors except one, which seemed to have a Formica finish. Tiffany motioned for me to be quiet, placing a finger to her lips as she tiptoed to the room at the far right corner of the hallway. When she got to the door, she beckoned me to come. I took wide silent steps until I was by her side. She pushed the door open and pulled me in with her.

"Whew!" She said. "We can talk now."

I was stunned by the luxury of her room. It was rugged all through just like the living room. Her bed was covered with a huge pink duvet with cartoon characters. She had a cute little dresser that was decorated with lotions and perfumes and more pictures. In one corner was a wardrobe and not far from it was a door.

"That's my bathroom." She said when she noticed my eyes fixed to the door. "All the bedrooms have private bathrooms."

I was impressed but that earlier feeling of loathing was slowly tugging at my conscience. I was now more aware of my wretchedness. My skin felt dry and parched all at once. The fabric of my dress felt thin and threadbare. I wanted so much to hide in shame from her and return to my own squalor, which I had grown accustomed to and could face with so little trepidation. Why had she brought me here to confront my shame?

"So, how old are you?" She asked. She was sitting by the dresser now and looking at me pointedly.

"Fourteen." I answered shyly.

"Really? I am fourteen too." She said with doubt dripping in her tone. "I was fourteen two months ago. Are you sure you are not older?"

"I am fourteen." I said almost defiantly. She had sounded as if being fourteen was an exclusive privilege for her kind alone.

"How come you have big breasts?" She asked.

I looked down at my chest area in reflex. My eyes were drawn to my breasts. They were full unlike hers, which looked like the skin around her upper torso had been pinched out to form tiny puckered mounds.

"Have you been to London before?" Tiffany asked suddenly, drawing my attention back to her. "Do you want to see the pictures I took in London this summer?" She asked, rifling through her dresser's cabinet with glee.

I watched her in awe. I was still reeling from the first question she had asked me regarding my breasts and now it was London. She had done the same earlier when she asked about my hair and without waiting for a reply asked if I would like to see her room. Two seemingly unconnected statements. I didn't know what to make of this creature.

"Here, look at this one." She was by my side shoving a photograph in my hand. "That was taken at Trafalgar Square... That's me by the fountain."

In the photograph she stood by the huge water fountain and her brother was beside her. In the background was a monumental-looking building and the famous red two-tiered bus. I was intrigued. I caressed the glossy sheen of the picture with my thumb and wondered briefly what it would be like to be in London.

"It's beautiful." Tiffany said as if reading my thoughts. "I will be going to school there soon, for my university education."

What do I care about that? I thought to myself. Of what significance would her schooling in London be to me? This made me want to loathe her some more. Was she deliberately mocking me with her wealth? Why, then, was she treating me to her room and acting as if I were part of her inner circle of friends? Her eyes mocked me. Though she smiled with affection at me, her eyes betrayed pity and embarrassment. They seemed to say, "You are beneath me."

"I have to go." I said worriedly. I had already spent more time than I had planned to. "My aunty will be waiting for me and I still have to give this envelope to your mother."

"Yes, yes," she agreed, "you have to go... but you will come back and visit."

I had no reply to that. I did not know for sure if I ever would return to this house again. I wasn't sure if I even wanted to return there. I had felt a cacophony of feelings all within minutes from the moment I stepped into that house—hate, envy, joy, shame and sadness, all making me dizzy and disoriented. Why would I want to feel like this again?

She led me back downstairs and made her way to the living room, where she continued with her "raindrops on roses". I was forgotten. She didn't invite me to join her. I didn't belong.

I dreamt of London.

For many nights after visiting Tiffany, that was all I thought about. Images of the weird red bus filled my thoughts with wonder. Was all of London like Trafalgar Square—clean paved floors and fountains with giant lion sculptures? And all those pigeons that seemed at peace with people! In my dreams I was Tiffany. I wore pretty dresses and beautiful shoes. I danced and smiled and sang of raindrops on roses. I was completely enraptured by all this, intoxicated. How could I not be?

It had been easy up till then to simply acknowledge that the Okoros were wealthy, but their wealth had no real meaning to me. Yes, everyone saw the cars, we saw the good clothes, we even caught glimpses of the jewellery Mrs. Okoro wore—but from a distance. It is so easy to admire when you are not compelled to stand side by side with the source of your admiration. But I had. Not only did I stand by Tiffany's side, I felt her touch, smelt her disdain and saw close enough what money could get you. How could I not want to be her?

Maybe those few moments with Tiffany was the day I began to dream. I began to want. I wanted bigger things than everyone told me I could ever have.

I found myself back at the Okoros not long afterwards.

It was different this time. I was invited. It was a hot Friday afternoon and I was sitting in front of my uncle's house. I couldn't stay indoors because we hadn't had electricity for the past two days and the humidity inside the house was stifling. I had some free time since I had finished up with all the chores. I had prepared dinner; I had cleaned the toilets and the compound was neat. My aunt had travelled to see her sister but was expected back the next day. The sun was out but the natural breeze made the heat bearable. I was alone at home.

A car pulled up in front of the Okoros. It was a new car. I knew it was new because I had never seen it before and because no number plates had been attached to it yet. It occurred to me then that the street would have something fresh to talk about in the next few days. I was about to look away when I noticed Tiffany walk out of the house. She looked at the car with not much interest and then looked around until her eyes caught mine. Without hesitating, she gestured for me to come over.

I don't know why, but I found myself crossing the street and joining her in front of her house. She looked different that afternoon, different from the girl I saw sitting in front of the television the first time I was in her house. I wasn't quite sure what it was until she spoke to me and then I noticed she was wearing red lipstick and her eyes were made up.

"My father just bought another car." She said dryly. "I don't like the colour. I told him to get a red car but he bought this grey one."

She spoke as if buying a new car was an everyday occurrence. I wanted to tell her that the only car my uncle owned had been bought second-hand five years before after the last owner had used it for three years. I couldn't even remember what the original colour of the car was —blue, green, yellow?

"It's a nice car." I said to her.

"What?" She asked sounding puzzled.

"Your father's car is nice." I repeated.

"Oh that?" She said absentmindedly. "Let's go up to my room. I have something for you."

"I'm the only one at home." I protested. "I have to be around when my cousins return."

She rolled her eyes at me.

"Didn't you hear what I said?" She said. "I said I have something for you."

I stared at her suspiciously but my curiosity won. "What do you have for me?" I asked coyly.

She smiled victoriously, grabbed my hand and pulled me towards the door of the house.

"Well," she said, "if you want to know what it is, you will have to follow me and find out."

This felt like a game, like playing *"Follow the Leader"*. To play this game, a group of kids linked hands together and followed the child at the beginning of the chain who screamed "Follow the leader" at the top of its lungs until they reached a dead end and it became someone else's turn to be the leader. For some odd reason, the leaders were always boys. I never did understand the futility of it all. It only showed how easy it was for us to be led once we have someone who claims to be leader. We follow. Many times I, along with the other children, was led into murky waters and what did we do? We laughed and kept following with our dirty feet and soiled clothes. We followed.

I followed Tiffany to her room. This time we were not as quiet as we were the first time she took me to her room. I imagined her mother was not at home much like my aunt was not around. I wondered briefly if she was scared of her mother like I was of my aunt. I only wondered but never asked.

"In the bathroom." She ordered.

I followed her into her bathroom and was again mesmerised by the sheer luxury even this part of the house exuded. The tiles used here were not the common white ones found in almost all homes and few public latrines. The tiles here were peach-coloured and had daffodils design on them. There was a bathtub, a toilet, and a sink with a huge mirror above it and still enough space.

"You have to sit down by the bathtub and wrap this towel round your neck and shoulders." She ordered pointing to a towel hanging by the bathtub.

"Why?" I asked.

"I want to make you beautiful." She answered.

"What?" I said. "How?"

She smiled and retrieved a white container from the cabinet beside the wall mirror. She dropped the container in the sink and removed a black comb from the cabinet.

"I am going to relax your hair for you, so it will be as fine as mine." She said.

"No, no, no…" I began to say. "I can't do that. My aunt would kill me."

"Don't be silly." She admonished. "Of course she can't kill you. All girls our age are relaxing their hair, you should too."

"I will be in big trouble." I said quietly.

"We can always plait your hair once we are done and no one would know any better." She added.

I was doubtful, but silently watched her approach me with the comb and the white container that read "Relaxer". This was a bad idea, I kept thinking. As an African girl, my hair was an integral symbol of my innocence and youth. This was drummed into us at school during Home Economics and Etiquette classes. Young girls were meant to keep their hair natural and neat or plaited in a simple-enough style to reflect good grooming, my teacher, Mrs. Pedro, used to say. I used to giggle at the back of the class because of her funny accent. She was a Nigerian married to a Brazilian and she had studied in Europe.

She placed her tools down and quickly wrapped the towel securely round my neck and shoulders. I cringed in pain as she began combing my hair out.

"Stay still!" She sighed reproachfully as I raised my shoulders in an attempt to push her hand away from my hair.

And then I felt it. A coldness at the front of my scalp

that quickly spread to all sides of my head. It was soothing at first but within minutes I felt my scalp burning up. It felt like my head was on fire and it burnt from within.

"It's burning me!" I cried, reaching for my head.

She slapped my hands away.

"Don't touch it," she said sternly, "it's supposed to hurt you for a while."

"It's really painful." I cried.

"Not really," she countered, "I will soon be done."

She let the chemical sit on my hair for another ten minutes before she agreed it was time to wash it off. I cried in relief as she shampooed it out of my hair. After towelling my hair dry, she led me to the mirror.

I was stunned by my reflection. It was me, but it wasn't me. I looked like an adult. My hair was stretched and dishevelled but refined, just like a white person's hair. I almost cried out in panic. I knew I was surely in trouble.

"I told you I would make you beautiful." Tiffany said with obvious satisfaction with her work. "But I am not finished yet."

She applied some lotion to my hair and styled it with her brush. When she was done with my hair, she applied some lipstick to my lips and eye shadow to my eyelids. When I saw the finished look I was truly afraid. How would I walk out of this house looking like this? How would I walk the streets? How would I face my uncle and aunt? I didn't even want to think of what they would do to me if they saw me like this.

I stared at her smiling face in the mirror and I hated her. At the same time another part of me was saying, "Yes, yes." I should have stopped her before she did this to me. I should have said "No!" but I didn't have the courage to do so. Without wanting to admit it to myself, a part of me secretly wanted her to do my hair and make me more like her. But this did not stop me from hating her at that moment.

Using the back of my hands, I wiped off the lipstick and cleaned off the eye shadow with my palms.

"You ruined it!" She shrieked.

"I have to go home now." I insisted.

"There's one more thing." She said as she dashed off into her room. "I really have to go home now." I said, following her into the room.

She retrieved a little nylon bag from her wardrobe and pushed it into my hands.

"What is this?" I asked.

"That's your gift." She said.

"What is inside?"

"If you must know," she said dispassionately, "they are some old clothes of mine. I thought they would look pretty on you... I don't wear them anymore."

"I can't accept this." I said pushing the bag into her hands. She didn't take it from me.

"Take them." She said gently. "They would only be thrown away or stolen by the housemaids... if you have them you can dress like me."

"Don't you need to ask your mother before giving away your things?" I asked.

"My mother doesn't care." She said quietly. I almost didn't hear her. "Just take it and go."

"Thank you." I said and hurriedly fled from her room.

I dreamt of London.

I dreamt that night and in the dream I was walking the streets of London with the wind in my hair—my new hair—blowing the silky threads of this new crown ever so seductively into my face. I was dressed up like a lady in a new dress that had no tears or had never been stitched before. But in my dream I walked on my bare feet and soon my feet began to bleed. There was a lot of blood everywhere. Bucket-full. The trail of blood followed me even when I was sure that all this blood couldn't have come from me alone. I ran to one of the fountains and dipped my feet into its water and suddenly the water turned blood-red. I looked up and the stone lion came to life and roared at me.

I woke up drenched in sweat. I couldn't sleep for the rest of the night. I was worried and rightly so. How would I begin to explain my hair to my uncle and aunt, especially my aunt?

When I returned home that afternoon, I had quickly tied my head with an old scarf. Luckily my cousins had not returned yet. I would not have been able to bear the scornful remarks I knew they would hurl at me and then the continued taunts and threats of telling their mother what I had done to my hair.

All seemed well that night. My uncle left me alone. My cousins were uninterested in me, so after dinner I retreated to the little storeroom where I slept.

When Aunt Rosa returned the next afternoon, I rushed out to meet her as she got out of the taxi. I greeted her and took hold of her bags out of respect. I noticed she looked at me funnily. I knew somehow she was trying to figure out what was different about me, but I didn't stay long enough for her to finally comment on why I was covering my head with a scarf. I prayed she wouldn't pay me much attention that day. But things usually happen quite differently when we so desperately pray for the opposite. It must have been the way I carried myself all day, like a hunted prey. I jumped at every sound and kept touching my head to make sure the scarf was still there.

I was rinsing some mangoes in the kitchen when it happened. She had instructed me earlier to get some of the mangoes she had brought back from her little trip. I had asked her how many and she told me to get ten so she could give some to Mama Sunday who had dropped by to say hello. Mama Sunday stayed in the flat opposite to ours. She was a good friend of my aunt's. Her son, Sunday, came around all the time to play with Nomso, my cousin.

"How long will it take you to wash mangoes for me?" My aunt asked as she entered the kitchen.

Her entry was so unexpected and sudden that I dropped

the mango I was rinsing and as I bent down to pick it up I unconsciously touched my scarf.

"You are totally useless!" She spat at me. "You can't even wash mangoes."

"I am sorry, Aunty." I said.

"Sorry for yourself!" She said back and finally her eyes found my scarf. "And what is that scarf doing on your head?"

I stood frozen.

"Don't you have mouth?" She asked in Igbo, our local language.

I couldn't speak. I began to shake. She eyed me suspiciously and then yanked the scarf from my head. I saw her eyes widen in shock as she stared at my relaxed hair.

"Chi'm o!" She screamed; my God!

"What is it?" Mama Sunday called out from the living room in worry.

"Come and see what this wretched girl has done to her hair." My aunt shouted.

Mama Sunday made her way into the kitchen and she, too, stared wide-eyed at me. I looked at them both and tears welled up in my eyes.

"How old is she?" Mama Sunday asked.

"She's only fourteen." My aunt said. "She has started mixing with bad company. The next thing will be that she is pregnant... God forbid! Not in this house. It will not be in my house that this will happen."

"These young girls don't know any better." Mama Sunday added.

My aunt sighed loudly.

"If only Kachi had listened to me before bringing this ungrateful child into our home!" She added. "Go and get me my scissors in my room."

Crying and snivelling, I dragged myself to her room and retrieved her sewing scissors. I thought of my mother then. I thought of my life before I moved to the city to live with my father's brother and his wife. I felt a cold fear when I remembered my father and my old room. I hated remembering. Memory was a bad place.

My aunt was in the living room waiting for me. She ordered me to kneel down after I had handed the scissors to her. I did as I was told and moments later, I watched pieces of my hair drop on the floor just like the tears dropped from my eyes.

There must have been a time in my life when I was extremely happy. I really don't remember when exactly but when I do probe my heart for an instance, I remember raindrops, roses and favourite things.

5

Without Walls

My second night in London and already I could tell it was going to be a very cold night. James was in quite high spirits and I wondered if it had to do with his taking me out that night to meet his friends. He seemed to think that with a few kisses from him, everything was fine.

I was waiting for him to say something regarding the tidy state of the house, the clean bedroom and the scrubbed floor, but he acted as if this was the same house he left that morning. I should have drawn his attention to my efforts, but I didn't.

"So who are these friends of yours we are meeting?" I asked after he had changed clothes.

"Just friends." He said without looking at me.

"I cleaned the house today." I added slowly. I could not keep it in any longer.

"Really?" He mumbled as he fumbled with his belt. "You really should be getting ready love, we are going out."

"I didn't see any pictures of your family or find anything on your family." I said.

I noticed his shoulders tense up and suddenly there was tension in the room.

"You went through my things?" He said under his breath.

"I was cleaning the room." I said lightly. "I was only

hoping to find a photograph or something."

He slammed his fist violently on the door of the cupboard and I jumped in panic. I could see the blood rush to his face and the vein in his neck swell. I was scared.

"You have no rights to search my things." He said in a harsh tone. "You get it?"

"I'm sorry." I whimpered. "I was just cleaning…"

"Just bloody dress up and let's go." He said and then stormed out of the room.

I thought of home then. I thought of packing up my things and leaving the very first chance I had. In fact, I had definitely made up my mind to do just that. I walked up to the door and peeped into the hallway. It was empty. Slowly I closed the door and went straight to my bags. I checked for my passport. It was not in either bag. I looked into my handbag. Nothing was there as well. I stopped to think of the last time I had seen the passport and my mind was blank. Apart from the airport, I could not remember seeing my passport again. Like my money, my passport was now missing. I was shocked. I had no money of my own and now my identity was missing as well. Obviously, James must have taken my passport as well, but I could not possibly think of asking him for it, not after the way he had just behaved.

Thomas was with him in the kitchen when I came down. They were both smoking and the smell of it was sickening. Thomas was sitting on one of the chairs in the kitchen with his feet on the table. James sat opposite him and between them were an ashtray and two cans of beer. Thomas saw me first.

"You one fine woman, Erika!" He said and winked at me.

I found that gesture vulgar and rude. There was something unsettling about him. I had sensed it the night before when James had introduced us and I felt it again when he looked at me. For a moment I remembered Providence and almost pinched myself when I realized that I would have wanted him to be here this minute. I knew he had been rude to me earlier but now I felt I would be safe if he was around me. He was black like I was. He wouldn't let anything happen to me.

"You are beautiful!" James said.

He stood up to meet me by the door. He took my face in his hands and began kissing me in front of Thomas. I was really uncomfortable. I tried to pull away but he pressed me against the door with his weight and grabbed my buttocks with his free hand. Why was this man doing this? I remember thinking. Why was he acting like he didn't just shout at me only moments ago? Why was he touching me like this in front of another man?

I stole a glance at Thomas and he was looking at us with a smirk on his face. One of his hands was cradling his crotch. Our eyes locked for a moment and he winked at me.

"I'm sorry." I heard James whisper into my ears. "I'm sorry I yelled at you earlier."

Was this enough? I remember smiling when I should have been crying and keeping silent when I should have been screaming. I remember thinking for a long time that it is so much easier not to feel anything. I remember. I remember. I wanted to tell him that I was afraid of him. I wanted to ask him what he had done with my passport but there was that unstable look in his eyes that warned me not to. I smiled into his eyes and told him it was okay.

I remember the noise mostly. It was a deafening repeated thud mixed with a harsh bass, continuous chink, voices, beats and booze. I remember thinking, I cannot hear myself think. Then there was the kaleidoscope of red, blue and green light. And dark corners. Very dark corners. This is how I remember *Haven 7*.

I have often wondered why James had thought it fitting to bring me to a disco club on our first night out together. When he had said "meet my friends" I had imagined a

private affair with six or seven of his intimate friends—
perhaps dinner. I had imagined candlelight, red wine and
maybe even soft jazz playing somewhere in the background.
Pipedreams! In Nigeria when a young woman goes out for
the first time with the man she is going to marry it won't
be to a nightclub. It would be somewhere special and if
his friends must be there then it would be a place where
conversation would flow easy and everyone would have the
opportunity to assess this new bride-to-be. Such an outing
would be a crucial point in their affair.

But it wasn't quite the thing on my mind that evening.
I certainly didn't care too much about that. I had other
things occupying my thoughts.

I had hoped that I would catch a glimpse of the James
I had painted in my mind after our exchanges. I had
pictured things differently. The truth was I had wanted a
more quiet life, a private life. Ever since I could remember,
my life had never been mine. There had been too many
intrusions. There had been too many walk-ins and
walkouts. It had seemed for a very long time that my life
was open to everything, like a room with no walls and no
doors and no windows.

It is amazing what I remember now; all the minute
details of that night in the club—the sights, the sounds
and the smells. For instance, I remember the beefy red-
faced man at the door who looked pointedly at James and
then me before letting us in. I remember the white girl
who was dressed in a chain of strings who gyrated in the
middle of the room while this very black man jiggled her
barely concealed breast from behind. I remember the smile
that broke out on James' face when his eyes caught this
too and he said, "Wicked!" I remember also the waiflike
blonde woman with black lipstick and black nail polish
who rushed up to us and embraced James warmly.

"Darling, you made it!" She said her eyes fixed on me.
"And who is that?"

James disengaged from her hold and turned to me.
He was smiling but I could not determine whether it was

a smile of pride or a conquering smile that adorned his face.

"This," he said holding my shoulder, "is Erika from Africa… Remember I told you about her, Sam?"

"Oh my God!" She said and embraced me. "It's so nice to meet you."

"Thank you!" I said thinking; so this is one of his friends.

"I'm Sam." She said. "Samantha… but everyone calls me Sam, love!"

I felt James' arms slowly wrap round my waist. It was clearly a message. I didn't feel warmth or loved by this gesture, but instead felt like a possession. As we had walked in, I noticed many eyes on me, many male eyes. Perhaps because I was a new face there. Perhaps.

"She's gorgeous!" Sam said to James. "Do you guys want anything to drink?"

"I'll take a beer." James said. "The usual, okay!" He looked at me.

"I'm not thirsty." I replied.

Sam stood still. She looked at James expectantly and I was a little confused by all this. Then she stretched out her left hand. James sighed, dipped his hand into the back pocket of his jeans and squeezed some money into her outstretched hand.

As she dashed off to the bar, my eyes trailed her and for a long minute I was able to take in my environment completely. I remembered the few times I had gone out with Princess and Uloma in Lagos to clubs and bars at Palm Groove or Victoria Island whenever we needed to let our hair down and dance off all our stress. Princess had always said that dancing was therapeutic and I believed her. The three of us, Princess, Uloma and I used to go to the middle of the dance floor, link our fingers together to form a chain and then spin round and round and round until we were intoxicated with dizziness. We usually ended up on the floor, laughing hysterically with tears in our eyes and our worries kept aside for another night. Yes, this place reminded me of the club at Palm Groove with its 80's disco music blaring from the overhead speakers even when the 80's were long gone.

At that moment a revamped version of Donna Summer's "State of Independence" was blaring out of the speakers. Men and women swayed together under electric lights. I watched them dance and it struck me that no Nigerian I knew back home would dance with such reckless abandon. We hadn't reached that state of independence yet. Not with our bodies. Not with our minds.

James found us a space on an already crowded table. Everyone there seemed to know who James was and thus I became the source of their amusement. One girl in particular seemed keener on me than the others. She had brown hair that fell to her shoulders and I could not tell the colour of her eyes under so many bright lights. She was rather plain-looking and was not as slim as the other girls on the table.

"So you flew all the way from Africa to meet James?" She said above the noise of the blaring music.

I could only smile and nod my head.

"Really?" She continued. "So you are going to get hitched and then file for citizenship!"

Someone coughed quietly. Eyes avoided mine.

"You Africans should really stay back in Africa." She continued, smiling as she spoke. "Don't you agree with me?"

No one spoke immediately. I felt James' hand stroking my knee. I could no longer hear the music.

"You do have a point Siobhan." One of the men on the table said. One half of his hair was coloured purple and he had a ring through one of his nostrils. "Africans and Indians are taking up all the work here… Everywhere you go it's black or Indian chaps working and we Brits can't get any decent jobs."

"Thank you Derek." Siobhan said, smiling at him. "But it's not just our jobs they are stealing; apparently they are stealing our men now. I wonder what next they will want."

I looked round the table; everyone was staring at me as if waiting for an answer. I looked at James and he was smiling crookedly as he puffed on yet another cigarette. I looked Siobhan and I saw clearly a determined odium flash through her eyes.

"Is it true about African men," she said, this time looking at the group, her eyes resting on James, "that they are well hung and better in bed?"

"Okay, Siobhan." James finally said. "Enough already!"

"I was just kidding." She said eyeing me slightly.

"Who wants to dance?" James asked abruptly.

"Let's go." Siobhan said as she got up and linked hands with James.

I watched them stumble to the dance floor and a mixture of relief and shame washed over me. I was relieved that interest in me seemed to have waned as almost everyone departed for the dance floor. I wondered if all of James' friends knew my story of coming to London to get married and become a citizen. I was ashamed of how cheap I felt. I imagined how shallow and needy they must think of me: the poor African trash looking for a better life by using one of them. Was that why Siobhan had spat her disguised venom at me? Was that why most of them had politely refrained from saying anything that may be viewed as politically incorrect? I felt so exposed.

"There you are." Sam said. She was standing in front of me with a drink in her hand. "Let's go to the ladies' room and freshen up."

"I should wait for James." I said looking worriedly at both James and Siobhan on the dance floor.

"Come on." Sam said. "From where I stand, James is alright and we will be back before you know it."

I got up and followed her. She led me past the bar and we got to a staircase that led to a basement floor. There was a separate dance floor on this basement level and when we got to the toilet entrance, there was already a long queue of white women waiting. It was strange standing in this line of white skin. I noticed some of the women looking at me and then turning away abruptly when I caught their eye. It was almost like I wasn't supposed to be there. I felt a passive hostility and for the first time in my life, I marvelled that one could sense hostility from the backs of others.

Choking cigarette smoke filled the hot humid air and I felt myself getting sick. On a closer look, I realized that almost everyone dancing on this basement floor was black or of African descent. There were a handful of whites but it was quite glaring, the apparent racial divide within the room. This was what made me notice the black man on the top level who was dancing with the white woman when I entered the club—he stood out because of his colour. Even the music here was edgier, almost angry.

"That Siobhan is such a tosser." Sam said. She was standing in front of me in the queue to the toilet. "I can't really stand the bitch."

I said nothing. Something told me Sam would keep talking anyway.

"You know, she used to date James." Sam said. "That was before she got pregnant..."

"She had a baby for James?" I asked in surprise.

"No, no." Sam said between lighting a cigarette. "She was sleeping with Derek at the time as well and so she had no idea whose child it was anyway."

She paused to blow out smoke.

"She had an abortion." She added. "No point having the little bastard anyway. But she's still a slut."

It was soon our turn and we both entered the ladies' room with two other women. As soon as we entered Sam rushed up to one of the mirrors in the room. There were four such mirrors each flanking a toilet stall. She opened her small purse and retrieved a lipstick. It was the same black shade she was wearing.

"I'm happy James is through with her." Sam said shortly. "I'm happy he's with you now, even though you are black. But you are so light-skinned, you could be white yourself."

She offered me some lipstick, which I politely declined. She replaced the lipstick in her purse and removed mascara. She began to apply that to her already heavy eyelashes.

"You have to be careful too of James." She said slowly. "He has his moments."

"What moments?" I asked. I really wanted to know if there were any more surprises from James.

She paused before saying, "You'll see."

See what? I wanted to ask. I wondered also how come she seemed to know so much about James' private life. Was this how it was in London? Everyone seemed to know everything about everyone. Was this what I was to also expect from my life with James? Our private life would suddenly become an open book and I would have to bid goodbye to any form of privacy.

I looked at Sam's reflection in the mirror and she smiled at me. For a fleeting moment I had a strong urge to grab her by her neck and shake out some answers from her. I didn't and she kept smiling.

The next morning, James disappeared as early as he had done the day before. I pretended to be asleep when he got up and I stole peeks at him while he noisily dressed. He didn't take a bath; he just changed into jeans and a shirt, ran his fingers through his hair and lit a cigarette. After a few puffs he grabbed his knapsack and walked out of the room. I remember hearing the thud of the front door opening and shutting.

How come he didn't bother to bath or even brush his teeth? I found this strange. In Nigeria, taking our bath was something we never forgot as well as making sure our teeth were clean and brushed. Why was it different for James? This show of neglect and nonchalance bothered me in more ways than I could imagine.

I was, on the other hand, quite surprised that he had got up at all that early in the morning. We had returned from the club late—about 2 a.m. To my relief, James had fallen on the bed and snored off. It was I who took his shoes off and made sure he was covered while he slept. I looked at him then and willed my heart to love him, but my heart had already begun to slowly turn. I was glad that he wasn't going to make me love him that night. Letting him touch me that way was something I was not mentally prepared for, not after meeting Siobhan. She had given me the impression that they were still sleeping with each other and in the course of the evening she had disappeared with James for about half an hour. Where had they gone? What did they do?

James was gone for about an hour before I got out of bed. I only got up because I needed to use to the bathroom. I put on my cotton night robe, which was hanging on a hook by the bedroom door.

The bathroom was situated at the end of the walkway that flanked the three bedrooms. James' room was closest to it and I was silently grateful for this. I carefully made my way there, cautious not to make any sounds that may disturb the household. As I was about to open the bathroom door, it suddenly flew open.

In front of me was a naked man. Like a sponge soaking up water, I took in all his nakedness in that one instance; the almost hairless body of this full-grown adult man. It was Thomas. I looked down to avoid his mocking smile and I was assaulted by his turgid maleness. I looked back up into his eyes and he winked at me suggestively.

"Hello, love!" He said.

"I'm sorry... I'm sorry." I stuttered in abject embarrassment. "I didn't—"

"Yes, love." He said carelessly throwing his arms into the air. He was even more exposed to me now but didn't seem to care. The look in his eyes confirmed how much he was enjoying my discomfort.

"Oh God!" I muttered under my breath.

I was shocked and angry at the same time. I looked into his eyes again and I felt him silently challenging me to look at his manhood. I had sensed his vulgarity the night before when he kept winking at me and now again he was flaunting his nakedness in my face. He stood proud, legs together and ultra-confident. I noticed that when he breathed, he puffed his chest out to make himself seem taller and bigger. I couldn't help but think that he was trying to convey a message to me. And then I saw it. His very action pointed like his penis to the fact that he was a man and he believed he was the superior being. How arrogant men are! How vulnerable I was! He may have been nude but I was the naked one. Was he expecting me to fall on my knees and worship him?

In spite of how my heart was racing I willed myself to hold his stare. Just then I heard clapping behind me. I turned round to see Providence standing in front of his room, grinning like an idiot and clapping away as if applauding a spectacular parade.

"Hehehehe!" He laughed.

But was he really laughing at the precariousness of the moment or something else, for his eyes seemed to look coldly towards Thomas? I felt like a prey trapped in the middle of two rival lions and my only hope was that the veiled abhorrence between the two would far outweigh any interest either of them would have in me. I managed to catch Providence's eyes briefly and I saw it—reassurance. Reassurance from what? But he looked away as quickly as I caught his eyes. It was almost as if he wouldn't let himself look at me for too long so that he could concentrate on Thomas. There was unmistaken tension in the room, only Providence was laughing albeit cloaked with salient hostility.

I was confused and didn't know what to do. I dare not turn back to face Thomas' naked body yet I felt the heat emanating from him. I knew both men were staring at me and waiting for my next reaction, I could feel their lecherous eyes upon me. But at the same time there was that foreboding that I was in the middle of something far bigger than myself: two men, one naked the other fully clothed both standing their ground as equals. Without much hesitation I fled into the bedroom and quickly latched the door shut. Oh God! Oh God! Oh God! My mind kept screaming. When I closed my eyes, the twisted image of the naked Thomas and the laughing Providence frightened them open. I could clearly hear both men laughing from the other side. It didn't sound like they were laughing with each other but rather laughing on their own, the quality of each laugh ascertaining its masculinity.

Soon the house was quiet again. Their laughter had faded away and the tepid noise of the waking morning began to filter in—a truck honking in the far distance, chirping of birds, the wind whistling softly, neighbours moving about in their flats, sound from a television set. How different morning breaks in Nigeria! The cock always crows and then like clockwork, the *imam* from the mosque across the road would blare out his *"Allah Akhbar"* from the public address system, which could be heard two streets away—all these before the usual noise from traffic jams and vendors selling everything from fresh bread and fried bean balls to the morning newspapers. I closed my eyes and longed for Lagos.

I began to relax when I heard someone leave the apartment. But I wasn't sure if I would leave the room again.

Knock. Knock. Knock. Someone knocked on the door. I stared at the door frightfully and stifling a scream. I held my mouth with my hands and breathed deeply.

Knock. Knock. Knock. Just like the wall clock in the room ticked, ticked, and ticked.

"Come on, Erika." Providence's voice boomed from the other side of the door. "I know you are in there… Open up for me."

What did he want?

I remembered the look in his eyes when he stared at Thomas. They were cold and animal. Was he protecting me? Or was there a history between the two men that I was not aware of?

"Erika," he said, "I just want to talk… Thomas is gone, okay?"

I remained quiet.

"Ok!" He sighed after waiting for about a minute. "I'll have to talk through the door then."

I heard some movement from the other side. It sounded like he had walked away and then returned to the front of my door. His movements sounded subtle like a predator and I could almost feel him touching the door, caressing it. I felt a bit relieved that he was close by and at the same time I wished he wasn't behind my doors.

"James should have warned you about Tom." He said. "Hell, I should have warned you yesterday that he enjoys walking around naked sometimes…" He paused to giggle. "That mad boy loves to show off the only black thing he inherited from his black father… I've even walked in on him screwing his chick on the sofa."

He stopped then for a second and I heard him curse quietly.

"I shouldn't have said that, right?" He said. "But you have to understand that there is hardly any privacy here… doors always seem to be open here… except this one now." I heard him laugh lightly. "I saw you go out last night with James. Where did you guys go?"

I walked to the door then. I was drawn to it against my will just like I was drawn to Providence against all reasoning. I had seen a side of him that chilled me. That whole display with Thomas was like witnessing the beginnings of a battle. And yet how could I deny the strong appeal I secretly felt towards him? He was Nigerian after all. He was somebody from home and there was something soothing knowing that and feeling protected by that knowledge. I felt a need to bond with him, yet I was afraid of him and very suspicious of him as well. It was strange that I felt this way and more strange that for the first time since I met him I could admit to myself that I wanted him to like me. I wanted him to like me. If he liked me, he would not harm me. If he liked me, he would protect me. Yes, I was surely drawn to him, but I cannot say that I liked him or even wanted to like him. It seemed like I was fighting a tug of war within myself whether to open the door and let him in or keep him on the other side.

His voice had a soothing effect on me. It sounded like home, the Nigerian feel and texture of his words. Listening to him speak only made me realize that maybe I had left Nigeria in much more hurry than I should have. I was truly homesick.

"Did he take you somewhere classy?" There was scepticism in his tone.

"He took me to a night club." I found myself saying.

"Ah!" I heard him sigh. "These white boys don't know how to treat an African woman. So you met his friends then?"

"Some." I said.

"No business of mine." He said. "But did you enjoy yourself? Do you even like this white boy?"

I thought about his questions on the other side of the door that divided us and like the door, I believed that there should be a wall to divide and protect private issues. I couldn't answer him. I wouldn't. I wouldn't start pulling down the walls that housed my feelings.

"Anyway," he said after a short pause, "I have to go now or I'll be late for work. Be careful of Thomas. And James."

Those were his parting words. When I heard the front door slam shut I remembered I felt totally abandoned. When he was behind my door, I didn't want him in but now that he was gone, I suddenly wished he was nearby.

Something else worried me. Why had he warned me to be careful of James? Sam had also warned me to be careful.

No one was saying much but I was already beginning to feel very apprehensive about James. This feeling worried me. It reminded me of a time in the past when another man had been the cause of much apprehension and uncertainty… I was suddenly thinking of Uloma and the man she loved.

6

Reason to Believe

I had never seen Uloma cry before. She always seemed so strong and quick-witted, but that evening when Princess and I returned from the market we found her on the floor of the living room weeping.

She looked different, smaller and very fragile like a young child who was crying for food. Princess thrust her bag of groceries into my hands as she quickly rushed to Uloma's side. When she bent down to cradle Uloma, she gestured to me with her head. I nodded and walked quietly to the kitchen. After staying with both of them for two years already, I knew when they needed a private moment, when I was not necessarily wanted. This used to bother me in the earlier days; it still bothered me, but not as much as before.

I removed the *ugwu* leaves from the bag and placed them on the kitchen counter, the oranges I stacked in a plastic bowl and the fresh fish, I kept in the fridge. I also packed away the *garri* we bought as well as the little bag of rice. It took me less than five minutes to finish this and then I moved over to the door, so I could see and listen to what was happening in the living room.

Uloma was sitting up now on the floor, Princess sat across her and was holding her hands. There were tears in Uloma's eyes and her forehead was creased with worry.

"Pius has been missing since last night." Uloma said.

Her voiced was cracked. "I spent the whole morning looking for him."

"All is well." Princess said consolingly. "I was a little worried when you didn't show up at the salon. I thought you were only going to be gone for a short while this morning."

"He was supposed to meet me last night, but I suspected he might not come because of this impending strike the labour unions are planning."

Uloma's head turned towards the kitchen and I moved back to avoid her seeing me. I felt sorry for her as I knew how worried she was about her lover's whereabouts in those uncertain times. Pius was very involved in the labour movement. He had become more so involved after the government and the Petroleum and Gas conglomerates had once again increased the price of fuel, gas and kerosene. The price of everything went up; food, transportation, rent—everything.

The labour unions had been threatening to go on strike for over a week now if the government refused to reverse their stand and subsequently, the police had announced that any form of strike would be looked upon as illegal and anyone involved would be apprehended and arrested. There had been so much tension in Lagos. Everyone covertly supported the call for strike. Things were hard enough in the country. In the market that evening, Princess and I had bought a paint bucket-full of garri for seventy naira— it had cost thirty naira only two weeks before. It was like that with everything else, prices had doubled and even tripled in some cases. But the market had been full as it seemed everyone was trying to buy up all they could before the strike took effect and the streets would completely be deserted.

I decided to come out of the kitchen. It was getting too hot in there and I wanted to hear everything that was being said.

"Have you finished putting everything away?" Princess asked as soon as I walked into the living room.

"Yes." I said, sitting on a stool close to them.

"Why don't you go and prepare something then?" She added.

"Let her stay." Uloma said before I could protest. "There's no gas to cook anyway and the boy selling firewood hasn't passed by yet."

"So, we are back to firewood again." Princess sighed.

"Uloma, Pius will be alright." I said gently.

"How do you know?" She asked. "If he is alright, then where is he?"

I kept quiet and Princess shot me a warning look.

Just then there was a slight knock on the door and before anyone of us could say anything, Alero, one of our neighbours who lived across the street entered. Alero was the neighbourhood gossip and regular busybody. She was the harbinger of scandal and anything that did not concern her.

"Ah! You are all here." Alero began, as her eyes travelled to every corner of the room and finally rested on Uloma. "Good evening-o."

"Alero," Princess said, "I hope all is well?"

"It is well with me." Alero said. "I just came to find out if you heard of what happened to Bello and his boys."

"What happened?" Uloma asked swiftly.

I noticed the alertness in her eyes and the almost satisfied expression in Alero's own eyes.

"It's so unfortunate." Alero said, shaking her head. "I heard it happened last night..."

"What happened?" Uloma asked harshly. One could tell her patience was running thin.

"I heard the police came for him in his shop and took him away with his workers." Alero said.

"Oh no!" Uloma said.

"Yes," Alero said, "everyone knows he's active in the Labour Congress and the police have been locking up their members."

"How do you know this for sure?" Princess asked doubtfully.

"Segun said so." She answered. Segun was her brother. "You know his shop is just opposite Bello's, so he saw everything himself."

"Are you sure that was the reason Bello was taken away?" I asked. She eyed me. "Bello and his boys are always harassing people on the street and he has been linked to some robberies in the area."

"I'm only telling you what I know." Alero sighed. "Anyway, I thought it would interest you since Pius is also an active member of the Labour Congress."

"Thank you, Alero." Princess said. "Please if the boy selling firewood passes by your house tell him to come over here."

"Okay," Alero said, "I will. Good bye."

As soon as she left, Uloma sighed deeply.

"That woman," Princess said, "she can be so annoying."

"I know Pius has got himself arrested." Uloma stated. I could hear worry in her tone.

"You don't know that." I said.

"The police are arresting unionists." She said. "Before Alero came, I already had heard that… now with the arrest of Bello…"

"Seriously Uloma, you can't possibly be grouping Pius with a scoundrel like Bello?" Princess asked.

"The man is just stubborn." Uloma said. "Why does he have to be involved in this trade union thing? Why can't he leave the braveness and righteousness to others?"

"It is who he is." Princess said.

"To hell with that!" Uloma spat. "All I want for him is to marry him and have his children—that's all I want. Does he give me the time or even propose? No."

Both Princess and I remained quiet. We had heard this argument before.

"Sometimes, I just hate him." She said. "He's turning me into this nervous, bitter woman who worries all the time. One day I would get a knock on the door and the news would be delivered to me; your man is dead. It would be my father all over again."

"What?" Princess and I said together. We hadn't heard that before. Like me, Uloma hardly spoke of her father.

"My father was killed by the military some years ago." She said. "He was always protesting with the trade unions and the labour unions and he was always in and out of prison. My mother never understood it because he was not a leader but he made sure he was always in the forefront of protests along with the leaders. One day my mother sent for me and when I arrived she calmly told me that my father was dead. She had got a knock on her door early that morning and one of the unionists had informed her that he was found dead in front of one of their members' home with bullet wounds on his body. The police dismissed it as a robbery case when it was reported."

"Oh my God!" Princess cried.

"I'm so sorry." I said.

"My mother just got tired of worrying." Uloma continued. "But she never recovered from his death. I don't want to be that woman who worries after a man. I can't be that woman."

Yet she had fallen in love with a man just like her father, I thought.

We heard gunshots on the streets early the next morning. In spite of warnings of dire consequences from the government against any civil servant who didn't show up for work, people stayed at home. It was not just the civil servants; it seemed all businesses remained closed.

We heard the gunshots around 8 a.m. Princess, Uloma and I rushed to the window to stare. A bonfire had been set in the middle of the street—a commercial bus had been set ablaze. We could only imagine that the bus driver and his conductor were hoping to make a quick buck by transporting people regardless of the warning from the labour unions and all other factions. There were men, women and children on the streets, running in panic to avoid the coming police vehicle and the gun-totting rascals called policemen.

"How will I go and look for Pius now?" Uloma said. Her tears had long stopped but her resolve still remained unshaken.

"We may be able to move around in the night." Princess said.

I remained quiet as I watched the police van stop close to the burning vehicle and the men in uniform and bullet-proof vests jumped out. The street had become truly chaotic now. Some angry youths wielding machetes, broken beer bottles and sticks stood in one corner jeering at the policemen. The policemen pointed guns at the youths while in the background we could hear women screaming and pleading.

"These boys will get themselves killed." Princess said fearfully. "You can't beat bullets with sticks and stones."

"They have cutlasses too." I said.

"Even with cutlasses," Princess said, "these policemen have no moral conscience. They have no qualms in shooting these boys."

"You have your government to blame for that." Uloma said. "After all, these policemen are suffering the same thing we all are suffering and worse still, they don't get paid."

"But why kill your own?" Princess said.

"The government equips a hungry and frustrated man with a uniform and a gun and what do you expect?"

There was another gunshot. We ducked. One of the policemen had shot into the air. We heard people running outside and soon a funny smell invaded our living room at the same time that our eyes began to water and hurt like pepper had been rubbed into them.

"Tear gas!" Princess said. "Let's go into my room and stay there."

We went to her room and she gave us handkerchiefs to tie round our noses. We all sat on the floor, our backs against the bed.

Soon after, the electricity went off and so did the water, we discovered later. It seemed the government really wanted to show its might. It was a very hot day and yet no one could go outside or even open the windows for fresh air.

"I hate this country." I finally said at about noon.

"Is it because of this little thing?" Princess asked. "It will be over soon. The price of fuel will stick and what the unionists will have achieved will be yet another holiday that yielded nothing and life would go on."

"I just hate this country." I said.

"What do you want to do about it?" Uloma asked.

"One day, I would leave this Godforsaken place." I said.

"And where would you go?" Uloma asked.

"London." I said. "I would go to London. I used to live next to this girl who always travelled to London for holidays. She showed me pictures of gardens and red double-decker buses and Trafalgar Square."

Both Princess and Uloma burst out in a laugh, the first that whole day.

"Who dash you London?" Uloma laughed. "How will you get the money and visa to travel? You don't even have a passport."

"I'll save and get a passport if I have to." I said stubbornly. "I'm just tired of this country."

"Running away doesn't solve problems." Princess said.

"It doesn't." Uloma agreed. "That is why I have to find Pius. I can so easily say that I don't care; after all, we are not married, but I won't. I have to find him or at least know what has happened to him."

We were back with the Pius issue again. I forgot my dreams of travelling to London then and worried with Uloma and Princess about Pius.

✴

The streets were deserted as well the next day. There were no buses or taxis on the empty streets and everyone stayed locked inside their homes. It was difficult to know what was happening in other parts of Lagos as the electricity wasn't restored and there were no newspaper vendors on the streets either. We could not watch television, listen to the radio or get hold of newspapers. I felt trapped in those two days. I kept thinking of the conversation we had about hating Nigeria and wanting to leave for London. Maybe they were right, maybe London was too much of an ambition, if someone offered me a ride to Cameroon or Ghana, I would gladly accept and leave behind this country with all its troubles.

On the third day, people started moving about early in the morning. Words filtered that the strike had been called off as the labour union had reached an agreement with the government. That morning, electricity was restored and as soon as the lights came on, Uloma told us that she was going to the police station to enquire about Pius. We offered to go with her.

We went to Sabo Police Station first but he was not there. One of the police women there told us to go to the station on the Island, a lot of young men were being held there she said. We got there at noon. We were not the only women there. Mothers, wives and daughters were all there in search of their loved ones. For the most part, we were ignored but later that afternoon one of the policemen came around to take names and descriptions from us as well as service money, as he called it—bribe, we all knew.

"What if he's not here?" Uloma whispered to us. There was no much talking here.

"It would be brutal for them to keep us here this long if he's not here." Princess whispered back. "And they have taken all the money we have."

"If he's not here, where then could he be?" I asked.

No one answered. We continued with our silence. Soon we heard a little boy crying. He was hungry and his mother was trying to shush him.

"Woman, better quiet your boy or we go throw you commot from hia." The policeman behind the counter said harshly.

The mother pleaded with the policeman with her eyes. She wiped the tears from her son's eyes with her wrapper and when he didn't stop crying, she lifted him up on her lap and then whipped out one of her concealed breasts. She pushed the nipple into his mouth and the boy began to suckle. I looked away. The boy was at least four years old.

At 4 p.m. we were told to leave. Just like that, without warning a scrawny-looking sergeant came to the waiting room wielding a whip and barking at us to leave.

"Why now?" One woman cried. "What about our money wey una collect? I just want my husband abeg..."

"Sharrap!" The policeman shouted. "I say make una go. Come back tomorrow."

He began to whip and shove us outside. I felt smelly, sweaty bodies pressed against me as we were pushed out of the building. All this for a man, I thought. All this, because of Uloma.

"What do we do now?" Princess asked, once we were together.

"Let us go." Uloma said, quietly.

"Go where?" I asked.

"Home." She said.

Without saying anything further we left the police station. We walked home.

There was a loud knock on the door very late that night. I was already in bed, nursing my slightly swollen legs after the long walk home.

I grudgingly got up and made my way to the living room. Since I was the youngest among them, it had always been my duty to see who was at the door. We had all retired early, after returning from the police station. It seemed there was nothing to talk about. I suspected though, that we all had something to say about our treatment at the station as well as not knowing anything about Pius' unknown fate; but these things are sometimes better left unspoken.

"Who is it?" I asked when I got to the door.

"Open, it's me." A male voice said.

I recognised the voice. Quickly I unlocked the door and threw it open. Pius stood in front of me. His body was framed by the darkness outside and immediately I noticed how haggard he looked and how unkempt his hair was. There was a cut in his lower lip and both his eyes were swollen.

"Pius!" Uloma screamed.

I turned round and saw her standing in the narrow hallway that led to the bedrooms. She ran quickly, knocking me out of the way, and flung herself on Pius. He held her tightly but at the same time, I noticed he was wincing as she pressed herself tighter to him.

I shut the door and moved away to give way to the two. Princess had come out of her room as well. She was watching from the hallway. I noticed she had tied a wrapper across her breasts to cover her nightgown.

"What happened to you?" Uloma cried into his ear.

"The police came and took us away from Pa Jimoh's house." He said. "This was Sunday evening. They released some of us this evening."

"What are you doing with Pa Jimoh?" Uloma asked. "I have told you to leave those troublemakers alone."

"Pa Jimoh is not a troublemaker." Pius said as he pushed Uloma aside. "He is a great man. He fights for the rights of the people."

"Please, spare me your union babble." Uloma sighed. "Is it until you get yourself killed before you leave that bunch alone?"

"We are fighting for what is right." Pius said. "We challenge the government to make sure the right thing is done for the people."

"Charity begins at home, Pius." Uloma said. "If you want to do what's right, then start from home. Do the right thing by me. Or don't you agree?"

She looked towards Princess and me. There was that sparkle in her eyes that said we should agree with her. I remained silent, so did Princess.

"Woman," Pius said, "you should be happy to see me after the ordeal I went through, instead of attacking me like this."

"Ordeal!" Uloma spat. "You don't even know the meaning of the word. I've spent sleepless night worrying about you... I walked from Ikoyi to this house because of you. Do you know how many hours that walk was?"

"What do you want me to say?" Pius asked. "What do you want from me?"

"If you don't know by now, then maybe it is not worth it." Uloma said.

She turned away from him and left him in the living room. Pius dropped himself on the sofa and sighed deeply. I watched all this. I watched as Princess moved to join him on the sofa. She rested her hand on his shoulder and patted him softly.

"She loves you." She told him. "She's just upset right now."

"Upset with me?" Pius asked.

"Not really." Princess answered. "She was worried that something terrible might have happened to you."

"The way she goes on, someone will think I was cheating on her."

"Maybe you are." I said from where I stood. They both looked up at me. "You are cheating on her with your time. All she wants is time with you, yet you spend it with your union buddies."

"What we do is important." He said. "If not for us the government will keep doing what they like until the common man cannot survive in this country."

"We understand." Princess said. "But go to her. She needs you too."

Pius stood up. He walked to the hallway where I stood and paused for a moment before entering Uloma's room. When he shut the door, I heard her tears. Long into the night after Princess and I had retired back to bed, I could still hear her muffled tears mixed with sighs of heated passion.

7

Unbridled

Gate E55. London Heathrow.

That was where the lady who checked me in told me my plane would be as she handed me my boarding pass and my red passport. She was a pleasant lady. I could see faint traces of the strain of working over the counter on her face but she covered it up nicely with her smile. Her name tag said "Sue".

The family she had checked in before me, an overweight Yoruba man and his equally overweight wife and three preteen children, seemed to have been sent from hell specifically to torture the poor Indian lady behind the check-in counter. Between the five of them, they had fifteen bags instead of ten, which they believed they were entitled to. The ensuing drama they created was like watching a rerun of *Mind Your Language*. No matter how the lady behind the counter tried to explain to them that they were entitled to only two pieces of luggage each, both husband and wife acted like they could not understand her English. Eventually she had to call her supervisor who settled everything but not after the man had called her the vilest names he could think up. I was somewhat relieved he had said them though in Yoruba and not English. Sue had smiled through the entire tirade not knowing any better. Ignorance, they say, is bliss, but as a woman, I know there's always something intrinsic about wanting to know.

As I made my way past immigration and through the duty-free shops, my eyes hardly registered all the temptations placed strategically for travellers like me, enticing us to discard the last few pieces of change we had on us or to swipe our plastic money cards through their machine that made us forever prisoners of the system. Unlike in Nigeria, it seemed everyone in England owed money. They lived on mounting credit while in Nigeria everything was done with cash. If you had no money, you had no hope.

I looked up finally when I felt a tap on my shoulder. This woman in front of me was smiling into my face. She was looking at me with a vague sense of recognition in her eyes but I could see it fading away as I gazed at her.

"I'm sorry." She said. "You look so much like a friend of mine."

I smiled at her and noticed an infant on her right hip, straddling her while she held on to another toddler as well as her handbag and two bags from duty-free. She was obviously Nigerian.

"Jeremy," she said sternly to the toddler, "do not pull down the chocolate, okay?"

I noticed Jeremy was trying to wrestle himself free from her grip and grab the Mars bar that was on the nearest display shelf. The mother dropped the bags she was holding in order to keep him still.

"He is not normally like this." She said to me. "I don't know what devil has possessed him today—Jeremy, stop struggling around!"

I smiled at the little boy and he smiled back at me, exposing his gums and the few teeth that had managed to sprout.

"He likes you." The mother said to me. "Would you please hold on to him for me?"

She handed him to me, and surprisingly the child held on to me happily. I smiled at him again and he smiled back.

"God, you are a blessing!" The woman said. "You really

look like one of my friends. Are you related to Tokunbo Dabiri?"

I shook my head. She picked up her bags.

"The resemblance is uncanny though." She said. "I'm Tope."

"Hi Tope!" I said warmly. "I'm Erika."

"Are you also on the 10:40 flight to Lagos?"

"Yes." I answered.

"You don't mind holding Jeremy for a while, do you?" She asked as we exited the duty-free area. "I didn't know how I was going to drag him from here to the plane... His father should have been here with us but he had to leave a couple of days before us. Men! I'm sure he was happy not to be burdened with his child... Jeremy is a handful. Do you have kids of your own?"

It seemed like she couldn't stop talking. I remember meeting someone like her years before. I told her I had no children.

"Are you married?"

"No." I answered and could not miss the pitying look that momentarily crossed her face.

"Oh well," she continued, "I'm so looking forward to returning to Nigeria."

I smiled at her and tried to avoid specks from the spit bubbles Jeremy was blowing.

"I have been here for just over a month." She said. "Annual leave... after the first week, I was craving to go back home. Isn't it just crazy?"

I smiled at her to express my agreement and understanding.

"Now, when I get back, it is going to be me and the three men in my life... Jeremy Senior, Jeremy Junior and of course baby Joachim here..."

She kept talking and soon I blanked out her words. My mind could only focus on this statement; the three men in my life.

I strongly believe that there are no coincidences in this life. If you look closely enough you see all the dotted lines.

When I think of it now, I realize that there's nothing stray about strangers meeting and making a connection like I did with Tope. There must be a reason I have met this woman, my mind whispered to me. She may be useful to me somehow, if only as a trigger to help me remember. I was doing it again, consciously working out in my mind if someone I had just met was going to be useful to me now, or in the future. Am I a calculating schemer by thinking this way? Or have I been conditioned by past experiences to be this way? I don't know but as I walked down the unending aisle to Gate E55 with Tope I couldn't help but remember another stranger I had met years before. I also could not help but remember when there seemed to be three men in my life.

James. Providence. Thomas.

These three men occupied a huge part of my life. Even now I still try to make sense of everything that happened eventually. At nights when I wake up drenched in sweat with my heart beating fiercely, I remember those three men. I remember how different they all were and the terrible game my coming into their lives set in motion. I also remember how alike they were—they were men after all and there was always the underlying attitude of pride and the sick sense of ownership they lay claim to when a woman is involved.

I had been in London for weeks by now and every morning James got up early and disappeared until late evenings. Sometimes I never saw him until the next day. When we saw each other, we talked. We talked about his big plans for us—which translated to his marrying me and then filing for my papers, just like we planned when I was still in Nigeria. There was something missing, though, in all this. There was no passion involved. It was more like a business arrangement. We went out some nights but it was to the usual bar or nightclub where I met more of the people he called friends. Mostly I was like a side attraction because I was from Africa. Everyone could tell because of my accent no matter how I tried to sound English. At first it was quite upsetting hearing people ask me about Africa as if Africa were some jungle state with war and famine or that Africa were one big mass of land with no boundaries dividing the different countries. Also disturbing was the general vibe I had picked up from them that Africa's peoples are one and the same. How silly it all sounds when one listens to white people discuss Africa. I have often wondered if it ever occurred to them that an Ethiopian is as different from a Nigerian as a Briton is from an Irish. I eventually got tired of explaining to them that Africa is a continent and not a country. In all this, James simply sat back and watched while I was grilled and embarrassed by his friends. Was he enjoying this or was he also using this to discover more about me and where I came from and how my mind works?

Any time I tried to find out more about James' family he would clamp up and go into a vile mood. Slowly and effectively, boundaries were being set. And I began to see the patterns.

I was a prisoner in this house. It was quite easy to see that. I didn't know any place in London or anyone to take me around. I had no money even if I had wanted to explore London on my own and I couldn't leave James. Where would I go? I still couldn't find my passport but I knew James had it, just like I knew he took the money I brought to London with me. Most importantly, I noticed that James was finding ways to fight with me constantly. When I reflect on this now, I see it as a ploy to put me in my place and intimidate me. I often wonder if there was more to it than I presupposed.

One Saturday morning I had decided to clean up the entire house and reorganize everything. It was my opportunity to rid the bedroom of some of the nasty magazines James had stashed away in every corner and if I am truly honest, I was hoping to find where James may have hidden my passport. It took me two hours and 18 minutes to finish up and when I was done I made myself a cup of coffee and slumped in one of the dining chairs in the kitchen.

Moments later, Thomas made his way into the kitchen. He had a blanket draped round his body and my guess was that he was naked underneath. This no longer shocked me. It was clear from the groggy way he looked that he had just woken up but that didn't stop him from winking at me. I looked away.

He sniffed the air.

"That coffee smells good." He said with a yawn. "Can you make me some?"

I was taken aback by his request. It did occur to me then that he expected me to naturally acquiesce because I was a woman and it was my place to serve him because he was a man. But I was not his woman and I was under no obligation to do anything for him. It was almost as if I had no value to these men since I started living in that house. James came and went sometimes without uttering a word to me; Thomas still walked around naked most of the time and Providence… I didn't quite understand Providence. Sometimes he went into praying fits where he spoke in tongues and invoked the spirits right in front of anyone present. But there was something about him that had a calming effect on me. Unlike most men, I was not afraid of him. Even when I thought he was quite mad in his fits of Biblical righteousness. I was not afraid of him.

"Come on now." Thomas said. He sat on the opposite chair to me. "Make me some of that coffee, Erika."

"You have hands." I said. "Nothing stops you from putting the kettle on and making yourself coffee."

"Come on love, stop being a wuss." He whined. "I bet if Providence had asked you, you wouldn't mind making him a cuppa!"

I looked sharply at him. He was smiling lewdly at me with a knowing look in his eyes that made me more unsettled. What did this man mean? My first instinct was to get up and leave the kitchen but it seemed like I was fastened to the kitchen chair. From the look in his eyes, he clearly had more to say.

"It is so clear honey that you have taken a shining to the Jah-man." Thomas continued. "I reckon because he's black."

He paused and leaned closer to the table to lock eyes with me.

"Hell, I'm black too." He said. "I've got black blood running through my veins just like him. Why are you not taking a shining to me then?"

His tone was no longer pleasant but had turned slightly bitter.

"Oh, I see," he said as he leaned back on the chair, "he comes from your home country, is that it?"

He looked away towards the kettle and I remember thinking that he was trying to bait me. He wanted me to say something, either to admit or deny his accusation. I found myself doing a mental check on my actions and attitude whenever Providence was around me. Was I really any different? Was I less aloof with him than I was with Thomas or even James? Most important, if Thomas had noticed something, was it possible that James had picked up on something as well? Eventually I had to discard Thomas' wild allegation. There had been no time I had knowingly treated Providence any better than I would treat him. At least Providence didn't walk around the house naked when I was there.

"Where the hell did you put the sugar?" Thomas said. He was by the sink now, pouring water into the electric kettle.

"On the top drawer by the left with the tea bags and milk." I answered.

"Woman," he sighed, "you've turned this place around... can't say I like it, can't say I don'."

I left the kitchen. I wasn't about to spend any more time with him knowing he would only further upset me. Today, when I look back to that moment with Thomas,

I begin to understand more of what was going on in his head. He wanted me like a child craves sweets, and like a child, he wanted me for all the wrong reasons.

I was surprised to find James in the bedroom when I entered. I looked round and was stunned to find the room had been turned upside down. Clothes were on the floor, the bed I had carefully laid was in disarray, the wardrobe was strewn open and its contents scattered. It seemed like a tiny hurricane had swept through the room leaving behind chaos and disorder. James turned round to glare at me as soon as I shut the door.

"I didn't hear you come in." I said carefully.

"What the hell have you done in here?" He screamed. "Where are all my things? I can't find anything."

"If you tell me exactly what you are looking for, I can tell you where to find it." I said.

"Woman," he said sternly, "I don't need you to reorganize my things. I like it the way it was before… Do you understand me?"

I did. Clearly. "I just thought since it's our place, it would be nice to have some order in here." I said.

"It's my place!" He shouted. "What's it with you women? You move in and the next thing is you want to change everything about the man."

I couldn't believe he said that. It was his place. I had no say here. So what was I to him? What was I doing here?

I watched him scatter more things, walking from the bed to the wardrobe and back. He lifted things, discarded others and sighed through the whole process. I wondered what it was he was looking for but I really didn't care. I made for the door but his voice stopped me.

"And where the heck are you going?"

"Outside." I answered quietly.

"Yeah, just go." He sighed.

I walked down the stairs with many thoughts running through my mind, most prominently the thought of escape. I had to somehow run away from all this madness. But where would I run to? I had nowhere to go.

I walked past the kitchen and stepped outside. Children from the neighbourhood were playing in the fenced playground across the building and some of their nannies or parents were close by either conversing or sharing a smoke. The sun was out and it wasn't so cold. After a minute I rested my head on the railing and began to weep silently. This was much too hard for me. I felt so alone and trapped and what was worse, it seemed like there was nothing I could do about it.

"No need to start crying in front of everybody, sis-te." A matronly voice called out to me.

I quickly wiped my eyes and looked up. It was Bessie, the black woman that lived in the next flat. She was the first neighbour I saw the first day James brought me here, the big African woman who strained her neck from her kitchen window to catch a glimpse of me. I had heard her name called by her husband through our thin walls. I had heard her speak before and she sounded Ghanaian. I imagined that was why she pronounced her words differently.

"No man is worth a woman's tears you know." She said soothingly.

I stayed quiet. I didn't know what to say to her. She was still a stranger.

"I hear your man shout all the time." She sighed. "James—he is the man you come for, right?"

"I don't understand." I said.

"You left whatever country you come from to meet a proper British man, right?" She said. "You are from Nigeria… you sound Nigerian."

I nodded. She shook her head and looked on into the distance.

"I have seen many girls like you." She said. "You come here hoping to meet Prince Charming and then—poof—you realize things are very different in this country."

"It's not what you think." I said defensively. "I just have a headache… I wasn't crying."

"Really?" She said doubtfully. "You could have fooled me."

Just then, a little girl ran up to her and grabbed one of

her stocky legs. She must have been about three or four years old and there was no mistaking the resemblance. The child had her eyes and full lips, but unlike the mother, this child was light-skinned. Her father was white.

"Whenever you are free come and have tea with me." Bessie said as she scooped the girl into her arms and walked into her apartment.

I was having tea with Bessie that afternoon as soon as James had left the house. Her home was much like the house I lived in. It was of the same decor, the same dimensions, the same floor space, the same design. The differences were in the choice of wallpaper used—subtle cream with faint green stripes. The curtains were of rich voile, its subtleness matching the wallpaper. I could sense her touch all over the place. It wasn't exactly a perfect house, three little children saw to that, but it was a home that exuded harmony and warmth. There was a pink child's bicycle in the passage-way to the kitchen. And in the kitchen there was a red ball. In a corner, between the washing machine and the fridge, a plastic fire truck. On the walls were pictures; some were real old-fashioned black-and-white pictures with what seemed to be Bessie's Ghanaian family and there were pictures of Bessie and her children and husband, her white husband.

From the moment Bessie let me into her home, I felt like I had stepped into another world entirely. I had longed for another woman to speak to. Another African woman who was more like me and who wouldn't judge me for the choice I had made to come to England to marry a stranger so I could become one of them; a make-believe British with a red passport and a new life.

"I have always wondered when you would eventually leave that house and start getting to know your neighbours." Bessie said as she cradled a hot mug of tea close to her lips. "How do you expect to know anyone if you stay locked up in that house?"

I watched her much the same way a child would watch an adult, with awe. She was wearing one of her African print dresses with a matching headscarf. In the background, I could hear her children singing along to the music from the television programme they were watching in the living room.

"So," she said, "are you here for holiday or you are here for good?"

I felt a chill when I considered her question and its implication. What would my life be like for good? The thought of being with James for good was no longer appealing to me.

"I don't know." I said finally.

"Sis-te, that is not a good thing." She sighed. "If you don't know what you want, why don't you go back home?"

"I can't." I said quietly. There was really nothing to go back to.

"Do you want more tea?" Bessie asked.

"No, thank you." I said.

Bessie got up all the same and walked over to the kettle. She poured herself another cup of hot water and dipped a used teabag into it. After several dips she discarded the teabag in the waste bin and returned to the kitchen table where I was still sitting.

"I don't know you but I worry for you." Bessie said tensely. "I worry that you live in that house with three men and you never seem to come out. At first I thought maybe you came for Providence, he is Nigerian too, but I listen through these thin walls… You came for James."

What is wrong with James? I wanted to ask. I had been looking for someone to ask that question ever since Sam warned me to be careful of him.

"I have seen that white man with more black women than I can remember." She said, almost as an answer to my unasked question. "But you have stayed the longest. I don't know why."

"Why did you do it?" I asked.

Bessie must have sensed my evasion as she stared at me. She looked straight into my eyes and there was something almost magnetic that kept our eyes together. I felt she was searching my soul through her eyes, looking for the truth and this made me uneasy. I was not ready then to confront the truth nor was I ready to hear it in her voice or see it through her eyes. I felt shame creeping up on me and I knew no matter what I said my eyes would always speak the truth.

"Do what?" She asked.

"Marry a white man." I said. "Was it to become British?"

"No, no, no, sis-te." She laughed heartily. "I was already a British citizen before I married Nicolas. I was born in England while my parents were students here. They returned with me to Ghana when I was three years old and I moved back here six years ago. Nicolas is Romanian. He only became a British citizen after he married me."

I was speechless momentarily. It never occurred to me that an African woman could be the one to validate a white man's national identity.

"The problem isn't marrying a white man. It isn't even the motivation for marrying one." Bessie said. "The problem is men."

She looked at me intensely then and smiled. At that moment one of her sons wandered into the kitchen. Unlike his sister, he was black through and through. This was not the product of mixed parentage.

"Mummy," he said, "can I go outside and play with Terrence?"

"Make sure you stay within the playground so I can see you, okay?" Bessie said. "And make sure you wear your jacket."

"Yes, Mummy." He said before leaving the kitchen.

"I used to be married to his father." Bessie continued after he had gone. "Back in Ghana. He used to hit me all the time. He complained about everything. One day

I was too fat, the next day I was lazy. I did everything to please him… I thought if I loved him enough he would change."

There was sadness in her words as she spoke to me. "We are the chameleons." She said reflectively. "Men don't change especially not for women. But women always make adjustments and changes to suit men. The day Kwesi hit me in front of our child, I packed my things and I left him."

Chameleons. I could understand that. Up until that moment I had been constantly adapting to situations dictated by the men in my life. It started with my father and gradually as I matured into a woman I had allowed men to define who I was.

"Why are you telling me all this?" I asked.

"If you find your man," she said, "you wouldn't have to change who you are or even try to change him."

A silent moment passed between us then. But just as sudden, it was like someone switched back on the noise and I could hear the television from the living room. The voices of the children playing outside filtered in and I could hear my heart beat.

8

Snakes and Ladders

I once thought I was in love. If love was sweaty palms and armpits, giddy feet and short breath then it must have been love I felt the first time Gerald Okoro graced me with his eyes. Two years had passed since when I first saw that family portrait with his parents and sister, Tiffany. I recall thinking how good-looking he was with his dark, mysterious, bespectacled eyes. It was two years since my aunt cut all my hair off and left me looking like a defeated bald ostrich, but my hair had grown back and I was no longer afraid to walk the street and face the constant jeering from the other children. It had been two long years.

I would never have come face to face with Gerald had it not been for his sister, Tiffany. She remained, in a strange way, my friend over those two years. We were both the same age and I found out that she secretly despised her overbearing mother much as I disliked my aunt. Tiffany had been horrified when she saw me the next day with no hair at all and she lamented that her handiwork had been brought to ruins. This seemed to be all that mattered to her, not how I felt. But we didn't see much of each other after that day. She returned to boarding school, but some odd weekends I would spy her from the window of her bedroom or from the balcony of her home. It occurred to me then that maybe she needed to distance herself from me since I was now bald and she had no more use of me as her dress-up doll.

This conviction of mine was further enhanced after she returned for the Christmas holiday and my hair had grown back enough for me to plait it. She beckoned to me to come to her house that first weekend when she returned for the holidays when she noticed me sitting in front of the gate to my compound. She was on her balcony wearing a red-chequered pinafore dress. I shook my head as the outcome of my last visit to her house had caused me untold anguish that was still very fresh in my memory. I could almost sense her stubbornness when she still beckoned to me to come. I continued to refuse. My aunt was in the house and she could call for me any time. What excuse would I give her if I missed her call? Secretly though, I wanted to run off to meet Tiffany. I wanted to be a part of her rich world again and maybe dream even for one moment that my life was different.

"Why wouldn't you come to my house when I asked you to?" Tiffany stood by me with her hands on her hips and her face masked in a scowl. It seemed she had decided to meet me at the front of my house when it was obvious I wouldn't come to her.

"I can't visit you." I explained. "My aunty is at home and she would be crossed if I wandered off."

"That is not a good excuse." She sighed.

Looking at her face then with the anger that contorted it, I realized that she was not to become a beautiful woman later on in her prime. Her skin may have been smooth, her hair relaxed and styled elegantly, her eyes made-up lightly and her lips shining from the lip-gloss, but she was not beautiful like I had imagined her to be. She was pretty but there was a hardness to it all.

"I'm sorry." I said. "But my aunty will be calling for me any minute now…"

"How come I have never seen you wearing any of the clothes I gave you?" She asked cutting me off.

Not for the first time her sudden change of topic had thrown me off guard with not enough time to say something sensible.

"You really are daft sometimes." She added after waiting for a response from me. "I only asked a simple question."

I wanted to tell her to go to hell. But I didn't. The truth was that when my aunt had discovered the clothes she had threatened to send me back to the village if she discovered the clothes were stolen. Once I told her they were cast-offs given to me by Tiffany the day she relaxed my hair, my aunt seized the dresses and that Sunday and every following Sunday her daughter wore them to church.

"Anyway," Tiffany continued, "I have some more clothes for you at home. Come and pick them up."

"I can't." I said. "I really can't come with you this time."

She actually stamped her feet and made a snarling noise from deep within her throat. For a second I thought I saw tears creep up to the surface of her eyes but she looked away abruptly.

"I hate you." She said coldly.

I was quiet. I did not understand this girl. I never was sure if she wanted me as a friend or as someone she could use for her amusement. In a way, I had always felt pity for her. Even now.

"I hate everybody." She continued.

"I'm sorry." I said quietly.

"I wanted to go, too." She said fiercely as she swung round to face me. "I wanted to go, too."

"Go where?" I asked in my confusion. What was she babbling about?

"England." She said. "Gerald is leaving tonight. He's going to Cambridge."

When she mentioned his name I instantly recalled his face in the picture. And then images of picturesque London filled my head once again.

"He's going and I will be left here alone with her..." She said solemnly.

"With whom?" I asked.

"With my mother." She said with venom in her words.

"She's jealous of me and that's why she hates me."

I didn't understand this and I wasn't ready to find out anything more. It was strange to me that a girl from such a privileged home who lacked nothing and travelled abroad at least once every year could be unhappy and even hate her mother. She had no right to be unhappy! I could understand why anyone in my position would be unhappy but certainly not a girl like Tiffany Okoro. I was happy when I heard my aunt call out for me.

"I have to go inside now." I told her. "My aunty is calling me."

She said nothing to me in return but slowly walked away. That was the last time we spoke to each other during that Christmas holiday. I saw her some other days with her other friends—those girls that looked like her and acted like her with their made-up faces and expensive, grown-up dresses. I caught glimpses of her sometimes when she went out with her mother or when she gleefully sat with her father behind one of their chauffeur-driven cars. And yet, she was lonely and depressed.

We didn't have another intimate moment until nearly two years later. That was when Gerald came back home. I was 16 then and so was Tiffany. It was yet another Christmas holiday and it seemed Tiffany felt charitable towards me again. This time she was the one who came knocking at my door. I was stunned when I saw her standing in front of me holding a Christmas hamper and smiling widely.

"What are you doing here?" I whispered worriedly.

"I've come for you." She said excitedly.

"Are you crazy?" I whispered back. "You have to leave here... my aunty is at home."

"It doesn't matter." She said. "You are coming with me."

"Who is at the door, Ngozi?" My aunty shouted from the kitchen. "And what are you still doing there?"

"Please go." I pleaded with Tiffany.

"Are you deaf?" My aunt's voice called out loudly. "I

said who is at the door?"

She leaned out of the kitchen so she could spy. Just then, Tiffany stepped forward and smiled at her. I thought I was surely going to pass out.

"Good afternoon ma!" Tiffany said looking her straight in the eye with that superior smirk on her face.

"Ah, Tiffany how are you?" My aunt greeted her.

"I'm very well." Tiffany responded.

"And your mother, how is she?" My aunt asked. By now she had stepped out fully from the kitchen and was wiping her wet hands on the wrapper tied round her waist.

"She is fine." Tiffany said. "She said I should bring this for you."

Tiffany showed her the hamper and I noticed how my aunt's eye lit up in greed. That was the first and only hamper we got that Christmas.

"Oh, thank your mother for me." My aunt said as she grabbed the hamper. "I will have to come and thank her myself this evening."

By now my cousin, Chioma, had come out from the living room and was staring from the corridor. She was a year younger than I but we never got along. She eyed Tiffany openly and then went back to the living room.

"My mum said I should tell you that she needs to borrow Ngozi for a few hours." Tiffany lied.

"What for?" My aunt asked suspiciously. The smile on her face was suddenly gone and she cast her evil eye on me. "Why would she want her?"

"One of our maids is sick and had to go home." Tiffany said easily. "We need an extra hand to scrub some of the floors and help clean out the storeroom."

I was amazed at how easy it was for her to lie. I looked at my aunt again and noticed that the tense look on her face had relaxed a bit.

"I see," my aunt said, "that will be no problem. Ngozi can follow you as you are leaving."

"Thank you, ma." Tiffany replied.

"Tell your mother that she can stay as long as she wants

until the work is done, okay?"

"I will tell her." Tiffany replied.

I watched this little drama with wonder. I had always believed my aunt had a sixth sense in knowing when she was being manipulated but this girl had her wrapped round her fingers. My heart was beating fiercely and I thought that any minute from now my aunt would discover the deception but minutes later I was out the door with Tiffany and soon we were across the street.

Tiffany burst out in a choking laugh as soon as we got to her doorsteps.

"That was funny." She laughed. "I couldn't believe she believed that story."

"Who taught you to lie like that?" I asked, not quite comfortable with this new side of her.

"That wasn't lying." She said. "That was acting. After all we are women; it is what we do best... Use what you have to get what you want."

"Did your mother really send that hamper over to my house?" I asked.

"No." She answered.

"What if my aunty comes over to thank her this evening?" I asked worriedly.

"She wouldn't meet her and even if she does my mum would be so confused she would think she sent one over in error." Tiffany answered. "We get hundreds of these hampers every year from people seeking my father's favour and spend half the time giving most of them away anyway... I have five already in my room for me alone."

I can't remember if I was impressed or jealous.

"So what do you want from me this time?" I asked. After all we hadn't spoken for close to two years.

"My brother is back." She said. "I want you to meet him."

And she threw the door open to let us into the house. Much had changed. It was even more beautiful than I remembered. The furniture had changed as well as the positioning of the new majestic sofas. Even the pictures on the walls had changed. There was a new family portrait with all of them now looking older and more dignified. Tiffany was in a silk off-the-shoulder peach gown with a pearl necklace round her neck. She had grown some breasts but mine were still bigger. Gerald was no longer wearing glasses and had a regal look. I felt my heart skip several beats.

"Let's go to his room." Tiffany said grabbing my hand and pulling me. It all felt like *déjà vu* to me. I remembered my first time in her house and how she dragged me to her room.

I followed her without complaining. Instead of going up the stairs, she led me through a corridor past another parlour and finally, to a door that opened up into a lavish apartment. It was a big room with a king-size bed in one corner and a sofa that faced a huge screen television on top of an oak shelving unit. The room was rugged all round and the wood used for the huge wardrobe matched with the other wooden furniture items in the room. There was a huge picture of Gerald above the bed.

"Gerald," Tiffany called out, "Gerald... I wonder where he is."

My eyes darted from corner to corner, trying to take in as much as I could within the few minutes I believed I had. It never dawned on me that I would ever be in the same place that Gerald slept.

"You have to wait here." Tiffany said. "I'll go look for him."

She dashed out and I was left alone. I didn't know what to do, whether to keep standing or find somewhere to sit. I wanted to touch his bed and his clothes and go through his wardrobe, but I didn't.

"Who are you?" A male voice asked.

I spun round to face Gerald. He had a towel round his waist and his body was still slightly wet. I noticed a trail of water that crawled from his chest slowly down to find a resting place on his navel. It seemed he had come from the door behind him, which I guessed was his bathroom.

Every room in this house had its own private bathroom Tiffany had once told me. He was looking curiously at me and I stood speechless.

"You must be that girl Tiffany talks about sometimes." He said with a smile. "How did you find my room?"

"Tiffany brought me here." I said nervously. "She left to look for you."

"I see." He smiled playfully. "Turn around unless you want to see me naked."

I turned round and instinctively closed my eyes, but I heard all the movements he made. I knew when his towel came off, I knew when he walked to his wardrobe, and I knew when he slipped into his trousers. I heard it all and remember thinking of only one thing: I wanted to run away from there.

"You can turn around now." He said after a short while.

I didn't. I was much too aware of his eyes on me.

"So what is your name then?" He asked.

Before I could answer him the door to the room flew open and Tiffany entered. She stared at me for a second before she looked over my shoulder at her brother.

"I was looking for you." She said to him.

"I was taking a shower." He replied.

"So you've seen him." She said to me. "Let's go to my room, I have something to show you."

She grabbed my hand again and dragged me out of Gerald's room but not before I had looked back once more at him and noticed with excitement that he was still looking at me. As she led me through the passageway that took us away from Gerald's room and up the flight of stairs to her bedroom, I could not quite get his smile out of my head. I had memorised every detail of his face from the dimple in his cheeks when he smiled to the birthmark under his left eye.

Desire is such an overwhelming emotion, but I have learnt that desire is an instinctive emotion that only needs little pressure before one yields. A baby cries. A mother feeds it. She instinctively knows what the baby wants and the baby knows how to get what it desires. I was intrigued by Gerald because he had awakened in me something I believed was dead. There was a burning desire within me and maybe, just maybe he could quench it.

I have always been suspicious of men. I even believed I hated them. So why, then, was I so enraptured by Gerald Okoro? Two years earlier he was nothing to me but a boy and now he was a man. The first brief encounter with him a week ago revealed that much to me. His voice was a deep baritone and a faint moustache defined his upper lip. I had allowed myself to dream childishly that he was the one who had requested Tiffany to bring me to his den because he wanted to see me. I knew this was not the case however, but I allowed my imagination to wander.

As for Tiffany I really began to think she was indeed a troubled child. Her erratic behaviour and impetuosity seemed to increase the closer I got to her, which was pretty close judging by the circumstance—who would have imagined that a spoilt rich girl would want to hang around me? She found a way to get me to come to her house almost every day, which entailed constantly lying to my aunt who was already becoming rather suspicious, but she always seemed to let me go anyway if it meant I would be subjected to menial labour.

The more I saw of Tiffany, the more I realized that her confessed malignity for her mother could be measured on a parallel with the blind adoration she had for her father. She never stopped talking about him. Eventually I got tired of listening to her and when she spoke I would fantasize about Gerald.

Some days while I was in her room, he would come in briefly to say something to her or drop something there and each time he would smile at me and I would shyly look away and pray he did not hear the giggle that almost always escaped me. Sometimes, I felt strange tingles in different places—my belly, my feet and my heart. It was a hotness, like a sudden sunburn. My heart would race, even though I was sitting still and trying my best not to look at him. And then one day I was left alone with him.

It started off like any other day. Tiffany had come for me that afternoon and not long after we got to her room she was showing off her new designer wristwatch her father just bought for her. It wasn't long after that Gerald came in to inform her that she was expected to meet with their mother at Ikoyi.

"I don't want to go." Tiffany protested.

"Stop this." Gerald said sternly. "Mum is expecting you and the driver is waiting in the car for you."

I watched the two siblings, feeling very uncomfortable witnessing this subtle family face-off. Eventually I noticed Tiffany's shoulders slump and I knew she had conceded.

"You have to go now." She said to me.

"You can stay." Gerald said to me. "I don't mind, really!"

Tiffany looked at him for a moment and then at me before she sighed. What could she have been thinking? I felt an urgency that moment. It felt very much like a battle of wits between the two was taking place. Who would have the upper hand? Who had the stronger will power?

But why this? What interest could Gerald possibly have in me? Why was it important that I stay behind? All these questions passed through me in no particular order and strangely, I felt special then. These two people battled to have me on their side. I was secretly curious to find out who would claim me. I knew whom I wanted. I closed my eyes and made a wish.

"Whatever." She hissed. "Please leave, I have to dress up."

I stumbled out of her bedroom and to my surprise Gerald took my hand and led me down the sprawling stairs to his room on the ground floor. The experience walking down the stairs with him was very different from all the time Tiffany had led me up and then down these very stairs. I tried counting the steps in my head but I couldn't; instead I felt like I was floating down a long ladder and had his hand to guide me. He said nothing to me until we were inside and he had locked the door with its key.

"Do you want something to drink?" He asked.

I shook my head. It was almost like I had forgotten how to speak. Why had he locked the door with the key?

"Are you afraid of me?" He asked mildly.

"No." I answered timidly.

"OK!" He said. "Tell me about yourself."

He propped himself on the bed and gestured for me to join him. I sat by the foot of the bed instead with only one half of my buttocks making contact with the mattress. I was as nervous as a rabbit and as much as I tried to focus on what he was saying to me, I was also trying to understand why he wanted me here with him.

"I see you looking at me all the time." He teased.

"I see you looking at me too." I said quietly but nervously.

"I like you." He said moving closer to me.

I like you. I felt myself swooning to his words like a drunk. I felt his hands on my shoulder, then his hot lips smouldering my neck. I felt the tingles and the pricks; I felt hot breath and hands touching me in places. I became congested and stopped breathing at one point. Movements, touches, noises, hands, feet and clothes seemed to spiral out of my control. It was as if time did not exist. The only thing I would not forget, though, was when I felt his welcome intrusion in me and when he exclaimed, "I am not your first!"

I am not your first!

He had said this as a statement of fact. It was not said out of shock or surprise or even contempt. It was just an acknowledgement. But I am sure that somewhere in the recesses of his mind he must have wondered how a simple girl like me would have experienced that kind of passion between my thighs before. Like other men he was curious to know, but I was not telling. We never spoke about it again. There are some things best kept as secrets.

I have often wondered if my life would have taken a different course had I not met Gerald that first time in his room. But I would still have been thrown out of my uncle's home; I would still have met Princess and she would have helped me and I would have ended up in London with James. That is destiny.

So what happened next must have been fate. Or could it have been my stupidity and carelessness? There is a common saying in Nigeria that you don't bite the finger that feeds you—but I did. I started seeing less of Tiffany and more of Gerald, sneaking off secretly to meet him. He showed me a back entrance to his quarters through the backyard and those days when my aunt was not at home and I had nothing better to do, I would find my way to Gerald's room. The first time, I was scared that someone would find me out but nothing had happened, and after a few more times I was totally relaxed doing this.

Tiffany became suspicious when it seemed I suddenly was never available for her. One day she cornered me on the street. I was returning from Madam Goodwill's where I had gone to buy some soft drinks for my aunt.

"I don't see you these days." She accused, blocking my entrance to my compound.

"Hi Tiffany!" I said. "My aunt is waiting for me inside please."

"You didn't answer my question." She pressed.

"What question?" I asked.

"Clara tells me that she has seen you with Gerald." She said accusingly. Her eyes held mine challengingly. I could not look away.

"That's a lie." I said weakly. I felt a sudden need to use the toilet.

"What were you doing with my brother?" She accused

brazenly. "I will find out, you know!"

"I didn't do anything." I said worriedly. "My aunty is calling me... I have to go." I squeezed through the gate and left her standing there.

As a child or young adult without privileges, the experience of impending doom is so real that it is almost tangible. I was terrified of Tiffany finding out what I was doing with her brother and was more terrified of what she could do with that knowledge. I was so scared I could not sleep at night.

At sixteen I was acutely aware that what I was doing with Gerald was wrong. He was twenty and much more mature and worldly than I was. I did go to church and Bible study classes some Sundays, so I knew that my body was a temple. But my temple had long been desecrated and it had nothing to do with Gerald. I have since come to realize that it was as much my choice what happened between us, as it was Gerald's pleasure. It was a dangerous game we were playing and I could see he relished it completely.

He came up with a signal, a rather simple one really. On the days he wanted me to come over, he would walk past my compound and drop white gravel he had picked up from his house in front of my gate. He only did this if he knew I was sitting on my balcony and watching. Two pieces of gravel meant he was not alone in the house but I could come. Three or more pieces meant he was practically home alone. After dropping the gravel he would slowly trace his steps back to his house using the backyard.

I was nervous about it. What if someone saw me?

"You just have to be careful." He said. "If anyone asks, just say you are meeting with Taffy."

We met like this twice a week for three weeks. And soon the excitement wore off for me; it was replaced by pure dread. What if we were discovered? And I began to see the resemblance between Gerald and Tiffany... not their physical similarities—they hardly shared any—but the similarity in the way I felt when I was with them. Tiffany used me as a tool for her amusement. It never seemed to bother me then, but I can't say I got much satisfaction when I was with her. I can't say I got satisfaction from Gerald either. Even though I didn't know what satisfaction meant, something was certainly not right.

Something was certainly not right one fateful evening as I snuck out through the backyard after my private moments with Gerald. It wasn't even five o'clock and the clouds had suddenly turned dark. It was a heavy wind and I knew it was going to rain. I hate rain, as surely as I hate snakes. I thought I caught a glimpse of Tiffany as I manoeuvred my way round the bushes at the back of the house. I thought I saw her by the rear window in the living room; she had her yellow flower dress on. I looked back in panic but only noticed the voile curtain fluttering from the effect of the strong wind.

By the time I got to my front door, I was already a little wet from the light drizzle. I adjusted my dress, smoothing it with my palms down my body before I opened the door. Standing in front of me was my aunt. She seemed taller and fiercer than I could ever remember seeing her and I thought I could see fire in her eyes.

"*Ebe ki je, Ngozi?*" She demanded.

I was tongue-tied and too afraid to speak. I shook uncontrollably.

"Ngozi!" She shouted.

"Yes, ma." I muttered.

"Can't you answer me?" She said with her hands on her hips. "*Ebe ki je?*"

"I—I was with Tiffany." I lied

"Asi!" She screamed. *Liar.* "So you have not been with a man?"

"No, ma." I cried hopelessly. I knew she knew I was lying.

"*Ebe ki je, Ngozi?*" She repeated.

"I was with Tiffany—"

Before I finished my statement I felt her hard bony hand on my face, followed by a continuous rain of blows from both her hands. When I tried to shield my face from the assault I felt her drag me by the hair and pull me towards her room. I was screaming. She was shouting and cursing. It thundered loudly outside.

"Aunty, please." I begged. "Aunty… please…"

"Shut your mouth." She spat back. "First it was your hair… we would see today… Uche, bring me the dried pepper."

Uche was my other cousin, her son. I noticed him from the corner of my eye standing by the doorway of her room. He was holding the transparent plastic container where she usually put the blended dry chillies. He dropped this by her bed and jumped back to watch me. I pleaded with him with my eyes as heavy tears rolled from them. My aunt pinned me down. It felt like her entire weight was concentrated on the knee that held me still to the floor. And then like a skilled fisherman scaling the fins off fish, she undressed me.

"Aunty… *biko…biko*" I cried and pleaded.

She got off me and ordered me to lie on my back and spread my legs. I obeyed, knowing what was coming next. My aunt had threatened me with this many times in the past, graphically detailing what she would do to me if she suspected I was sleeping around with men. I closed my eyes as I felt her finger slip inside me to examine me. It felt wriggly and foreign. I then heard her cry out.

"Ngozi…Ngozi…Ngozi!"

She grabbed the jar of pepper, opened it and stuck her fingers into it. I watched in pure horror. Everything in the room seemed to dissolve into the background; it was just those fingers and me. I tried to get up but she slapped me down and parting my legs with one of her knees, she stuck her peppered thumb inside me.

My screams must have been heard in the entire neighbourhood despite the sound of thunder that competed to be heard. My body must have fought back instinctively because I can't remember doing so. I pushed, scratched and struggled to be let loose. I registered the bewildered look in my aunt's eyes when she realized the newfound strength in me. I remember looking at my nails briefly and seeing the scrapes of flesh buried underneath them. I must have scratched her because there was a line of blood on her neck. I was crying and burning inside… I was surely going to die from this pain.

"You attacked me!" My aunt said baffled. "Ngozi, you made me bleed… You… you slapped me!"

I was dying. I was burning up. I understood nothing of what she was saying.

"You attacked me in my house in front of my children." She was saying. "No… No… you cannot live here anymore…"

I ran out of the room and into the bathroom. There was a bucket of water by the tap. I squatted down and used my hands to scoop water over my private part. I cried. My head was filled with so many things. I thought about my mother. I had a mother, too. She would never do this to another human being. Why was this happening to me? Why was I so cursed?

I heard a loud bang on the bathroom door that made me jump.

"I want you out of my house." My aunt shouted from the other side. "Get out of my house… you hear me!"

I left my uncle's house that evening and I never went back.

I have often wondered why my uncle never came looking for me. I also wondered about Gerald. Did he go up to my gate the next day and drop his gravel in hope that I would come meet with him for our little intimate moments?

9

Borderline

Brixton was very cosmopolitan to my inexperienced eyes. There was more life here and more people. People here walked very fast, as if they were hurrying to an appointment, very much like the people on Broad Street, the business district in Lagos. I was fascinated by this, as well as the endless cobblestones on the walk- paths. But soon, after my fascination had worn off and I had managed to buy all I needed, I became suddenly conscious of the time and worried that James would get back before I did.

I heard Bessie sigh when I looked at my watch. It was 5:45 p.m. and it would take us at least thirty minutes to get back to the house by bus. It was Bessie's idea that we visit the African shops in Brixton. She wanted to show me another side of London that I had not seen before. It sounded like a good idea when she mentioned it. I was dying to get out of the house. I also needed to buy some fresh vegetables, chillies and some nutmeg, which I had run out of.

"Why do you keep looking at your watch?" She finally asked.

"I need to get back before James does." I said.

"Why?" Bessie asked.

"I just have to be home." I said. "He may need something to eat or need me to do something for him."

"Something like what?" Bessie probed. "If he's hungry

he can always look inside the refrigerator and use the microwave. He is not a child, sis-te."

I wanted to say something back, but there was nothing to say. I was afraid she was right. I had been at James' beck and call ever since I arrived in England. If he wanted something, I was there to give it to him. I was always in the house, waiting for him to return. Never questioning.

We stopped at the bus stop. It was full. There was nowhere to sit, so we stood, huddled together with the other commuters. There were two buses parked in front, picking passengers, but they were not the one we wanted. Bessie said we needed to look out for bus 73.

"I know he is your man," Bessie said suddenly, "but you have to be able to do certain things for yourself, without being constantly afraid."

"I'm not afraid." I lied.

She waved my comment off. "Of course you are afraid of him." She said. "You need to be a little more independent. As a woman, you can't be too accessible to a man. I'm like this with Nicolas and he respects me more."

I wanted to tell her then that her situation with Nicolas was different from mine with James. James had the upper hand—he was British, he worked. I depended on him for money. In her case, she was a British citizen. It was as simple as that. While she had the ability to be inaccessible to her man, I didn't.

Bus 73 arrived. We joined a small queue. Before we entered, we presented our bus pass to the driver. I was still very impressed with this transport system—I couldn't quite get over it. In Nigeria, you had to equip yourself with the correct fare before fighting for room in the bus.

"What are you good at?" Bessie asked, once we were seated.

"I don't know." I answered. "I don't have a degree or anything like that."

"I don't mean that." She said. "There must be something you enjoy doing that can fetch you some money."

I thought real hard. Princess had taught me how to

plait and braid hair and I used to help her out sometimes in her beauty shop when she was a girl short. I became quite good at this and I told Bessie.

"Really?" Bessie said excitedly. "You are wasting your talent doing nothing. Sis-te, people pay a lot for hand labour in this country and finding a good African hair stylist is rare."

I was sceptical and unsure of my ability. Bessie heard nothing of it.

"Sis-te," she said squeezing my forearm to get my attention, "in them salons, even the really cheap ones, women are paying as much as ten pounds to have their hair braided. If you charge six or seven pounds you can make some good money and not have to wait on your man to provide you with every penny you need."

I saw her point, but it wasn't as if I had a shop of my own or even had money to set up a business like that. Most important, I didn't know anyone who would trust me with her hair.

"I will let you plait my hair when we get home." She said. "If it's that good, I will show it off to my Ghanaian friends, okay? And you don't have to worry, you stay in that house alone most of the time, we ladies can always come over when we need our hair fixed."

The thought of this thrilled me, but only for a moment. I was more concerned about getting home before James did. I was in a constant state of apprehension until the bus stopped at Belham Close.

"Go ahead." Bessie said, indicating that I could leave her behind. She never walked fast, always taking her time as she moved around. It was almost as if she believed that there was no hurry in life.

"Thank you." I said, picking up speed. "I will come later and do your hair for you, okay?"

I was panting by the time I got to my door. Taking deep breaths, I dropped my shopping bag on the ground and searched my handbag for my key to the flat. Just as I was about to slot it in, the door flung open. James stood in front of me.

"Where have you been?" He asked.

"I... I was out, shopping." I said, breathless. "You scared me, James."

"Shopping!" He snarled. "Who with?"

"Bessie." I said. "You know, our neighbour."

He looked at me. His eyes squeezed up, their green becoming darker. I heard him take in air, his chest heaving up and outwards with the effort. I waited for the reprimand, but instead he stepped aside, giving me room to pass. With my head cast down, I picked up my bags and entered the hallway.

"I don't want you spending any more time in that house... or with that woman!"

James, of course, was referring to Bessie's house and Bessie. Bessie had become a real friend as the weeks and months ran by. She had a part-time job that took her away most of Saturdays and Sundays and a couple of hours during the week but she spent a whole lot of time at home with her kids when they were back from school or the childminders. I spent whatever time I could with her.

It was better than staying in that house alone when the men had all gone out. It was certainly better than watching Thomas bring in his women from time to time or having to endure the noise they produced while in his bedroom. It got to a point when I believed the rumpus they made was intentional, to get my attention. It had its patterns. With white girls he was more discreet, almost quiet. But when he came with a black woman or a woman who was mixed race like himself, there was an effort to make a show for me. And then there was Providence who burnt my ears with his stories of woe and the visions of God he claimed to have. He also always wanted to talk about the things he remembered most about Nigeria. I could not quite reconcile his two sides though. When he spoke of God he seemed to be somehow on a philosophical high with his eyes wide open and his arms stretched out in an orchestrated demonstration, but when he spoke of Nigeria I saw a different picture. He spoke of the women, booze and the partying he enjoyed while he was still there and confessed to missing it all.

I was in the hallway that led to the kitchen and the staircase. James was taking off his jacket as he spoke to me and his face, carrying the burden of his entire day plus the greenness in his eyes, was harshly fixed on me. Before, I would have been afraid if he gave me a direct order like he just did, but not that day. I was tired of all that. I was also changing. He must have noticed.

"I mean it this time." He said to stress his point. "I don't appreciate your spending time with that woman."

"James, she's harmless and the only friend I have here." I said.

"What do you mean only friend?" He asked. "I have loads of friends you can hang around with... Sam seems to like you... and—"

"Bessie is more like a sister to me." I said. "Your friends are... *your* friends, James."

"She's not a good influence, believe me." James said, his voice taking up a hard tone. "There's too much black in her... some of the guys around here believe she indulges in juju. You can't say you haven't noticed all those native beads she wears. Even her husband is afraid of her. He can't seem to control her."

"Her husband doesn't need to control her, James," I said, "because he respects her. For heaven's sake, juju!"

Silence.

"I'm just saying." James said eventually. His eyes had turned icy even though he managed an unconvincing smile. He touched my chin and his fingers felt very cold against my skin.

"I am black too, James," I whispered, "in case you haven't noticed."

"You are different, okay?" He said. "I don't want you to

become her… I liked you the way you were before." Before
I met Bessie I thought—powerless.

He kissed me on the lips before he made his way into
the living room to catch up with the football match that
was about to begin on the television. I looked into his eyes
and saw the hardness in them that dared me to challenge
him again. I stood still, alone and visibly upset. I can't say
I didn't see that coming, it had been apparent the moment
I realized that without James, I could still do something
for myself; Bessie had let me see this.

I heard a roar from the living room and I sighed.
They were all there; James, Thomas and Providence. And
James had one of his other friends over as well. Eugene,
I think his name was. They all were enjoying their silly
game of football with their beers and their hypnotised eyes
glued to the television set while I was left thinking how I
would continue my friendship with Bessie without James'
intrusion.

I made my way into the kitchen and put on the kettle.
Why I did that, I don't know. It wasn't as if I needed tea
or wanted hot water for any particular reason, I just had
to do something with my hands. I opened the fridge and
slammed it shut almost immediately as well. I paced round
for a bit before I reluctantly sat down in resignation by the
kitchen table. I felt trapped. There was simply no way I
could do away with Bessie just like that. She had become
a good friend and it was because of her that I was able to
make some little money. Two months had gone now since
I did her hair. She had loved the Ivorian braids I did for
her that evening and soon her friends started trooping in.
It was hardly a business. The most I saw was maybe four
of her chatty friends in a week but mostly it was usually
one or two. But it was something. I was able to start saving
some money of my own.

"Useless game, man!" Providence said as he entered
the kitchen. "Chelsea is not my team anyway, neither is
Newcastle… What's the matter woman?"

He propped himself on the seat facing me and lit a

cigarette. I looked away. I was in no mood for him that afternoon and I was tired of being referred to as "woman" as if I had no name of my own. James did this some days and now both Providence and Thomas had picked up on it and it seemed they all had forgotten I had a name. Why was it difficult to call me by my name? Did they think that by calling me Erika—which wasn't even my real name— that I would assume the same status as them—an equal? Or was this a way to remind me that I was not a man and would not be addressed as an individual?

"Talk to me," Providence continued, "I know something bother you when you sit like that with your face all squeezed up."

I took a deep breath and made to stand up but felt an invisible force push me back down. I had nowhere to go.

"I hear what James tell you." He said in a playful whisper. "Is that why you fretting like this? Talk to me woman!"

"God, leave me alone." I sighed deeply.

"Don't use His name in vain, woman." He said raising his eyes up to the ceiling. "Didn't your mother teach you nothing?"

"Erika," I said harshly, "that's my name—or you can call me Ngozi since you have no problem pronouncing it."

"Okay," he smiled, "this 'woman' business upsets you… I'm sorry, Ngozi. So talk to me."

I eyed him but only momentarily. It would have been so easy to let loose my tongue—but not to him. I had so many feelings pent up inside that screaming at the top of my lungs would have been a better option.

"What do you want, Providence?" I asked.

"I want you to let me in." He said suggestively, in a whisper. "You have to trust me, I can help you."

"How?" I asked. I knew I shouldn't have said anything to encourage talk like that, but I wanted to know what he had on his mind.

"How long now have you been here?" He said.

"Nine to ten months." I said, doing a mental calculation.

"And you're still waiting for him?" He said in a low tone.

I was afraid where this conversation was leading and was more concerned that James wouldn't hear us. But he had a point. What was I waiting for, really? Over the past months I had discovered a few truths about James like the lies he had fabricated about his family over the Internet and his inheritance, which never existed. Yet I waited. Going back to Nigeria was not an option for me. Even if I had my passport, my visa had long expired and the thought of starting over again back home was not appealing to me. I knew others had come before me to England and had made some successes with their lives. Yet when I thought like this and looked at Providence who had been here longer than I had, cold fear and uncertainty would grip me.

"What are you trying to say?" I asked also in a hushed tone with my eyes darting quickly to the door.

"I'm saying you need a friend like me around you." He answered. "You have to let me in… you can trust me, you know."

Could I indeed? I got up and walked to the sink to pour myself a cup of tea. I did that so I could have my back to him and he wouldn't be able to read my face and know that he had planted an idea in my head. I was not quite sure what that idea was, but I was aware of some possibilities, not the least leaving this house and James.

I had to juggle a number of emotions and conflicts all at once, as I made tea. There was the issue of not seeing Bessie, which I knew I was not going to abide by. Then there was James and the total feeling of suffocation I was going through with him as well as the ever-enclosing wall of losing my identity and sense of self. I also had to deal with the fact that I was now an illegal alien in London.

"You hear what I'm saying?" Providence said softly. He had crept up behind me to whisper into my ears and I could feel the outline of his body behind me as well as his breath on the back of my neck.

I was slapped out of my thoughts and felt panic at his closeness.

"What are you doing?" I whispered worriedly. Though I could not see his face I could sense him smiling.

"Uhhhh... what is going on here?"

I pushed Providence out of the way and spun round to see Thomas staring at both of us from the kitchen doorway. He was balanced sluggishly against the doorframe with his arms crossed over his chest and his eyebrows raised questioningly.

"Nothing... I—"

"Nothing going on here, boy." Providence cut me off. He smiled at Thomas. "Erika here was just making me a cup of tea, weren't you, sweetheart?"

He looked at me then and his eyes seemed to convey to me to remain calm and play along. He then smiled at me and took the cup of tea already in my hands. I was speechless.

"Thanks, love." He said and sipped from the cup. He looked at Thomas once again before he headed for the door.

Thomas seemed to hesitate before he stepped aside for him to pass and then he followed Providence with his eyes until he was out of sight.

"You were making him tea, huh." Thomas said. "Is that all it was, Erika?"

I sensed the mockery in his tone, which only made me worry about how much he may have heard and seen. He walked slowly and deliberately towards me and stopped directly in front of me. His body movements seemed curiously feline—calculating and suspicious.

"So, how about making me some tea, then?" He said glibly.

I spun round without hesitating, if only to look away from his interrogative eyes, grabbed a mug from the top shelf, dropped a tea bag in it and then poured hot water into the mug.

"Don't forget sugar and milk, love." He added teasingly.

My hands were shaking as I added two full teaspoons of sugar and some milk to the brew. Once my hands had stopped shaking noticeably, I turned round and offered him the mug.

"Thanks, love." He said mimicking Providence's accent as he took the mug and then he made two clicking sounds with his back teeth and winked at me.

Thomas left stirring the tea in a slow calculated fashion like the panic that was slowly stirring within my mind.

The best form of defence is attack, they say; attack first before you are attacked.

I had this on my mind that night as I restlessly waited for James to interrogate me on what Providence and I were doing in the kitchen. I was almost certain that Thomas would say something to him. Not knowing if Thomas had heard anything, or how much he had heard or deduced from my little encounter with Providence, kept me in a perpetual state of worry the whole day. It didn't help that every time I passed Thomas, he would look deeply at me, disarming whatever guard I may have put up to shelter my feelings. If his aim was to unsettle me, it worked, and I knew I had to be careful around him.

But nothing dramatic happened that afternoon. The men finished watching the various football matches on the television, they had their post-match debates and amateurish strategy analysis of what the teams and their coaches could have done differently. I was left pretty much alone to make dinner and worry. Many times I was tempted to leave the house and go to Bessie's but I didn't, not because of James' earlier warning, but because I wanted to be around if Thomas decided to say anything. I wanted to be around to deny whatever he said before

James had enough time to react or find any semblance of truth or possibilities in such gossip.

In bed that night with James, I noticed he handled me differently. There was a conscious effort from him to give me pleasure. He touched me gently and stroked me with care. He kissed my intimate parts with a gentleness that would have been rewarded by another with satisfactory moans and unconstrained surrender, but my body responded differently. It seemed like my insides were tied up in knots, preventing my senses from responding. My body was alert and ready for an assault and his teasing touch only perpetuated its suspicion.

"You like that, don't you?" He said from between my thighs and I grabbed a handful of the bedding and squeezed tight. It wasn't from pleasure that my body tensed up just then, but from dismay. It seemed James was reading me all wrong.

"We need to talk, James." I said eventually.

"Not now." He muttered.

"We need to talk about Kwame." I said. This was my attack.

"What? Who?" He stopped and looked up at me.

"Kwame." I said. "Your childhood friend."

"What the hell are you talking about?" He said with obvious irritation. He pulled himself up to a sitting position and I did the same.

"It's about what you said regarding Bessie." I explained tactfully. "That she is too black and probably practises black magic."

"What the hell is wrong with you, woman?" James said. His face was red and I could see the thick vein that ran across his forehead. "Who is Kwame and why are we talking about her and Bessie?"

"Him." I corrected. "Kwame is a he. You said you had a Ghanaian friend while growing up called Kwame when we met online; Bessie is Ghanaian too. Or was that a lie? I thought you were comfortable with black people."

I could see the look of confusion on his face even in

the dark room; the lights were switched off but light from the moon filtered in creating a faint white-blue fluorescent glow. Something flickered in his eyes and I caught this. This was the moment, I thought. This was the moment to know if Thomas had said anything to him. If he had, James would come all out and say something to deter me from exposing his lie. Men do that when they feel trapped, they turn the table around.

"This is shit." He cursed. "You had to spoil the moment with this rubbish!"

So I was convinced that Thomas had said nothing to him. I experienced a brief moment of relief but was awakened to another apprehension. Why had Thomas not said anything to James? Yet. Could it be that he was waiting for the right moment to corner me or perhaps use what he thought he knew to get something else from me?

"This is shit." James repeated. "You see what that woman is doing to you—she's turning you into a frigid bitch like herself."

"She's my friend, James." I said.

I turned to touch him but he pushed my hands away and turned over so that his back faced me. He heaved the duvet over his shoulder as he positioned himself to sleep. I could feel the barrier that had been created between us on the bed as surely as if it were a solid wall. In a way I was thankful for this. I was too distracted to engage in any physical intimacy that night with James. The relief I had sought for knowing that Thomas had not said anything to James was only short-lived and my mind was slowly patterning new evils Thomas' silence might pose in the dire future.

I was awake most of the night with my worries and James' snores as companion. And just before I felt myself finally succumbing to sleep, it struck me that James didn't say anything about Kwame.

The following week felt empty for me but at the same time I could sense the tension building up like a time bomb ticking towards its final moments of explosion. Nothing changed outwardly but everything changed. James still came and left like he did on most mornings and late nights, but he wasn't talking to me much. He hardly ate anything I cooked and seemed to survive solely on the cigarettes he smoked endlessly. On some nights he didn't come back at all. This was not new to me but the frequency was. I had tried talking to him to let him know that I was no longer interested in the Kwame story, but he wasn't even trying to listen to me.

Why did this bother me? What did I fear most? I wasn't missing the few times we enjoyed a few laughs together. It was not knowing what was coming next that terrified me.

It suddenly became a rather gloomy house. Even those few moments I used to have with either Providence or Thomas seemed to disappear with my seeing less and less of them. I suspected they had both picked up on the rift that seemed to exist between James and me and had made a conscious effort not to be stuck in the middle of it. The few times I encountered Thomas either in the hallway, the kitchen or by the bathroom, his eyes seemed to tell me that he knew my secrets, haunting me long after he was no longer in the house. I thought I could find some sort of solace from Providence, but like the other men, he kept his distance. His eyes told me things too. They told me to consider what he had said.

This was the state I was in one afternoon while I was plaiting Bessie's hair in her apartment. We were in her bedroom and she was sitting in front of her oval dressing mirror and I stood directly behind her, parting her hair to get a straight line that ran from her forehead to the back of her head so I could have two identical halves of hair. I knew James would be quite upset if he knew I was still seeing her, but I needed some form of company, especially as I wasn't getting much in that house.

For some reason, my eyes were drawn to the beads she

wore round her plump neck. James had said she practised juju and the beads were an attestation to that. I looked briefly around the room looking for anything that would point to juju practice; earthen pots with tiny baby skulls in them, strange idol gods carved out of wood or anything fetishistic—but there was nothing.

"You seem so far away." Bessie said staring at my face from the mirror. "What is the matter?"

"Nothing." I lied.

"It's your man again." Bessie said. "He's still not talking to you is he?"

"I was just wondering about your beads." I said evasively. "Why do you wear them all the time?"

I noticed her hands instinctively went to her throat and caressed the necklace slowly.

"I've been wearing beads for as long as I can remember." She said reflectively. "I don't know about Nigeria, but there are certain coming-of-age rites that a young woman must perform to mark her entry into adulthood back in Ghana. My parents made me partake of the Bragoro rites since I am Ashanti." She stopped to smile. "I think because they felt a little guilty that I was born in England and they wanted me to have some sort of connection to Africa as well."

She stopped again and closed her eyes. I sensed she was fighting an unpleasant memory.

"We were required to wear these beads—lots of them for what they symbolised; beauty, purity, pride and all that! It was during that ceremony I met Kwesi." She said. "Beads... I wear them to remember home and also to remember that I am beautiful."

She stopped again and remained quiet for a long while. I knew she was transported back to Ghana in her mind and I could tell that she didn't visit that part of her soul frequently. There must have been many unpleasant memories there. The first time we had met she had mentioned briefly how her Ghanaian husband abused her psychologically as well as physically. I imagined that at that moment she was back there with him, listening to him tell her that she was ugly.

I looked into the mirror at the beads again and they were beautiful just like she was. The beads were made from fine stones. Each bead looked more exquisite than the one before it. I noticed her hands were still caressing them gently.

When I left Bessie, I wasn't feeling any better. I missed home. I just wanted to go back and leave behind all this misery. I remembered my last telephone conversation with Princess a week earlier when she had asked me if I was okay and if everything was what I had expected. I lied and told her it was. I told her that James was a real gentleman and that he was treating me like a fine lady buying me beautiful things and taking me round the country to all the wonderful places we only saw on television.

"I'm so happy for you." She enthused over the phone.

But if only she had seen the tears in my eyes that moment. I had to lie to her and to everybody else. I could not tell her that things were not right and that the fairytale world I had hoped for was only a dream. I could not tell her that being in England was more difficult than anyone could imagine especially if you had nothing. Money was so hard to come by and friends were even harder to find. I could not tell her that James was a big mistake. I did not want pity.

Providence was already in the house when I got back. I heard some noise in the kitchen and discovered him there trying to heat up some food with the microwave oven. He smiled at me and I noticed he seemed relieved.

"Where've you been?" He asked. He looked away from me to adjust the timer on the oven. "I was looking for you when I got in."

"I was just outside." I said. "Taking a walk."

The timer went off. Providence retrieved his meal and set himself up on the kitchen table. I watched his actions with ardent interest.

"So what's going on between you and James?" He asked

after taking a few bites.

"Nothing." I said, surprised that we were actually talking.

He shrugged. "You still don't trust me, do you?" He said.

I said nothing. I just stood by the doorway and watched him. Once he was through with the food he lit a cigarette. Through the cloud of smoke that shielded his face briefly, our eyes met and locked. Something happened then that I couldn't quite explain—even until this day. I wanted to be loved. I wanted to feel something other than the anguish that was going through me. I wanted the ugliness that I was feeling inside to go away.

Providence abandoned the cigarette in the ashtray. He got up and came up to me by the door. He took my hands into his and squeezed gently. He pulled me closer and I didn't resist him. When my breasts were pressed against his chest I could feel his heart beating away fiercely. I felt his hand pressing against my buttocks and his cigarette breath on my face. I was aware of his hardness against my soft thighs and as he kissed me, I succumbed. We said nothing but kissed anxiously.

It didn't go any further than the kiss. When it was over I felt strangely ashamed. I could not look at his face or speak to him even when he tried speaking to me. I left him in the kitchen and raced up to the bedroom. My head was throbbing with the riot of thoughts that ran through me. I kept thinking, "What have I done? What have I done?"

10

Crossroads

I was roused from my sleep. The captain had just announced that we would be landing in Lagos in the next thirty minutes. It had been a fitful sleep for me. Like my life, it was in halves; half asleep, half awake throughout the flight. I was seated in the middle row of the plane. I had a young man to my left on the aisle seat next to me and on my right I had two more people. To my immediate right was an elderly woman with thick glasses that made her eyes seem like they were ready to jump at you when looking at her face. To her right was a teenage boy who seemed to be her grandchild. They shared a resemblance except that the young boy wore defiance on his face like an armour. I had gathered early that this trip was not what he would have chosen to undertake if he had had a choice. He didn't see the point of spending his holiday with an extended family of uncles, aunts and cousins he didn't have much in common with anyway, and that lived in Nigeria. I was intrigued to pick up the disgust in his words whenever he said Nigeria: "Ain't Nigeria a backward country, ma?" or "Can't one die from one of 'em mosquito bites in Nigeria, ma?" or "I heard that a foreigner is kidnapped every other day in Nigeria, ma... Why do we have to go?"

Sometimes we have to go back to our roots to discover the truth about ourselves. This is what I wanted to tell the young man as well as giving him a good lecture of the rich

African heritage he took so much pleasure in condemning. But I didn't. I, too, had come to terms with the reality of my going back to Nigeria. It was a pilgrimage I knew I had to undertake to reconcile my immediate past with my beginnings and then my present. And in thirty minutes I would be taking the first furtive steps in that journey.

How will Erika, the woman I am now, fit into Ngozi's world? As much as I would like to believe that I have changed in many ways, I still see strong traces of Ngozi in almost everything I do. Why is it that when I am in deep thoughts, it is Ngozi that still speaks in my head and not Erika?

Traces of memories filtered into my head as I caught a glimpse of the waking sun from one of the windows. It was just a glimpse but it was enough to let me remember another family I would be returning to once I set foot in Lagos. It didn't seem so long ago...

Uloma saw him first.

It was late evening and we had just finished with the last customer at Princess' shop. It had been four months since I was thrown out of my uncle's house and I had started living with both Princess and Uloma. Time flew so fast, and gradually I had conditioned myself to this new family. It had not been easy at first. With three women living together under the same roof, things were bound to happen. There were some days when Princess would go into a foul mood and would snap at everyone for no obvious reason. There were other days when it would be Uloma's turn to assume the role of the irritable tyrant— a role she undertook well, by the way. Yes, those days I would feel completely miserable and blame myself for their ugly mood. I somehow would convince myself that my presence was already causing them some discomfort and that they were tired of having me around them but both Princess and Uloma would quickly reassure me (once they were better disposed) that my being there had nothing whatsoever to do with their occasional bad temper. I had to believe them; after all I too experienced bouts of ugliness that was in no way connected to either of them.

"Na who be this one?" Uloma had said in Pidgin English signalling with a tilt of her head at the boy who stood at the front steps of the shop. "We don close and na woman shop be this one."

I had been clearing away some plastic hair rollers from the top of the dresser but something other than her voice had made me turn round to look. He was staring fixedly at me and it occurred to me then that he had not changed since the last time I saw him, years before. I wondered if that was what the village did to him—stunting his growth, trapping a young man inside the body of what may seem to many as a growing youth. It was my brother, Nnamdi.

He stood there in dark brown trousers that were several inches above his thin ankles. His feet were dry and dusty in his rubber sandals. He was wearing a faded red T-shirt that accentuated the darkness of his skin. He looked every bit a villager who thought he was dressed up appropriately for the city. I was deeply embarrassed.

"Do you know him?" I heard Princess asking.

He pushed open the door and stepped into the shop, not once taking his eyes away from me. As the light from the shop illuminated his gangly frame, he seemed for the first time to flinch and shrink further into himself, yet his eyes stayed fixed on my face.

"Ngozi." He said. His voice was much bigger than he was; harsh and deep for his skinny frame but I recognized it.

"*Ke onye i bu?*" Uloma asked in Igbo.

He looked at her briefly, the expression on his face showing a hint of relief, but then his eyes trailed back to me. I stood frozen, unsure of what to feel.

"*Ke du ihe i cho?*" Uloma continued relentlessly. What do you want?

"Ngozi." He repeated my name.

Now I could feel all eyes on me. Three pairs of questioning eyes.

"Ngozi," Princess said, "do you know him?"

I remember taking a deep breath before I answered, "Yes, I know him."

He nodded his head at me and then broke out into a smile. He looked too much like his father and this unnerved me. I wondered why he was here and what he wanted. But more important, seeing him had triggered in me panic and fear of something I had long suppressed.

I asked him how he found me.

"*A jurum ajuju.*" He replied in Igbo and gestured with his arms in a wide circle.

"*Kemgbe i ji bia Lagos?*" I asked, curious of his journey.

"*A bia'aram nwanne echi.*" He said. Two days ago he had come; he explained that he had been staying at Uncle Kachi's house.

He moved closer to me and made to embrace me, but I backed off slowly. He stopped and I noticed the rage that seemed to be building in his eyes. I took another step back for good measures. Princess and Uloma watched both of us in silence, but I felt safe knowing that they would let nothing happen to me if things took a violent turn.

"*Ke ihe ina eme iba?*" He asked angrily, between gritted teeth. What are you doing here? I found myself unconsciously translating his words into English. "*I ma n' ina emevo anyi?*" Can't you see you are embarrassing the family?

"Who asked you to look for me?" I asked, intentionally speaking English.

"*Anyi nuru na isi n'ulo Kachi gbafuo.*" He replied in Igbo to show me he had nevertheless understood my question. We heard you ran away from brother Kachi's house.

"I can assure you that I did not run away." I said. "I was told to leave."

"*Ehe, ke ihe mere ilotaghi n'ulo?*" He asked, referring to my home and using Igbo once more to intimidate me and remind me of my roots. As he spoke, I imagined him

133

speaking in English so that I had control of his words.

"What are you doing here with these women?" He asked.

"I am home." I said.

"How can you say that?" He spat. "Don't you know what these women are? Don't you hear what people say about single women in Lagos?"

"Please go back to where you came from." I said quietly. "Tell them you did not find me."

My words may have sounded brave but I knew it was a huge contradiction to how I felt. I was quivering inside but I was determined not to let him see that. I watched as his face went through a series of emotive contortions and for a moment I was captivated by how easy it was to read his thoughts: bafflement, confusion, anger and finally pity.

"You will come with me." He said with quiet definiteness.

I felt all my tenacity crumble. I really did believe I would follow him like a defeated dog with its tail between his hind legs.

"She's going nowhere with you." Uloma's voice broke the spell I seemed to have been under.

She came up to me, standing between Nnamdi and me, and then it felt like my vision was restored. Behind Nnamdi was the sliding glass door of the shop. I could see through it that the darkness of the evening was slowly staking its claim where the scorching sun had once ruled. There was a young boy outside with a tray of peeled oranges balanced on his head and not far from where he walked there sat an old woman who had a smoking black pot by her side. She tenderly fanned the flames from the fire underneath; she was selling cooked corn and I was going to buy some from her before leaving the shop. In the far corner of the shop, there was a mass of human hair and fake hair that looked like a dingy black nest of dusty hairballs. All was illuminated, including Princess, who had joined Uloma in shielding me from Nnamdi.

"Ngozi," Nnamdi said impenitently, "won't you tell

them who I am?"

"Who are you?" Uloma challenged.

"Tell them." He challenged back.

Both Uloma and Princess turned round to look at me.

"He's my brother." I said in a whisper.

"Yes," he said exultantly, "and you are coming with me."

Silence.

Uloma and Princess still had their eyes on me. Silently their eyes conveyed their concern and probed to know if this was what I wanted. I felt Uloma's eyes especially, burning deep into me to know the truth and there was that moment of connection between us that many women have felt when their souls and spirits unite in one voice.

"No." She finally answered for me. "Ngozi is going nowhere with you."

She had turned round now to face him and I noticed for the first time that she was holding a large pair of scissors, the ones they used for cutting and styling customers' hair. She held it suggestively like a weapon.

Nnamdi chuckled wickedly, reminding me more so of his father. But he was not stupid; he did not attempt to move any closer to me or her.

"Abeg, go." Princess said in Pidgin English, she could not speak Igbo. "We no want trouble here, broda."

"Ngozi," he said, "let us go."

"No." I said.

"You are making a big mistake." He said. "Our mother wants to see you."

My heart told me it was a lie.

"Sister Rosa was right all along." He said shaking his head. "We have lost you to these prostitutes."

"Get out!" Uloma shouted at him. She walked up to stand eye to eye with him. I could feel the rage in her boiling over and the way she was wielding those scissors made me fear for Nnamdi.

He stepped back. He was still shaking his head when he turned round to push the door open.

"Ngozi!" He said finally before he walked out.

"That bastard!" Uloma fumed as she let the scissors drop to the floor.

"It's okay, it's okay." Princess said. She was holding my shoulders now and still looking at my face for answers. "What just happened?" She asked. The entire dialogue between Nnamdi and me and Uloma was in Igbo. Princess did not speak or understand Igbo.

"He called us prostitutes." Uloma said, but I knew Princess was referring to me and the history that instigated this episode.

While Uloma cursed in the background, I pleaded with Princess with my eyes not to push for answers. I didn't look away until I got a silent nod from her that told me she understood.

I felt my chest tighten when the plane started its final landing plunge. I gripped the handle of my seat tightly and closed my eyes to whisper a silent prayer. I hated that suspended, claustrophobic feeling that overtakes your body at a time like this. Babies and children started whimpering and crying from all corners of the cabin and suddenly my head was filled with noise from the children, from the engine, and from my apprehension.

I felt a thud as the tyres finally screeched on the tarmac and the plane began its initial fast break on the runway. My heart settled its pounding throb as I felt the plane slowly steady itself into its final halt. I sighed with relief as soon as the captain's voice beamed out to welcome us to Lagos.

We remained seated until the *fasten* seatbelt sign went off and then it was a fury of activity within the cabin. Everyone seemed to be up at the same time and retrieving luggage stored in the overhead lockers. I remained seated, breathing in and out slowly to settle my nerves and imagining what the Nigeria I left behind years before would suddenly look like. I had heard that many things had changed with the re-emergence of democracy in the society. Wonderful things had happened and were still happening to this previously abused and ambushed nation. When I left, we were still under the rule of a military tyrant and everything seemed to have fallen apart.

"Do you need help getting up?" The young man that sat beside me said. He had his hand luggage and was smiling at me.

"No, thank you." I said. "I'm alright. I just want to wait for a while."

"Okay." He said shrugging good-naturedly. "It's good to be back, right?" He didn't wait for an answer as he moved on towards the front, where the main exit door was located.

Was it really good to be back? I asked myself. It felt strange but exciting, yes, and there was indeed that part of me that had waited so long for this. I was back, now, and I must face whatever challenges awaited me out there. Who would I be now that I was back home? Whose voice would I speak in? Erika's? Ngozi's?

"Madam, do you need assistance?"

I looked up at the smiling male steward. He looked tired from the flight, but his smile was unwavering.

"Everybody is almost out." He said offering me his hand.

"No, thank you." I pulled myself up. "I just didn't want to be caught up in the rush out of the plane."

He stood aside for me and then handed me my hand luggage, which he had kindly retrieved from the overhead storage bin.

"Do you have everything?" He asked me.

I nodded.

"Mobile telephone, passport, wallet?"

"Thank you," I said, "I have everything."

I walked up to the exit door; there was no one there except the airline staff and some ground-handling agents. Everyone smiled at me as I stepped out of the plane and took my first lungful of Lagos' air.

When I stepped into the terminal building it hit me: Everything had changed. It was almost like being in another country's terminal building. I felt the cool chill from the functioning air-conditioners. Ahead of me the escalators were working. But most of all, it was the surrounding neatness that impressed me. How could I forget the airport I departed from all those years back? Then, nothing seemed to have worked. There was the epileptic power supply to contend with, the broken air-conditioners and the repugnant heat created from the suffocating smell of sweating bodies. There was nothing welcoming about the airport then. But now, I felt a certain pinch of pride.

There was a long queue at the passport control section. Two booths were for people with Nigerian passports, one booth took care of those carrying other African and ECOWAS passports, while the last booth was meant for people with non-African passports. This was the shortest line. I joined this line and withdrew my red British passport from my handbag. Ahead of me were five other people and I noticed the young boy and his grandmother were in this line.

When it was my turn, I walked up to the booth and handed my passport to the uniformed immigration officer. He screened my passport thoroughly, folding it this way and then that way and bringing the picture close to his eyes to scrutinize it and stare at me simultaneously. He looked again at the visa page and then at me suspiciously.

"So you be British?" He sneered condescendingly.

"Yes." I replied, not even bothering to be polite.

"You were born in England?" He asked with doubt dripping in his tone.

"No." I said. "I was born in Bendel State, now called Delta State here in Nigeria."

I noticed he looked at me with a hardened squint in his eyes. I wondered what he was thinking.

"But you just say you be British!" He said harshly.

"Yes." I agreed. "I am British by marriage and Nigerian by birth."

"Where your Nigerian passport?" He asked. I could at once sense he was trying to be difficult.

"I don't have one." I said. "Is there a problem, sir?"

He did not answer me, but instead signalled to another official to join him in the booth. I watched in silence as they both deliberated on my passport whilst sneaking peeks at me at intervals. After what seemed like five minutes the other official addressed me.

"Madam," he said, "we appreciate it when travellers are not rude to immigration officials."

"I was not being rude." I said. "He asked me questions and I answered him."

"What is the reason for your visit?" He asked sternly.

I paused to take a deep breath before answering.

"I have come to bury my father." I answered.

The hostile look in his eyes softened. "I am sorry for your loss." He said.

"Thank you." I answered.

He handed back my passport to me and let me through.

As I waited for my bags at the baggage carousel I experienced another bout of anxiety. Why was I feeling this way all of a sudden? Was it because I had finally brought myself to say it, to acknowledge that my father was dead and that was the only reason I was back here? Or could it just be nerves after being away for so long?

I noticed one of my red suitcases journeying to me on the carousel. The woman standing next to me had retrieved six huge bags, all stacked up in two trolleys and she had her eyes still fixed on the carousel, waiting for more. Some people travel light with the barest amount of luggage—I wonder sometimes if their life's burden is like their luggage, simple and light, or if there was more to it. Some other people carry tons of baggage when they travel. And me, how does my luggage measure up to the life I have lived so far? One thing was certain—like my red bag that journeyed towards me, my life had made a complete circle back to the land of my birth.

I grabbed my first suitcase and as I waited for the other one, I was forced to think about the people waiting outside to receive me. My family…

Nnamdi's unexpected visit marked a new level of respect I had for Uloma. I would never have known the strong spirit that dwelt within her. I would never have known that she cared enough for me to defend me like she did that evening.

I had always worried that she merely tolerated my presence and if not for Princess, she would have wished me good-bye and good riddance weeks before. But that evening when she stood up to Nnamdi, and challenged him on my behalf, I loved her much more than I ever thought I could.

Nnamdi's appearance caused me other worries—like what if he showed up again and this time prepared to really take me? Not even a scissors-wielding Uloma would stop him. What if he was in Lagos with his father? The endless questions and scenarios swam round my head causing me to be tense during the days and sleepless most nights.

"So, when are you going to tell me?" Princess asked me one evening.

It was a very hot night. There had been no electricity for over a week and the wind seemed to have gone into hiding. Apart from the half moon, everywhere was pitch-black except when lit up by moving headlights. Uloma was already sleeping half naked in the middle of the tiny parlour. She had laid out a mattress on the floor. She wore only her panties while the rest of her body was exposed.

"Tell you what?" I asked, knowing exactly what she was talking about.

"Why don't you want to see your family?" She asked.

I remember looking into her face briefly before looking

away and shaking my head.

"You keep more secrets than a Catholic priest." She sighed. "When will you start trusting me?"

"I trust you." I replied. I really did.

"But not enough to tell me what is going on." She added.

I laughed a little. She made it sound like some big conspiracy and it wasn't. But yes, there were things I hid inside and away from everybody; things I was ashamed of and things that had hurt me so much. It was then, under the half moon and smouldering heat that I realized that I didn't want to be Ngozi Akachi. Too many bad memories were associated with her. I wanted to be someone else with a different life and a different past. How does one begin to do that? I asked myself.

"There's really nothing to tell." I lied. Maybe denying it was the first step.

Just then, Uloma sauntered into the corridor. She had tied a piece of cloth across her breast to cover her nakedness up to her knees. She looked wild with her hair in disarray and a scowl across her face.

"This heat wan kill person!" She lamented.

She joined us and sat on the front steps of the apartment. Three of us huddled together in our barely covered bodies like the mythical Three Fates—*Clotho, Lachesis* and *Atropos*, under the hot moonlit night. In Greek mythology, they were the three goddesses who determined human life and destiny. They were also known as Moirai and they appointed to each person at birth a share of good and evil. I imagined I was Clotho, the Spinner who spun the thread of life. Princess would be Lachesis, the Dispenser of Lots who decided lifespan and assigned a destiny to each person and finally, Uloma would be Atropos, the Inexorable who carried the dreaded shears that cut the thread of life at the appointed time. Our decisions, like the three Fates, could not be altered, even by the gods.

We watched as other neighbours and passers-by complained about the heat and lack of electricity while the others had spread out mats in front of their pavements and prepared to sleep there.

It may have been unbearably hot but there was something calming about sitting out there with those two women. I found myself searching for their hands and without speaking we linked our fingers together and squeezed gently. We watched with interest at the comedy taking place across the street. A man laid out a mat on his balcony and had quickly disappeared inside. As soon as he was gone his overweight wife had dashed out with a pillow and positioned herself in a prime spot on the mat. When the man came out with his deflated pillow, much like his deflated male ego, we could sense his frustration as he tried to squeeze into the remaining small portion left while complaining bitterly to his wife that she was too big and had to lose *weight*.

I laughed. Princess and Uloma laughed too and it suddenly occurred to me that I was truly home. And this was my family.

11

Family Portrait

My father was well known in the village. I knew this because my mother used to tell me all the time. Not only was he well known, he was also a direct descendant of Akadike Akachi one of the greatest *dibias* that had ever lived in our village.

When I was still little, before my sister, Ofunne, was born, my mother used to let me play in her room. I found things there to amuse myself with, things like the metal portmanteau that she kept her things in. This was like a treasure trove for me. In it were trinkets and beads and valuable fabrics she called "George". I would scatter the contents of the portmanteau each time I was left alone in her room and when she returned, she would sigh and say, "Come out of there, you little rat! Next time I would lock you up inside." I would always laugh at this because I knew she never meant it and no matter how stern she tried to sound, she could not hide the smile that twitched at the corner of her mouth. I spent a lot of time in her room.

The only times I was not allowed inside her room were those nights when father would go there after supper and he would not come out again until day break. I never understood why he had his own room. Those nights I would cry for mother until Nnamdi would make me stop.

Nnamdi always knew how to make me stop crying. He would first tell me "Ndo," and then proceed to entertain me by miming the movements of apes and monkeys in the

143

forest. He would hunch his back a little and let his arms dangle at his side in a slight bow while he hopped around from one foot to the other making silly noises at the same time. This always amused me. And to end it all, Nnamdi would sweep me up in the air and then place me on his shoulders. I would laugh so hard until tears ran down my eyes. The excitement usually tired me and soon I would fall asleep in his arms.

The morning Ofunne was born mother had been so sickly that she was rushed off to the midwife's hut. I was home alone with father and Nnamdi but soon Nnamdi had to leave for the farm. Then I was alone with father.

He was sitting in the front yard on a cane chair chewing a stick. His skin was very black and he had hairs covering his chest and part of his big stomach. A wrapper was tied round his waist, and on his feet were a pair of rubber slippers. His legs were crossed as he chewed and spat.

I sat at the entrance of the house observing him. I was six years old then and was vaguely aware of what was happening with mother. I knew that when she returned home that evening, I would either have another brother or a sister. I also knew that her stomach would not be so big anymore.

My father turned to look at me. It wasn't often that he looked my way and so I held his gaze and even smiled softly. He smiled back.

"Come." He said, gesturing to me with his right hand.

I scrambled to my feet and rushed up to him. He looked at me for a moment longer before he lifted me up to his lap. He spun me round so that I was looking at his face. He stared deeply at me, touching my cheeks gently and using his fingers to straighten my eyelashes. He patted my hair and then rubbed its texture between his fingers.

"Beautiful." He whispered. "Beautiful."

"Papa" I said smiling.

"Yes?" He replied. "What is it?"

"Will mama come home with another boy or girl?"

"Only the gods can answer that." He said.

"I hope it is another girl who looks just like me." I said.

Papa shuddered. I felt it, just like I felt something else pressing against me. He said nothing more to me and I didn't mind. I only felt happy that I was in his arms and he had spoken to me. He played with my fingers and as he did this, I marvelled at how dark his skin was against mine. Later he set me down and went into his room. He remained in there until Nnamdi returned to inform us that mother had given birth to another girl.

"What does she look like?" Papa asked. His eyes were fixed on Nnamdi and his words sounded a little harsh.

"I haven't seen her myself." Nnamdi confessed. "But Aunty Ndidi told me to tell you that she will look like us. She will be dark."

Papa nodded and returned to his room.

Mama came back home that evening with my baby sister. I snuck into her room that night to take a look at the baby. She was a tiny, brown bundle. Her eyes were squeezed shut and her tiny fingers opened and closed anytime she moved. I was captivated by this tiny person, not even mother's portmanteau and its hidden treasures could tempt me away from her presence.

"She's beautiful." Mother said. She was lying beside the baby on the bed. "Just like you."

"What will you call her?" I asked.

"Your father and I have agreed to name her Ofunne." Mother said, quietly.

Mother held one of my hands and smiled warmly. I smiled back and gently touched Ofunne's wrinkled forehead.

12

Running Through Mist

The date was June 17. It was the day I started keeping a diary, my little blue book of secrets, which I kept hidden beneath the flat base of the bedside dresser. It had been exactly 227 days since I came to England. It had rained dreadfully the night before. It had been sweltering hot during the day and the rain had come as a sort of respite from the heat but I knew there was more to come. There was something about rain and the tidings it carried along with it that always seemed to unsettle me. All I could see was the endless string of water running down the pane like a "sheeted" waterfall.

James had slept late into the morning. This by itself was unusual. For the last weeks he had been very consistent with the time he left the apartment. I stared at him while he slept and realized that I did not love him. I did not even like him. But I wasn't ready to walk away from him and a life I knew I would certainly be miserable in. You see, misery wasn't the point. What mattered was that he offered me a new beginning.

I certainly was not expecting it then when his eyes fluttered open and he smiled warmly at me as if he had just had a beautiful dream with me in it. His piercing green eyes seemed to tear right through my concentration.

"Good morning." He yawned and stretched.

For many days he had not spoken to me directly in the

morning when he got up and I did not know what to make of this greeting but to stare strangely at him. He must have sensed my confusion for he smiled at me again.

"Come here, love." He said patting the space beside him. "Come join me in here."

He may have been smiling but there was something in his tone that was not asking me but ordering me and I found myself obeying. I unfolded my legs from the lotus position on the armchair and walked slowly to the bed. I watched him pat the bed three more times when I was near enough and I carefully sat on the space he had patted. He grabbed me and pulled me closer to him. I could feel the warmth of his body even when I felt no warmth in his embrace.

"I have been thinking," he said, "we should do it this weekend."

"Do what?" I asked.

"Get married." He said.

I must have frozen in his arms. Why now? Where did that come from? I must have asked myself a hundred and one variations of those questions in that split second it took for him to deliver his unexpected bit of news and the time it took for him to laugh in that obnoxious manner of his.

"Say something." I heard him say. "Aren't you happy?"

"I am happy." I responded robotically. "I'm just surprised... I wasn't expecting it."

He laughed again. I felt his fingers touching me and invading certain areas of my body—it made me feel sick.

"Well," he said, "I have decided that summer is as good as anytime to get married. I have checked with the local registry and they said we could be fitted into the weekend."

I wanted to tell him to hold on and wait. All this seemed to be happening too fast for me, and from his voice I could sense a deeper motive for this rush. I said nothing still, knowing that whatever it was would be revealed in good time. His time.

So when he finally left that morning, I was left feeling

confused and suspicious. The suddenness of his so-called proposal did not make sense to me. Even for James, it was too random and erratic. I stared at my reflection in the bathroom mirror as I brushed my teeth and thought to myself: Ngozi, you are going to be married! You are going to finally become Mrs. Erika King. But what did all that mean? Did that mean that I would automatically become a new person? Would that wipe away my past and offer me a clean slate?

I had no answers, but in my despair I could only think of Providence. Why? I don't know. Or maybe I did. Maybe it was because I now knew that soon my doors would be closed forever and there would be no letting Providence in ever again. If I said yes and went along with James, then there would be no possibility of Providence and I ever being together. I had tried not to admit this feeling I had for Providence, but after James' proposal, it was all I thought about. I hadn't completely got over the kiss I shared with Providence. I still smelt him when I closed my eyes and my insides cried in agony for him. But then again, how could I dismiss the other part of him—the almost savage part that had shown itself the first time I was confronted by Thomas' nudity? Or his swift duplicity when Thomas had almost caught us in the kitchen together? I couldn't overlook these. Yes, he had always begged me to let him in, but I had managed to keep him out. I was still free, but soon I would be free no more.

I wasn't sure if Providence was still in the house. In my shock of the morning I had not heard anyone leave except James. But based on the time, it did occur to me that I might be the only one left in the house. I felt wretched and desperately lonely. Most women would be dancing with joy when asked to be married by the man they had always wanted. Most women would not wait to share the news with their family and best friends. It was different for me. I had somehow waited for this moment for so long that now that it was here, it was almost as if I didn't want it anymore. I had waited 227 days for this moment and it had taken me that long to realize that what I thought was best for me might be a mistake. The little seed of doubt that had found its way into the depth of my heart had grown until it was a solid wall of suspicion and distrust. Too many things had happened, far too many things.

I paused for a very long time in front of the bedroom door before I walked unhurriedly to Providence's room. I heard every beat of my heart as I raised my hand to turn the door handle. The metallic material of the handle felt cold in my palm. I heard the tiny squeak as the door slowly pushed open. There was a moment of panic that quickly passed. I was trying not to make any noise, as if that would conceal any trace of my invading his private space. It felt wrong sneaking in here, but I had a strong urge to go through his wardrobe; I needed to see what he had in there and hopefully discover a part of him I was yet to uncover, maybe even discover a secret he had managed to hide, something dear, something personal, something other than the picture of the man he portrayed—I wanted a reason to keep my doors shut. I also wanted to smell his clothes; inhale the sweet maleness of him, his sweat and that distinct African scent he still carried with him. And finally when I was done with his wardrobe and his clothes, I wanted to sit on his bed for a while and forget about James and forget about marriage.

The door opened enough for me to enter and I entered. I thought I was alone in his darkness. Then I heard a voice speak. I knew it was not addressing me, but there was something in me that wanted to be spoken to by those words.

"Oh Jah, I worship thee with my whole heart." Providence was there, kneeling by his bed in prayer.

"Oh, I'm sorry." I whispered taking a backward step, ready to flee, but Providence unclasped his hands and motioned for me to stay with his right hand. I stopped instantly. I watched him cross himself before he got up and turned to look at me. It was only then I realized he was as naked as the day he was born. He did not try to shield his penis from me, nor did I look away.

"You want something from me?" He asked.

"I didn't know you were still in." I said quietly.

"So you normally come to my room when I am away." He said teasingly.

"No…" I said. "No… I just…"

"It's okay." He said. "Come right in."

I found myself walking further into darkness, as if I was somehow entering into Providence himself. Darkness itself had become a garment to wear, to experience.

"You are naked." I said, as if he was not aware of this fact.

"I sleep like this." He said. "Do you want me to wear something?"

I said nothing and so he reached out to me, pulling me further into the room. There was an ecstasy to the moment, but it was not sexual. I was not thinking of sex, in fact, I never did. I let him touch me. He held my hands and then touched my face, my lips, then my neck, and trickled his fingers down to my breasts. I did not fight him off. Not even when he raised my chin up to kiss me and then he unveiled me. I felt him once he was inside me but my senses only responded to that because of the dryness and tightness that ravaged my womanhood. He was very gentle with me and kept asking me if I was comfortable and if I was enjoying this. I said nothing. I was weeping quietly. Silent waves of tears flowed down my eyes. Was this what I wanted?

Something of my question must have registered with him for he stopped suddenly.

"Why are you crying?" He asked. "Am I hurting you?" He seemed only to sense the physical sensation of pain. "Am I too big?"

I said nothing. My eyes were closed and I felt him leave me.

"Hey!" He said. "I'm sorry. I thought you wanted this. I thought you wanted me."

"It's okay." I said quietly. But it was not okay.

"Are you sure?" He asked and I nodded.

"I have to go." I said almost immediately.

I remember how quickly I got up, picked up my nightdress from the floor, put it on and then fled from his room. When I got back to my room I latched the door shut and sank to the ground. Grey showers had become a storm. It seemed the rain in my eyes would never again stop.

I ran a bath of hot water and soaked myself in its scalding contents. The water was really hot and its vapour covered the bathroom in a swirling mist, making the outlines of objects barely visible. I sat upright in the tub, with my eyes glued to the mirror that hung just above the sink, and I could make out a blurred picture of my face surrounded by the cloud of mist. I was barely recognizable to myself. My sorrowful, heavy eyes stared blandly back at me. What had I just let happen? I didn't want to close my eyes, even for an instant because I knew there would be images waiting for me behind my eyelids.

A creepy silence surrounded me. I scrubbed my face repeatedly, also scrubbed my arms as if trying to remove an unseen tattoo.

I dressed up in black, a black blouse and a fitting black pair of jeans. When I got downstairs I noticed Providence was in the living room. He sat on the sofa. Our eyes met briefly and I quickly made a detour into the kitchen. As I opened the kitchen drawer to retrieve a cereal bowl I could hear sounds from the television set. Why is he still here? I recall thinking.

"Ngozi" I heard his voice from behind me. It sounded really close.

I turned round and he was in the kitchen with me. He stood by the edge of the kitchen table. I sensed his apprehension and was relieved that I was not the only one who was feeling peculiar.

"Ngozi, I need to tell you something," he said.

I noticed a nervous tick above his right eyelid. I didn't want him to comment on our earlier encounter. I prayed he wouldn't have to say anything about it that may worsen how awkward I already was feeling.

"I have to leave." He said slowly.

I stared on at him. I knew that, I knew he had to leave the house some time today despite the rain.

"James has asked me to go find another place to stay." He said.

"What?" I said, shocked.

"Yeah!" He continued. "He told me last night just as I got in."

"Why?" I knew there was more.

"He says he would be starting a family soon and needed the space." Providence said.

"So you knew!" I whispered.

"That he was going to ask you to marry him? Yes, he told me as well."

So he knew but still he allowed what happened between us that morning take place? I didn't know what to think. A part of me felt cajoled and manipulated but the other part, which far outweighed the first part, was visibly upset that James was throwing him out.

"What about Thomas?" I asked.

He sniggered and shook his head.

"Thomas stays." He said. "E be like say them don yarn about this thing before yesterday."

He pulled out one of the kitchen chairs and then sat on it. Without hesitating he lit a cigarette. I was still too stunned to sit down. So both James and Thomas had sat together to decide he was to leave the house? It immediately occurred to me that it was possible that Thomas may have expressed his suspicion about Providence and me to James. Could this be the reason for this sudden marriage? Was this why James wanted to get rid of Providence?

"Where would you go?" I asked suddenly.

"I have some friends around Kent." He said. "But I may end up in Leicester. Things are cheaper there and there's this Nigerian dude doing well there—Kelechi, he was a classmate of mine. The brother don make money for Leicester, he go show me the way."

I sat down and rested my chin on my left palm. "When do you have to leave?" I asked in a defeated tone.

"Don't know." He said casually. "I got the feeling he wants me out like yesterday... I'll be leaving before Saturday."

I watched him stand up. He adjusted himself by straightening his shirt, tugging here and there before he set out for the door. He stopped by the doorway and turned round to look at me again.

"You know you have a choice, Ngozi." He said. "You don't have to commit yourself to him."

I had no choice. What could I do?

"Come with me." He said. "I know say things dey hard now, but e go better."

He stood still, as if waiting for me to respond to his offer. I said nothing. He waited for a while longer before he turned round and left. I heard the front door slam shut.

He was leaving. I would stay—I somehow knew this. He wanted me to come with him. Was he serious? He could hardly take care of himself and he was clearly an illegal alien in this country. So was I. Why would I risk everything and go with him?

These thoughts came into my mind in no particular order but the stark reality was that Providence would be leaving. I would lose my one connection to home. I had always counted on his presence in the house. I loved the fact that he spoke with an accent that reminded me of the chaos of Nigeria. I loved the fact that he would speak to me sometimes in Pidgin English, knowing that I enjoyed the lyrical sweetness of it. I loved that he was black and Nigerian and not some half-mixed concoction like Thomas. And James wanted to start a family? A family comprising a father, mother and children? Was this really what he wanted or was he just making sure that Providence got the picture that he was not wanted in this house anymore?

What did James know about having and maintaining a family? Apart from my discovering that the respectable family background he had painted to me before I came to England was false, I had never heard him once talk about his family or an interest in building one. What about me? What did I know about having a family? I ran away from mine. Princess and Uloma were not related to me by blood but I considered them the closest thing to a family. I also could not see myself as a mother, certainly not a mother to James' children. This thought shook me. It was better left unexplored and much easier instead to focus on losing Providence. But how was I losing him? For me to believe I was losing him, I also had to confront the issue of his belonging to me. Someone once told me that you can't lose what you never owned. Did I covertly lay claim to him because he came from the same country as I did?

Bessie was home. She welcomed me into her house with a smile and a hot plate of *kelewele*, a traditional Ghanaian delicacy of cubed ripe plantain tossed in hot pepper, ginger and other spices.

"Nothing better than a plate of hot *kele*," she sighed gleefully, "for such horrible weather."

I followed her to the living room. She dropped herself on the seat opposite the television and balanced her meal on her lap. She was watching a game show. I wanted to talk to her but I was not sure exactly what I wanted to tell her.

"Sis-te," she said, "you are not eating."

I smiled sheepishly and then spooned some *kelewele* into my mouth. The sweetness stung me for a moment. Bessie dropped her plate on the coffee table and switched off the television with the remote control.

"I know you too well, Erika." She said. "Something is wrong. What is it?"

I took a lungful of air then.

"James asked me to marry him." I said.

She looked at me with her eyebrows raised.

"So with luck, you would become a British citizen."

She said. "But this is not what troubles you."

I took another lungful of air.

"He has asked Providence to leave the house." I added.

"Ahhh!" Bessie said with sudden realization. "The Nigerian man. I see… I see."

What did she see? I wanted to ask her but I was afraid that she would guess correctly.

"So, James wants you to marry him and he tells you Providence must leave first?" She asked.

"No." I said. "He asked me this morning before he left. Providence told me himself that James asked him to leave last night."

Bessie nodded thoughtfully. She picked up her plate and took a spoonful of her meal.

"When he told Providence he had to leave, he also told him that he was going to marry me. From what Providence told me, Thomas also knew and Thomas would still be living with us."

"I hear you, but I can't determine what is upsetting you the most." Bessie said. "Are you angry because it seems you are the last to know, or is it because Providence is leaving?"

I opened my mouth to respond to her but no words came out. My mouth hung open for what seemed like a minute and then I closed it. Her eyes were fixed on mine and suddenly I covered my face with my hands so she would not see the tears that were threatening to escape.

"Dear, dear, dear…" Bessie said. "Do you love him?"

She could have been referring to James or Providence; I was not sure and felt safe in remaining silent. I knew that if I kept talking, I would reveal to her what happened that morning with Providence. She had that effect on me; I could not lie to her or keep much away from her. I wiped my face and then dropped my hands so I could face her once again. With a fake smile, I picked my plate from my lap and began to eat again.

"You promised to teach me how to make this." I said, referring to the *kelewele*.

Bessie looked at me knowingly. It was obvious to her that I was being evasive. I sensed that she was battling whether to push me for answer but with a resigned sigh, she didn't push any further. She instead spooned my plate, as hers was empty, and smiled fondly.

"You need lots of hot chillies," She said. "Fresh ginger is a must and the plantain cannot be too ripe or not ripe at all..."

She went on to lead me into the kitchen and then made me assist her while she cooked up another small helping of *kelewele.*

Providence did not return that night.

13

It All Started Here...

Princess and Uloma were both there, just as I had expected, among the crowd of people outside the arrival lounge. Friends and relatives of arriving visitors were still not allowed inside the arrival hall area, but they could wait outside, close to the entrance. This area was visible through the glass doors. I had to restrain myself from jumping and running to meet them. And they had changed a lot in appearance over the years, just like I was sure I must have appeared different to them as well.

Princess looked fuller. She was no longer the slim woman I used to know then. Her cheeks were rosy and plump, which made her pleasant face all the more beautiful. She had written me two years earlier when she was about to get married and had sent me pictures of her wedding by email since I could not attend. It seemed marriage was good to her; she looked extremely happy and content.

Uloma stood tall and fiercely attractive. She was the less changed of the two. One significant thing I noted was the laugh lines that spread at the corners of her eyes. She still wore a lot of make-up and she had remained unmarried over the years even though she had two little children of her own now.

As soon as I pushed my baggage trolley through the automatic doors, I saw his head shoot out from behind the heads of other waiting families and friends of arriving passengers. It was Nnamdi. Our eyes met and he smiled at me. For a moment I thought I had just seen a ghost, but he was no ghost, he was still there even after I had blinked a couple of times. My first consideration was to turn back but before I could do anything, Princess lurched forward and before I knew it she was in my arms in a suffocating embrace.

"Ngozi," she cried, "Ngozi… God! Is this you?"

"Yes." I whispered back. "I'm back."

"Hey, I missed her too."

Uloma was suddenly by our side and the three of us were locked in a group hug. Tears flowed freely from our eyes and I noticed that people were staring at us and trying to avoid colliding with us as they made their way to their own waiting hugs and kisses. From the corner of my eye I also noted that Nnamdi stood still at a distance, observing us keenly.

"I can't believe that you are back." Princess cried.

"You are so yellow now, you almost look white." Uloma added. "Life must really have been good for you over there."

"You both look beautiful." I said in an attempt to forestall any further enquiries into my assumed life while I was in England. There would be enough time later to fill them in on the truth.

As we disentangled, they must have noticed my attention was divided between them and Nnamdi who stood some metres away. I noticed both of them followed my eyes and turned to look at Nnamdi as well.

"He knew you were coming back." Uloma said. "He came to Lagos yesterday and came by my house."

"He was at my place as well." Princess said. "He wanted to be sure that you hadn't arrived yet."

"Who would have thought he would come here?" Uloma added.

He stood there, a spitting image of his father. He was a fully-grown man now. I remembered our last encounter vividly. I was a different person too. Now I was ready to face him.

"I have to speak to him." I said to both Princess and Uloma. "Alone."

One of them took hold of the trolley with my luggage. They both stepped aside for me creating a clear space between my brother and me. At that moment it seemed the entire world had dissolved and we were the two last creatures left surviving. I walked up to him and when I was near enough the dissimilarity between us could not have been more apparent. He was night and I was day.

"Ngozi," he said, "*Papa a n' wugo!*"

"Yes," I answered, "I know he is dead."

"*Anyi a ma ro ma iga à bia!*" He said.

"I said I would come, you did not have to worry."

He sighed. I noticed his eyes were red and wondered what must have been going through his head at that moment.

"*I ma na papa na acho i'nwu mana I zitaro ego ka anyi we zur ogwu!*" His words were bitter. *You knew he was dying and still you didn't send money to help!*

I looked away, not because I was ashamed of myself but because I was disappointed that after all these years he would still try to blackmail me emotionally. Some things never change after all.

"Why did you have to wait for him to die before you came back?" He demanded. "Why did you hate him so much? He was your father too!"

It happened then. My silence was finally broken.

I looked sharply at him with all the hate I could dredge up and in my newfound voice I said brusquely: "How dare you accuse me?"

His face registered his shock and surprise at my perceived impudence.

"How dare you?" I continued in my rage. "How can you stand there and tell me that you did not know?"

I felt the tears begin to run down my cheeks and this angered me more. I did not want him to think I was weak. I was feeling quite strong, these tears were not tears of anguish, they just flowed out of my eyes and I had no control over them. But I did not look away or even try to wipe my face. I watched him instead until he looked away, his eyes betraying his own shame. How could he pretend not to know? I turned my question into his home language and let it hit home, with full force.

"*Nnamdi, k'a e tu I ga si na I ma ro?*"

✶

Memories.

It's amazing what sensations we retain in our hearts and in our heads; it is also amazing how we recollect them. As far back as I could remember my memories had always been clouded with shame, sadness and denial.

One of my earliest memories was my mother plaiting my hair methodically, double strands woven together, under the embracing shadow of the guava tree in our village-home. Ezi was a village in every sense, tucked away in the down southern region of Bendel State, in the beautiful Igbo-speaking part of my childhood land. I still recall the red earth that reliably left its orange stains under my bare feet whenever I chose to play outside, the profusion of trees, the numerous farms, and the long treks to a cool stream to fetch water. Most of the villagers lived in identical mud houses, only a few affluent families possessing cement houses with tin roofs. And of course I remember the missionary school where I learnt all that a child needed to learn. Or so I believed once upon a time.

My mother used to love plaiting my hair because it was naturally long, unlike hers or anyone else' in our family. She used to tell me that I was different. I was special, she would whisper into my ears as she plaited my hair.

"No one is as fair as you in this family." She used to say lovingly. "You can see that we are all very dark—I, your father, even your brother and sister."

"Why am I different?" I would ask.

She would sigh quietly and then proceed to tell me

about the heavy rain that fell the night I was born. By the time I was twelve years old, I must have heard that story over a hundred times. I never knew how much of it I believed, but she always told it with such conviction in her.

"It was a unique rain and no one had expected its ferocity, not even the village rainmakers who had all been worried about the absence of the rains and the devastating effects it was having on agriculture." She used to say while she plaited my hair.

"What is agriculture?" I would ask and she would shush me, telling me it was the farms and all the things that grew on them, like papa's cassava and yam farm.

She would go on to explain that it had been a trying period for the villagers and many had begun to worry that the land was cursed. And so that fateful night when traces of the coming rain could be smelt in the air, there had been some sort of euphoric fervour that swept across the village. This was short-lived however, for as soon as the skies opened up and the first wave of the treacherous rain came lashing down, all things fell apart.

I had been told that some lives were lost that day in the flood as well as property, farm animals and hope. Till the day I left Ezi, Nne Achili still mourned her missing five-year old, Amadi, who hadn't been seen since that fateful night. Like many other children of his age, Amadi had run outside in anticipation of dancing in the rain. That was the last anyone ever heard of him. He was not the only child reported missing after the flooding, but Nne Achili always stood out in my mind because she had lived close to my father's house and I had endured a childhood of scorn from the bitter old woman, who always glared at me with an evil eye and rolled her hands over her head and snapped her fingers at me in a curse whenever I passed by.

I had also learnt that I was the only child that was born that fateful night in the entire village. This had been the reason many believed that my birth was in a way tied to that rain. The village elders had all come to that conclusion and when my father had been summoned to their midst, they had warned him to be careful of that daughter of his. "The gods must have been angry when she was conceived, hence the catastrophic rain." They had warned him.

I used to go to bed at night feeling guilty. I would hear the voices of the missing children screaming for help in my head and I would also hear the bleating, mooing, clucking and braying of the lost animals. I had many nightmares as a child.

It was my mother who had named me Ngozi. Technically it should have meant "Blessing" or more appropriately "God's blessing". But what that name had always meant to me was simply "God's blight."

Memories could be such lethal things.

Then there was the day my life took a drastic turn. The morning started off like many other mornings with mother waking Nnamdi, Ofunne and me for what would be several trips to the stream to fetch water. The night before, I had hid some dried pepper underneath my pillow and when I heard mother shaking Nnamdi awake, I quickly retrieved the pepper and chewed a few. I knew the immediate effect would be to make my body temperature hot—someone in school had told me about this and how she used it to fool her grandmother all the time to avoid doing chores.

It worked for me for as soon as mother tried to rouse me from sleep, I complained that I was feeling sick and she was a little alarmed at how warm my body was. She allowed me go back to sleep but not before she informed me that she would be rushing off that morning to the next village, Ìsse'luku, to assist her younger sister who was to be wedded the next day. I was still awake when she finally left. Elder Chibike came for her with his noisy patched-up Peugeot pick-up truck, which unfortunately was the only cross-village transport service available to us. It coughed its way in and then out of our compound in a cloud of grey smoke. If that wasn't enough, I had to endure the very loud greeting between my father and elder Chibike who never failed to brag about how he was one of the very few noble ones to own a "motto". I never liked him. He drank too much, smelt badly of putrid saliva and always seemed to be scratching his crotch area. He reminded me of my father and I hated that too.

Not long after mother departed, I was about to drift off again, with the hope of catching at least one more hour of sleep before it was time to rush off to the missionary school. Though my eyes were squeezed shut, I still could not sleep. I felt I was being watched; I could sense an eerie presence that felt like an invincible weight on me. My inner spirit stirred, disturbed. I opened my eyes and immediately noticed my father by the doorway, staring at me. His eyes were like I had never seen them before. They looked hungry. Not hungry for food, hungry for something else. There was a raw animal longing in the depth of his eyes that scared me and I quickly noticed that his loincloth stood unnaturally at attention. Was that a staff he hid beneath his cloth? I dared not ask. I sat up abruptly when he entered the room but he said nothing, just kept staring at me like I was some ripe fruit or scrumptious meal waiting to be devoured.

"Papa" I called out. "Papa can I help you with anything?"

In what seemed to be a drugged voice, my father barked: "*Mecha onu I*—Shut your mouth. I'm not your father. You are a spirit child. You are not my daughter."

His tone scared me. His words carried no meaning to me. There was a claustrophobic sense of violence that seemed to hang around the little room and I was aware that there was nowhere to run to.

"You cannot be my daughter." My father kept saying. "No one in my family is light like you are. No one is yellow in my family neither is anyone in your mother's. We are all black... You are yellow."

"Papa, what do you want?" I asked as I made an attempt to rise and escape from him.

I was too late. He pounced on me and before I knew it, he had ripped off my wrapper and pinned me to the raffia mat on the floor. I screamed once. It was loud. It was piercing. It was animal. It was terror. He shoved one of his hands into my mouth to suppress my scream and I bit hard, drawing blood, which tasted salty and metallic. He withdrew his bleeding hand and hit me several times across the face until I stopped screaming and was reduced to subdued sobs.

I didn't know what was happening. All my senses were filled with the acrid stench of my unwashed father and the heat emanating from him. I was also aware of my nakedness and of his rough hands on my young forming breast mounds and the roving thick finger that played rudely with the opening of my womanhood. Was this the same man, who when I was younger would carry me on his lap and play with my fingers? His thick black fingers that tickled me once now violated me.

He muttered something as he took one nipple in his mouth and sucked hungrily.

"Papa no... Papa... Noooo!" I cried.

The tears ran freely down my cheeks as I went into some kind of shock. Momentarily it felt like I had somehow floated out of my body and was watching this terrible thing happen to a person that was once me. He suckled my breasts, biting hard on the nipples before discarding his wrapper and roguishly parting my tiny legs, stinging his way inside me. The pain tore into me, taking me to that faraway place that seemed better than death. All I could see were the cracks on the roof with the big cobwebs and red mud cocoons made by black wasps with the unusual maroon markings. I felt my father fully inside me and the pain brought visions of one particular wasp that always made its way into my room through the opened window. It was some sort of evil spirit, I believed. A wicked spirit that stole the souls of children when they played outside and hurriedly imprisoned them in the cocoons it built in the various corners of my room. I was always scared of this wasp. I felt another sharp, deep pain and I squeezed my eyes shut, trying hard not to scream. I had kept my eyes open an entire night before when that wasp had buzzed its way round and round my room with no hint of going away. I had been afraid. I had cried loudly and had begged my brother to chase the wasp away but he had laughed at me. Thus I had kept my eyes wide awake that night, crouching underneath my cover cloth and sneaking peeks through the little hole I created for my eyes. Through this hole I watched the wasp to make sure it made no attempt to come close enough to sting me through my sleeping cloth or steal my soul.

"*Ku ni!*" Get up. He ordered.

It seemed like no time had passed after all and at the same time it felt like an entire lifetime had washed itself over me while my body was defiled. It was over like it never happened and the only memento of the deed was the faint trace of blood that matted my pubic area and the obvious signs of struggle on the mat. I lay still while he walked away after tossing my stained cover cloth on my roughened frame.

That was not the last of father's visitations. Whenever mother was away and I was home alone, he would come to my room. He was the one who ordered my mother to stop sending me to the stream to fetch water with my siblings because "she's not as strong as the others," he would insist. He was the one who made sure that I was home alone as often as was possible. He was the one who said he would kill me if ever I told anyone what he did to me. I felt so isolated and afraid.

I was very certain that Nnamdi discovered what happened between father and me whenever I was left alone with him, but he said nothing. He let it continue. He never tried to protect me.

How did I know for sure that he knew? It was several months after the first time that father visited me. It was one of those days when mother had either gone to the market or farm and was not expected back early and I had returned from school, so had Nnamdi and Ofunne. Father had quickly sent both of them away on some errand to Obiaku's compound, which was a good twenty-minute walk. As they were leaving, I looked pleadingly at Nnamdi, my eyes trying to convey to him to not leave without me, but he had looked away sullenly. As soon as they left our compound, father was in my room. This time, he didn't stay long; he was finished after only a few minutes. It was usually like this whenever he was drunk. I left the room moments after he had departed, on my way to the back of the house to wash up. By then I had stopped crying after father's visitations, so it was with dried eyes that I stumbled out of the house and to my greatest shock, Nnamdi was standing by the entrance of the compound. Our eyes met once and he quickly looked away. Ofunne was not with him. I recall thinking; "Where is Ofunne?" and also, "God please, let her not have witnessed this!" She was still too young to know what her father was doing to her sister. But I was certain that Nnamdi knew exactly what had happened.

Later that night, while Ofunne was coiled up sleeping on her mat beside me, I decided that I would confront Nnamdi. Though he was much older than I was, a good seven years older, he was still my elder brother and as such, was supposed to protect me. I had little doubt that, despite his small frame, he would be able to face up to our father.

Nnamdi came into the room very late that night. I watched him in the moonlight as he prepared to sleep. His movements were very subtle. He made very little noise. It was as if he was trying hard not to disturb Ofunne and me, believing we were both asleep.

"Nnamdi," I called out softly. I heard him move on his mattress.

"Go to sleep." He sighed.

"I have to talk to you about Papa." I insisted quietly.

"I said, go to sleep." He repeated but this time I heard his voice quiver.

"Papa hurts me." I said in a voice so small I was not sure if he even heard me.

"Shut up." He said gruffly. "It is not a woman's place to complain about her father."

That was it. I didn't sleep that night. I was so disturbed. It was that night that I lost all respect for my brother and all men. It dawned on me that Nnamdi was like his father; he was a man. I wondered if he was protecting father or if he was just too much of a coward to challenge him.

I didn't have to worry too much after that night. Two days later I was sent to Lagos to live with father's younger brother, Kachi, and his wife, Aunty Rosa.

"I don't know what you are talking about." Nnamdi said.

I wasn't surprised. After he shut me up that night years earlier, we never discussed father's visits. I do not believe that it was a coincidence that after I tried to talk to him about father I was bundled off to Lagos like a bad omen to live with father's brother and his wife, who clearly did not like me. But I'm sure Nnamdi must have somehow convinced himself that he knew nothing or that nothing had happened between father and me after all those years of telling himself that lie.

"So let me tell you what happened then." I said. "When I was thirteen years old…"

"I don't want to hear your lies." He cut me off. "These are not things to discuss in the open. What is wrong with you?"

"Nothing, Nnamdi." I said. "But how do you know I'm lying if you claim not to know what I'm talking about?"

He said nothing. I wasn't expecting an answer.

"Why did you come here?" I asked.

"It was mother." He said. "She wanted to know if you were really coming for the burial. Are you?"

"I'm here." I said in response and then stepped away from him.

It felt like somebody suddenly switched on life. I was now aware of the air I breathed and all the noise and people around me, also the deep sense of love and protection that enveloped me from my two good friends.

14

Breakaway

The day Providence packed up his things and left, he squeezed a rumpled piece of paper into my hand. It was late morning and I watched from the doorway of my bedroom as he finally stepped out of his room, a huge canvas bag draped over his left shoulder and another slightly worn-out suitcase in his right hand. The suitcase reminded me of the type used to store those ancient typewriters. Following after him was another Nigerian man, his friend, I presumed. They had both come in together and spent less than ten minutes packing his things. His friend carried another bag with him.

"That's my mobile number." He said. "Don't hesitate to call me if you need anything… anything, okay?"

I nodded glumly. He had come in that morning after spending the last two days away from the house. As our lives had collided that first night when I came into the house almost a year before, he was gone with equal unexpected suddenness. Anguish surged through my soul the moment I heard the thud of the door shutting. I felt like a previously unknown part of me had been cut off and the separation created a painful anxiety. I wished I could cry, I wanted to, but I found no tears to shed.

I unfolded the squeezed piece of paper in my hand and looked at the numbers scrolled on it. He had also written a Leicester address. His handwriting was a series of long intertwining strokes, very artistic and mature. It held my attention for a long while, almost speaking to me. I felt like the whole essence of Providence had somehow been trapped within that little piece of paper. It was all of him I would ever have to keep, since having him in person was never going to be a possibility. I memorized the number and address and then hid that rumpled piece of paper in a place I knew James would never find it.

I was occupied the following days with the marriage arrangements. I had thought that getting a marriage certificate was as easy as it was back home in Nigeria, where one could simply pay a small amount to the clerks at the registry and all requirements would be waived and a marriage certificate would be produced within a day or at most two. But here, a lot more had to be done. One of the requirements was that both James and I produce our passports, birth certificates as well as a Superintendent Registrar Certificate. Before this we had to give notice of our intent to marry with proof that we had been resident in our district for at least seven days. We waited almost a month before we got a response from the Superintendent Registrar saying that our certificate was ready.

One night I woke up drenched in sweat and my heart was pounding fast against my chest. It had been like this for many nights, but this night had been different. I had a bad dream and in the dream, my hands and feet were bound in shackles and linked together with other black men and women as we were led to a port. In the dream I could not tell if it was an airport or a seaport, but it was clear by the stern faces of the white men who shoved and pushed us that we were being taken to a place where we would be returned to our home country. There was a lot of weeping but when I looked round I couldn't identify where the crying was coming from. Instead, I heard voices speaking in Igbo and Yoruba. I saw Princess in the distance beckoning to me and as we approached a bridge it was not Princess that stood there but my father and he said in a language that was not his, in a white man's voice, "No escape for you." That was when I woke up. James was still sleeping, undisturbed on his side of the bed. I got up and left the room.

The wall clock in the kitchen told me it was 2:17 a.m. I had only succumbed to sleep less than three hours earlier. I knew I wasn't going to fall asleep again, just like the other nights. What is the worst thing to happen? I asked myself as I put the kettle on the stove. Our request would be rejected. I would be sent back home. It could not be worse than that. Then why was I so worried? Why did my heart beat so fast and so hard?

Shhhhhhhhhhhhhhhhhhhhhhhhhhhhhhhh.

The kettle whistled, tearing me away from my worries. I switched off the stove and poured some hot water into my mug and then a silent giggle escaped me. It all seemed funny to me how, slowly, I was truly becoming British. The whole idea that all I could think of doing in a time of worry was to make tea was strangely comical to me. When had this change occurred? When a woman worried back home, nothing as trivial as a cup of tea could soothe her nerves and yet, here I was with my cup of tea.

"What are you doing here?" I looked up and James was by the door. "Do you have any idea what the time is?"

I turned to look at the wall clock. It was 2:43 a.m.

"I was thirsty." I said.

"For tea?" He said sardonically.

"I couldn't sleep." I said resignedly. "I'm so worried, James."

"Worried about what?" He asked.

"Everything." I said. "What if our request is turned down because I'm now an illegal alien?"

"I've told you countless times that I know someone in the Home Office." He grunted. "We are sorted. Now come back to bed."

I obeyed him only because I knew it had not been a request but an order. I was not comforted by his telling me he knew someone in the Home Office. In fact, I found it a bit odd that he claimed to know anyone there. James worked in the maintenance unit of the local council. He fixed leaking taps in council flats, repaired broken heaters and other such menial jobs. There was nothing posh about his job and it was very unlikely that he might know someone in the Home Office.

Surprisingly, everything turned out all right. We were issued with the Superintendent Registrar Certificate and were married the following weekend.

It was a very small private ceremony that took place in the Town Hall, actually in a small office within the Town Hall. Present were the officiating registrar, three witnesses that included Thomas, Sam and Claudia, James' sister, and of course James and myself. The entire ceremony lasted less than fifteen minutes.

Sam had been her chatty self. I recalled our first meeting at the nightclub. She had warned me then to be careful of James but now she seemed oblivious to all that as she smiled at me and squeezed my hands whenever she had the opportunity.

"This is really happening." She had whispered into my ears more than once.

I wanted to ask her if I still had anything to fear about James, but I stopped myself when I saw the excitement that tainted her eyes. I wondered whether it was because she was happy for James and me or whether it was simply the giddy excitement of a wedding, any wedding at all. Maybe women in England were like women in Nigeria who got excited by weddings; their minds got caught up in the fantasy of *happily ever after.*

I was very curious about James' sister, Claudia. In a way, they looked alike. They shared the same red hair and straight nose with the slight bump in the middle. Her eyes were a darker hue of green, almost black.

"Hello!" I said as soon as James introduced us. "It's so nice to finally meet you."

She looked in my direction and avoided my eyes. She said nothing to me but simply lifted her head slightly before turning away. I felt indignant at her behaviour because I had actually wanted her to like me. I had hoped that when I finally met with someone from James' family, I would warm up to them. One of the reasons I looked forward to this ceremony was to meet his sister and maybe, just maybe, bond with her. I did not expect to be snubbed so openly by her. I wondered what she thought of me. Did she only see my colour? Was I that desperate African woman who did not deserve her brother? I tried at various times to speak with her, but she made it pretty clear that she wanted nothing to do with me. Whenever I drifted to her side to join in a conversation she was having with either Sam or Thomas, she would look at me coldly before she turned away. She did this a couple of times before I decided not to bother.

Assessing her from a distance, I was able to get the answers I was looking for. She was no classy lady, nor did she ooze sophistication or show signs of any privileged upbringing. She was dressed in a drab-looking dress with floral prints, which did nothing to conceal her excess weight. Like her brother, she smoked a lot and everything that came out of her mouth was blemished by a swear word. But finally I had my answers to James' family. As I said my "I do," I realized that I was marrying a lie. James did not come from the background he had painted when we first started communicating and now I was certain of it.

"White men tell lies too." Bessie said dismissively.

We were walking to the open market to buy some groceries. It was a Sunday afternoon. I had just told her about the lies James had told me about his roots before I came to England. She didn't seem surprised at all, merely irritated that I had believed him in the first place.

"And why shouldn't he lie?" He continued. "He is a man after all. They all lie especially when they want something."

We stopped under a makeshift tent where fresh large

tomatoes and okra were on display. Bessie picked up a plump tomato and sniffed it. She frowned and I presumed she was still upset with me for not inviting her to the civil ceremony. I had wanted to, but James had been quite explicit about whom he didn't want in the wedding. Though Bessie had told me that it was all right, I sensed she was upset.

"So does Nicolas lie to you?" I asked and immediately regretted my cheek.

Bessie replaced the tomato gently, murmuring about how you must look out for rotten tomatoes in life, slipping her wise words in as gently as she rearranged the seller's display. Then she looked up to stare at me coldly. I opened my mouth to apologize for being rude, but with a brush of her right hand she hushed me.

"When Nicolas lies to me, I know." She said. "And it is not very often. All men lie."

"I'm sorry," I said, "I shouldn't have mentioned Nicolas."

"You apologize too much." She said, smiling suddenly. "Nicolas is a man, after all. He is one of them, but he knows better, he respects me and loves me."

The abruptness of her smile immediately lessened the tension that had been building up. I was relieved. I had other issues that were troubling me that I wanted to discuss with her and since she was the only one I had to talk to, it would not have been wise to upset her.

Ever since the wedding, James had become a different person. The day we returned from the Home Office after applying for my British papers, I had gone to the room to change out of the stuffy formal skirt suit. Bessie had helped me pick out that blue suit and pink cotton blouse from the sales rack at Matalan. It had cost £35 for the entire outfit. With the money I had saved from styling Bessie's friends' hair, I was able to afford it, and Bessie had encouraged me to spoil myself a little sometimes. Anyway, as I was hanging the suit in the wardrobe, James shouted for me from the living room. When I finally got there, he was stretched out on the couch with his feet crossed on the coffee table; his hands lay folded on his belly.

"What were you doing?" He asked. "I called you over five minutes ago!"

"I was changing, James." I said. "Did you want something?"

"Get me a can of beer from the fridge." He said.

"Is that all?" I asked.

He simply nodded.

"You could have just walked to the kitchen." I said. "You were closer to getting yourself a beer than I was."

"You are here now." He said.

I walked away and got him the beer. But it didn't stop there. He continued with this, waking me up late at night to fetch him something he had left in the bathroom or underneath the staircase. It didn't take me long to realize that he was doing everything intentionally. I saw the deliberate look in his eyes whenever I returned from one of his hopeless errands. Early this morning, before he left the house for work and before Bessie and I left for the market, he had woken me up to make him breakfast. The time was 5:45 a.m.

"James, what is going on?" I asked.

"I want something to eat." He said.

"You never want something to eat at this time." I said. "What has got into you? You treat me like I am some slave."

"You are my wife now." He said. "Wives serve their husbands. Is it any different in Africa?"

"What are you talking about?" I asked.

"I'm talking about how it never bothered you to serve Providence." He said. "You'd make him coffee and stuff and it never bothered you."

I stared at him with questioning eyes.

"Thomas told me about you and Providence." He said.

"What exactly did he tell you?" I asked.

Even as I asked that question, it struck me that the answer didn't matter. It didn't matter what Thomas may have told him, what mattered really was that James believed him. There was nothing I could say or do to make him disbelieve Thomas. This was why I needed to talk to Bessie. I knew she, too, had her suspicions about my feelings for Providence. I knew this because any time we talked and Providence's name was mentioned, she would look at me quizzically and knowingly.

"Bessie," I said as we approached another vegetable stall, "I'm not sure I did the right thing by marrying James."

"Why?" She asked. "Is it because he lied to you about his roots?"

"No." I answered. "He's been treating me like a slave lately."

"How, sis-te?" She asked.

We stopped by the vegetable stall and Bessie quickly exchanged some pleasantries in her native language with the Ghanaian seller. She picked up two large melons and mentally weighed them, her hands and body becoming a human scale.

"What makes you think he is treating you like his slave?" Bessie asked as she dropped one of the melons, the lighter one.

"It's just how I feel when I'm around him." I said. "All of a sudden he is commanding me all over the place. He would be sitting in the kitchen and I may be watching something on the television in the living room and then he would call for me to get him something on the kitchen counter or from the fridge. Other times, he would wake me up at night and demand I go bring him something he left in the living room earlier in the day. Or he would call me up during the day and ask me to make him his favourite mashed potatoes with peas, carrots and grilled chicken but when he gets back he would refuse eating that and demand I make him something else."

"Maybe he believes you are his slave then?" Bessie concluded. "He married you, didn't he? He believes he has saved you and wants you to accept that you owe him eternally."

"I don't know." I said, thinking instead that he was reacting to the things Thomas had made him believe.

"I know." She interjected. "I was once married to a man like James. He thought he was doing me a favour by marrying me. He would tell me I was fat and ugly when he was angry. No man would have stepped up to marry me if he hadn't, he would add. He told me this for so long that soon I started to believe it myself. Out of guilt-induced gratitude, I would jump when he asked me to, bend down like a bitch so he could have his way with me from behind and when he was done, I would say, thank you."

She had delivered her speech in a calm measured tone, only her eyes betrayed her true sentiment. I noticed her brows had knotted and her two pupils were like two black dagger points. It struck me that she might be right about James. In his mind he had done me the ultimate favour a white man could do for a black African woman, and that I was indebted to him forever. After all, what had been his answer when I asked him to reveal to me what Thomas had told him? He had merely shrugged and said it was no business of mine. What really could Thomas have told him? He saw nothing and knew nothing of Providence and me.

A long silence passed. Uttering anything immediately would have rubbished the impact of her words. The silence seemed almost deliberate on both our parts; it allowed her to release a bad memory that had been buried deep within her, while allowing me to see how easy it was for me to become the woman she once was.

I decided then never to tell her about what had transpired between Providence and me. This woman who had been through so many traumas in the hands of an African man would surely not approve of a fellow woman giving in to moments of weakness and debasement caused by a man. As much as I understood she did not like James, I also got the feeling that she did not think much of Providence either. And I had not allowed myself to reflect on what had happened between Providence and me that wet summer morning when James had asked me to marry him. My thoughts had died an unnatural death and I found myself refusing to awaken those memories with even a sprinkling of hope.

✶

It wasn't quite 5 a.m. when I heard the doorbell ring followed by a continuous banging on the front door. James had stirred in his sleep.

"What the hell!" He mumbled.

I got up and headed downstairs to answer the door. I figured it was Thomas—sometimes he forgot his keys and I had to let him in. As I made my way to the door, I was aware of the sickening silence that pervaded the atmosphere. It seemed that the entire city of London was asleep at the same time. There was no sound on the streets, even the birds had gone into hiding; everything was still. Then there was the doorbell again and the banging.

When I opened the door, I was surprised to find Bessie standing there. She was crying. Her eyes were red and swollen and a wet dribble ran from one of her nostrils. She was still in her nightdress, which she had managed to cover up with a bathrobe.

"Are you alright, Bessie?" I asked. My immediate thought was that something had happened to her or her children. I had never seen her cry before.

"She's dead." Bessie cried. "Haven't you heard?"

"Angela?" I said. Angela was her daughter's name.

"Diana." She said. "She's dead. The news is all over the BBC."

"Oh my God!" I cried.

I pulled her into the house and led her to the living room where I immediately switched on the television set. A picture of the princess loomed with a caption that confirmed her death in a car crash early that morning in Paris. As the correspondent's voice filtered in, Bessie's sobbing became a loud ominous cry. Even though I felt her pain, I was more worried then that she would wake James up.

"She was such a good woman." She cried. "I don't understand why this had to happen to her."

"Everybody loved her." I said soothingly.

Even as I said this it occurred to me then how I had never for once thought about Diana or how much of an impact she had on so many lives, especially women's lives here in England. Yet I felt pain, a real pain at knowing she was dead and this surprised me. Was I grieving because she was a woman? Or was I grieving because like me she had lived through a less than perfect marriage and just when she was on the verge of starting a new life, it was suddenly over? Was this also to be my fate?

We cried together as we listened to the highlights of what happened as Diana and Dodi Al Fayed had been chased into the tunnel under the Place de I' Alma in Paris by a group of desperate photographers. We were still crying together when Thomas yawned his way into the living room. As ever, he had no concern for anybody's privacy, just his own importance.

"Shit!" He said as he hurriedly tried to stop his swinging penis on sighting Bessie and tried to beat a manly retreat from her eyes.

We both stared at him, our eyes like batons chasing his truncheon. His shame was as evident as the awkward hands that covered his crotch. Any other time, this might have brought a chuckle, but that day it felt like something special between us had been violated...by a man.

Bessie left not long after that, still crying and with a resolve to lay flowers at the gates of the royal palace along with thousands of others. Sadness hung in the air that summer day like a dark foreboding cloud. England mourned the death of the people's princess and while I grieved with them, I thought about Nigeria and my dear Princess and how she had told me about the death of Fela, another beloved Nigerian icon. Only a week or so earlier, I had learned while speaking with Princess and Uloma on the phone that the radical Afro-beat musician who had in his time criticized and challenged practically all the ruling military Heads of State in Nigeria including the current one with his music, had eventually died of what many believed to be AIDS. Many in Nigeria loved him but just as many loathed his junkie lifestyle and numerous women. I was one of those who loathed that lifestyle despite agreeing somewhat with the philosophy of his lyrics.

Diana's death combined with Fela's shook me up in many ways that day. They seemed to tie my lives with the two countries together. I felt that halving; the split in me so painfully realized, and also joyously, for grief can sometimes open up truths. The world had come to know how unhappy and beautiful Diana had been, how the two existed together in a symbolic way and how she, like an Everywoman, mirrored other lives, even mine. Her private life became public in a way that allowed her to reflect some of the hope and despair that many kept hidden. The princess had felt emotionally starved. I knew that feeling. She also had her secrets. And here I was with my own troubling secret. Providence.

The next time I saw Bessie was two days later. She had been out on the playground across our building with her children. There were a couple of cement benches scattered round the ground and she had placed herself on the one underneath the huge oak tree. There were a couple of nylon shopping bags placed by her side and as I approached, I noticed she was reading a newspaper, *The Independent*. Her face still wore the gloom from Diana's death, but she was no longer crying.

"Hi, Bessie." I said as I sat down beside her.

"Sis-te," she said glancing away from what she was reading, "how are you?"

I told her I was fine and immediately she began talking about Diana as if she had known her intimately.

"They killed her you know. Men!" She said. "They just wouldn't let her be."

"She died in a car crash Bessie." I said.

"I know that." She waved the newspaper in my face, showing me a picture of the wrecked car. "But the car wouldn't have crashed if it wasn't being chased by those disgusting men."

"Photographers," I corrected.

"How many of those photographers were women?" She retorted.

I had no answer to that question. She looked away and I presumed her eyes were searching for her children on the playground.

"Men," she continued, "it's almost their unbridled ambition to destroy women. We are not their slaves, Erika. You must remember this. Even Diana had to let go. Her divorce was right. Women are life and we have to seek life. Don't wait until it's too late."

Her words resonated in my head for the rest of the day like a warning from a soothsayer, startlingly similar to Princess' warnings of years before.

I have often questioned what really happened the night James first hit me. What was it I did wrong? Was it really me? But most important, I had struggled to understand how he had changed to the violent man that he had become. I believed that his change was sudden and abrupt but now as I look back to that period in my life, I realize that there was nothing abrupt about his change. All I needed to do was to look closer and see all the warning signs.

That first night there had been a phone call from James' sister, Claudia. I knew it was her because I had answered the phone and when she told me who it was in a very curt manner, I handed the phone to James. That call must have upset him visibly. I watched his face turn crimson and between cursing at intervals and kicking the kitchen stool, he would pause to listen to the phone and then roll his eyes in rage. Eventually he walked out of the kitchen with the phone still glued to his ear.

"She's damn crazy for sticking with that old bastard." I heard him say from the passageway. "I don't bloody care anymore."

His words sounded quite harsh and his anger was visible when he made his way back into the kitchen and slammed the phone down. I had the urge to take him in my arms and quell his pain, whatever it was. I sensed it was a family issue and I was his wife now, an integral part of his family. That was the way it would have been back home in Nigeria. A wife would be there to tell her husband that things were okay. She would be there to put him at ease and take away his worry. I had watched my mother do this with my father many times when I was a little girl, long before my innocence was shattered. There were days he would come back home in such a foul and violent mood and it was mother's duty to soothe him. I had watched her and learned from her that only a wife or mistress had the power to pacify a raging bull.

"What was that all about, James?" I asked.

"Nothing." He mumbled.

He moved to sit on one of the kitchen chairs and was smoking a cigarette furiously. I had just finished washing my hands after cutting up some onions when I walked up behind him to massage his shoulders. He used to like it when I did that.

"James, you need to relax." I said as I clamped my hands on his shoulder blades, feeling the tense, knotted muscles.

"Frigging leave me alone!" He barked.

It happened then, almost like in slow motion. James shrugged my hands away from his shoulder, swivelling round at the same time. He shot out of the chair. His right hand was raised and then came crashing down on my face. His blow was so unexpected that I was knocked off my feet. I landed on my backside on the wooden floor with my back hitting the kitchen cabinet. I watched his foot smash into my sides repeatedly.

"See what you made me do." He said breathlessly.

"Please stop." I cried as I felt a kick on my back. "I'm sorry...I'm sorry..."

When the kicking stopped, I peeked through my arms, which had become a crossed shield to lessen the impact of his violence. I was not sure, but I thought I also saw what seemed to be traces of tears trapped in his maddened green eyes. His face was still very red and a network of veins interlaced his entire frame from his face to the exposed parts of his arms and neck, straining with his blood.

"See what you made me do." He sighed and then stepped back from me.

He stood still for a full minute in absolute silence and all I could see were his legs in the blue pair of jeans he wore and his white and black sneakers. I dare not look up at his face or eyes for fear of igniting another sequence of madness but my eyes were locked on his legs. His right one twitched in an uncontrolled spasm, rippling and creasing the fabric of the jeans and causing me to shudder as I imagined he would invariably launch another volley of kicks in my direction. Slowly, I watched his legs turn away and then he walked out of the kitchen.

I stayed where I was, crouched on the floor with my knees pressed against my chest and my arms cradling my frame in a solitary embrace.

15

Little Blue Book

November 11, 1997
  Dear Diary,
  It's the eleventh day of the eleven month. And it's yet another winter. I feel so cold. So alone. Another night and James isn't here. He didn't return last night either. We had another fight on Thursday. No. We didn't fight, he just hit me again. This time he had complained that I did not pick up his call in the afternoon. He wanted to know where I was and what I was doing. I told him I was probably asleep when he called, but he said I was lying. I was. He believes I was either with Bessie or with another man. I wasn't. He believes that I get visits from Providence. I don't. The truth was, I didn't want to pick up the phone because I knew it was him calling. I didn't want to speak with him or with anybody.
  I'm happy he is not home again. It's already past eleven. Almost midnight. I don't think he will be coming home again tonight.
  Maybe tonight I will sleep. I didn't sleep last night. I was afraid he would return in a fouler mood and start looking for another fight. I'm tired. I'm much too tired. Tonight I will sleep.

✶

December 10, 1997
    Dear Diary,
    I got a mail from the Home Office today.
    It was addressed to James. But I knew what it was. I recognized the envelope as the very same one we registered and sent off to the Home Office months ago with my application forms and marriage certificate. I opened it. I couldn't wait for James to come back. Inside were my new British passport and some other documents.
    I did not tell James anything about the mail.
    Tonight was quiet.

December 20, 1997
    Dear Diary,
    I think Bessie knows James is hitting me. She was looking at me funny today. She asked me if things were all right with me and James and I told her they were. I wish I could talk to her about this, but I can't. I know what she would say, and I don't want to hear it. I almost told her about my passport, but decided not to. I'm afraid if I talk about it, James will find out.
    I'm confused about James. Last night he was all warm and loving. He kissed me and then made love to me. This morning when I reached out to him, he withdrew. He looked at me coldly and left the bedroom.
    What does this all mean?

December 23, 1997
    Dear Diary,
    James is becoming suspicious. He asked me today if the parcel from the Home Office arrived. I told him it hadn't. It was frightening when he mentioned the passport. It was almost as if he knew. He kept looking at me intensely whenever

I passed him. It was unnerving. I even thought at a point that he had discovered the passport from where I hid it. If he had, he would have discovered you, Diary, as well. My life would have been over if that had happened. When he finally left the house, I hurried to the room to check. I was relieved, but also afraid. Should I hide my passport in another place? I don't think James would find it. He hates lifting things. He hated me moving the furniture around... I think I am safe. For now, Diary. For now.

January 01, 1998
Dear Diary,
It's a new year today!
It feels the same to me. I am supposed to be happy today, but I am not.
Thomas surprised me this morning. He got me a gift. He gave me a little bottle of perfume wrapped in a red gift paper. He said he thought I would like something. I kept the gift. I wanted to reject it, but it was the only gift I got. James got me nothing. He got me nothing for Christmas as well. So I accepted Thomas' gift. I wonder if he's feeling sorry for me. Is this pity? He has seen what James does to me. Unlike Bessie, I cannot avoid him. I cannot hide my scars from him.

February 14, 1998
It's Valentine's Day, a day for lovers.
James didn't come home last night and I don't think he will be coming home tonight either.
I broke up with Bessie today. I had to. She was seeing too much and asking too many questions. I am ashamed that she is seeing me this way. I don't want her to feel pity for me. Yet every time she asks me what's wrong or consoles me, all I see is pity in her eyes and I feel a rage I can't explain. She is my friend, but I don't want her pity. I hate it that every

time I look at her, I see a content woman with a happy home and wonderful family. Without knowing it, she makes me see what I don't have. Should I resent her for this? Should I resent her that my life is such a mess?

I told her the bruise on my left arm was sustained from a fall and immediately she called me a liar, in her usual, causal way. I was so angry with her that moment that I told her she was pompous and felt superior. I also called her an ugly fat woman and asked her to leave my house.

God, I feel terrible about everything I said to her. I wish I could take it all back. She has been nothing but good to me.

But this may be best, Diary. James had made some threats against her if I continued to associate with her and now with his erratic behaviour, who knows how far he would go?

I will miss Bessie. I will miss our talks and the times we spent together.

I'm sorry Bessie!

March 15, 1998

Dear Diary,

Things are getting worse. It seems every day now a new scar is added to the existing ones. Even when there are no marks to show, the scars inside me are widening.

This morning James started one of his pointless arguments. I could not take my eyes off the kitchen knife he was holding as he screamed at me. I was afraid that he was going to cut me with the knife. He didn't but I could see from the look in his eyes that he could if he had wanted to.

I am tired of being afraid.

I could leave him.

I should leave him.

I have my papers now. And passport. I am British now. I should leave him...

April 07, 1998
    Dear Diary,
    I saw Bessie from my bedroom window today. She looked well and alive. She was with one of her Ghanaian friends, Mekwa. For a minute I wanted to run out and join them. But I didn't.
    I packed my suitcases today. And then I emptied them again. This is the fourth time I have done this.
    It took only ten minutes to pack the two suitcases. I am sure I can do it in eight minutes if I tried harder. Ten minutes, that is all it took.
    James is sleeping in the bedroom. He reeks of alcohol. He smells like he hasn't washed in days.
    I hate that I have to write this in the bathroom.
    Ten minutes.

16

One-Way Ticket

There was a loud bang, as the front door was slammed shut. I'm not sure what grabbed my attention more, the banging of the door or the mouse that crossed from the washing machine to the hole in the cupboard by the cooker. The mouse's long tail was still visible as it made its way inside the cupboard. There were pieces of cornflakes still on the floor from previous days, a squeezed-up newspaper used to wrap fish and chips two nights earlier was crumpled on the floor by the bin—Thomas had made an aim for the bin and missed but still left the trash on the floor. On the stove I had clean pots and pans but in the sink there was a pile of dirty dishes.

I heard his footsteps on the stairs. There was another bang—the bedroom door. He had come back early today. It was only 8.12 p.m.; it wasn't even that dark outside. I stepped out of the kitchen into the passage and my eyes were fixed on the little store-away underneath the stairs. Some coats were hung there and some old boots and shoes were stored there, covered in dust and cobwebs. Only moments earlier I had hidden my suitcases there. It had taken me eight minutes this time to pack. I took only the necessaries. I wonder if James would notice anything. I was about to return the suitcases to the bedroom and unpack just before James returned. What would he have thought if he had seen me carrying those suitcases?

I moved away from the passageway and back to the kitchen. Old letters and bills were scattered on the kitchen table. I went straight to the table and sat on the chair closest to it. I heard the bedroom door slam again and hurried footsteps on the stairs.

"Christ!" James said as he entered the kitchen. "Why is the house so dirty?"

So he noticed, I thought to myself.

"Didn't you hear me?" He asked. "What were you doing all day? Why's the house so filthy?"

I stood up and began walking towards the entrance to the kitchen. My mind was fixed on my suitcases. What would happen if he discovered them? Ten minutes. Eight minutes. Five minutes… My head was counting minutes. How come time was getting shorter?

"I'm talking to you." James said, grabbing my shoulder. "Where the hell do you think you are going?"

"What do you want, James?" I asked, shrugging his hand off.

"Why is the house so dirty?" He demanded. "What is going on?"

"Nothing is going on, James." I snapped. "If you think the house is dirty, then maybe you can clean the damn place and while you are at it you can get Thomas to join you."

I don't know where those words came from but I saw the shocked look in his eyes and I experienced a sickening thrill watching him. For that one moment alone he must have wondered where I had found the courage to challenge him, but the moment quickly passed.

"F…k you," He shouted. "F…king shut up."

"No, f…k you, James." I shouted back, feeling adrenaline rushing through me.

I knew I was treading on dangerous ground, but I was past caring, there was a sickening exhilaration that seized me. I had never been confrontational all my life but as soon as I spoke back to James, I was more afraid to resume the role of the submissive servant. There was no going back.

So when James struck me, it occurred to me that I could strike back. Somewhere between his blows, I struck back. And when he hit me to the ground, I searched for anything I could use as a weapon. I found a brass handle underneath the kitchen chair and I reached out and grabbed it despite his kicks. I pulled myself up and wielding my weapon, I struck him squarely in the face. There was a piercing scream as well as blood everywhere—his and mine. He knocked the brass handle away from my hand and came at me again with renewed rage. I felt his blows deafening my ears, his kicks crushing my ribs and instead of crying and pleading for him to stop, I fought back. I had finally found the strength to fight back and cause him almost as much pain as he had inflicted on me.

It was not just him that I fought that night. It was all the men who had damaged me all through the years. It was my father; I finally took hold of his wretched manhood and castrated him. It was Gerald; I finally told him off for not making any attempt to find me after our last time together. It was Thomas; I finally told him that I would never have an interest in him and that parading himself naked in front of me would never change that. It was every man who had looked down on me because I was a woman; I finally looked them straight in the eyes and spat on them.

"Jesus!" I heard Thomas' voice amidst the bashing. "James, you are going to kill her."

I watched as Thomas thrust himself between us, eventually dragging James away from me. James struggled but Thomas had his arms firmly locked behind him. They were soon sprawled on the floor close to me, Thomas' legs held James down in a scissors grip. There seemed to be blood everywhere and the kitchen furniture was scattered all over the place. I looked away from the men and my eyes captured a woman by the doorway. She looked scared. Her eyes were wide and wild with shock as she stared fixedly at me. I knew her. I had seen her before with Thomas. She was one of his many black women.

"What are you trying to do man?" I heard Thomas whisper to James. "She's a woman… you don't hit women like that, man!"

"The bitch hit me." I heard James say.

"It don't matter." Thomas said. "Man, it don't matter."

Thomas released James only after he had promised not to touch me again. I watched him as he got up. He looked at himself briefly before he walked out of the kitchen, not looking at me once. I heard the front door slam shut and knew he would not return that night.

Thomas shook his head at me and sighed. He said nothing to me. Instead, he turned around to face his woman. Her frightened eyes were reluctant to look away from me even as he gently pulled her away.

When they were gone, I straightened out my rumpled dress and went straight to the store underneath the stairs and packed my suitcases.

"A one-way ticket to Leicester, please." I said to the man behind the glass-partitioned counter.

How strange it seemed to be saying that. A one-way ticket? When was life one way? When had I ever known of a life in one direction? After so much packing and deliberate secrecy it was hard to imagine I was here at last.

I looked at the man in the stiff blue jacket. The white shirt without creases. A life so immaculate.

"A one-way ticket." He said. It was so plainly-spoken, so clear as if it meant nothing. He then passed it so that it slid under the glass to my fingers. And he took my money without even looking. He didn't see my looks… I was buying back my life. He didn't see the bruises. Not even the lips, cracked like the pavement, like a crack on life's surface. It was a whirl, yes—a maelstrom. That was such a good word I'd picked up from Bessie's *Independence*. Maelstrom. Whirlwind. Male-strom. Male storm.

I calmed myself and picked up my suitcases like ballast

for balance. Swinging in my hands, I felt their propulsion. Soon I would be gone. But I was gone already. Here I was at St. Pancreas, at King's Cross Station, saying goodbye, to my king, James King. Now, there was an irony, one of too many. Everything in my way seemed to cut two ways.

"Goodbye Mr. King." I said from King's Cross, St. Pancras. "Goodbye Mrs. King."

As I looked at my ticket, I was already gone. But how far gone was I? A one-way ticket from His and Hers. A one-way ticket to somewhere that was nowhere. For what did I know of this place called Leicester? All that I knew was out of the whirlwind. And that, yes, that, that had to be good. Slowly I walked; how well that even sticks now. It adheres to the memory like a bruise on the neck bone. I walked to a bench and set down my luggage. I waited for the train with a mind firmly focused. Talking to myself as I tried to recollect what I had done. Was about to do. I sat on the bench and adjusted my body so not too much weight came near to my bruise and thought of Bessie and the letter I had left for her. Would it be enough to account for my strangeness, for I knew I had rejected her to conceal my escape. In the end I had trusted no one, not even myself. Not knowing if I was daring until the final minute. Had I left it too late? How long in my life had the train been gone? What would she feel when she read the farewell letter?

It had taken me eight months to realize that I had to finally let go. And it felt right. As I left that morning, I wanted to stop by Bessie's house and tell her goodbye, but there was no need for that. I noticed her from her kitchen window as I passed. There was something eerily familiar with the way she looked and I quickly realized that this was the way she was when I first saw her. I paused to stare and she finally looked up. Our eyes met and then she smiled. It was all I needed. I mouthed to her that I was sorry. She nodded and waved me goodbye. I slipped the letter I had written to her through the letter slot in her door, knowing she would find it and read it. Knowing also she would understand.

And so I sat with my one-way ticket securely in my pocket. The wind was blowing on the station as I checked the time of departure: 11:45 a.m., and I nervously fingered my ticket. It had cost £15. That was the price of my freedom. It had to be one-way. As I waited, clutching the old piece of paper with its phone number and an address; I finally understood what it meant to let go. And like many women, I imagined, who had been physically and emotionally abused by men, what letting go meant was to simply vanish into the shadows where the past could not catch up ever again with the future.

17

Finding Providence

New beginnings. That was what it felt like as the scenery from the train platform in Leicester hit me; long rail tracks snaking their way into invisible nothingness the further I looked in the direction I had come and at the same time new carriages appearing and disappearing into this same nothingness. Preceding this nothingness was the smoke of fog faintly creating its own illusions, at once a magician's prop for his disappearing act—one train appeared, two disappeared and then another appeared from the other direction. I watched this train-station trickery for a minute or so, marvelling at its almost trancelike repetition, before I felt my skin tighten from the chilling breeze. It was only then that I noticed the people around me, some hugging their warm clothing, some smoking and some like me, carrying a bag or two, all moving fast, in a hurry to leave the station and the cold. It struck me that there was one thing different from them and me: they all seemed to know where they were going. And while I knew where I wanted to go, I had no idea how I was going to get there.

I moved away from the train platform and followed the exit signs until I was inside the station building. It was much warmer there and much rowdier. I looked round until I noticed a pay phone. I dug into my pockets and retrieved Providence's note with his phone number and address inscribed on it. My heart pounded as I approached the telephone. Many thoughts flashed through my head, the most recurrent one being—suppose he didn't use that number anymore? He had given me the number months earlier and not once had I ever called him. What would he think if I called him now? Would he have forgotten who I was? He couldn't! He couldn't just have forgotten me like that. People don't forget people that easily. I knew because I had spent my entire life trying to forget certain people, hoping even that by not seeing them, I would certainly erase their existence from my memory, but alas! I could not forget them. Providence could not forget me.

I found a fifty pence coin in my purse and slotted it into the phone.

Providence had said I should call him for anything. Anything. Those were his words, his wishes and there had been no expiration date tagged to them. He had looked me in the eye and spoken with all sincerity. And I believed him.

I began dialling the number.

If Providence had changed his number, he would have found a way to reach me, to inform me that he had a new number. He would have known when it was right to call me, he knew I was always in the house and he knew when James was not there. He knew. He knew because he had lived in that same house with us. He knew when it was safe to speak to me, to touch me—like he did that morning…

I pushed the last digit.

What would I do if the call didn't go through? What if I got a programmed message informing me that the number was no longer in use? What would I do then? Or what if another woman picked up the phone? I would ask for Providence and she would ask why I needed to speak to him and what would I say? It had been months and I never called him and he never called me either. Why didn't he ever call? Not even once to say hello and find out how I was doing. And now I was here and expecting what from him?

"Hello?"

It was his voice. It was the way I recalled it, deep and manly with traces of the Nigerian flavour. I closed my eyes, his image filled my senses—the darkness of his skin, the firmness of his body and strong arms with the thick long fingers that had held me. I pictured his face and his deep meaningful eyes. I saw his completeness as if he stood right in front of me.

"Hello?" He said again and this time with less excitement. "Who is this?"

"It is me, Providence." I said.

"Who?" He asked and I heard the uncertainty in his tone.

"It's me." I repeated not sure what name he would respond to.

"Erika?" he said and then, "Ngozi?"

"Yes."

I'm not sure if I imagined the silence that followed, but it did feel like a quiet moment passed. In that moment my mind was conjuring up thoughts of rejection and regret for not thinking things through before I set out in search of him.

"I can't believe it's you, Ngozi." He said. "Where are you calling from?"

"I'm here." I answered. "I'm in Leicester."

"Where?" He asked. I sensed the restrained uncertainty in his voice.

"In Leicester." I repeated. "At the train station."

"You are here in Leicester, at the train station?" He repeated disbelievingly. "And where is James? Is he with you?"

"I'm alone." I answered. "I left James and I had nowhere else to go."

I waited for the expected excuses that this was not a good time, that he was still squatting with his friend or that he was living with a British girlfriend who had promised to marry him and my turning up would complicate things for him. I waited for the rejection.

"Are you okay?" He asked instead.

Was I okay? This was a question no one had asked me in a very long time.

"I'm fine." I said.

"Okay, wait there." He said, "There's a coffee shop opposite the station, you would have to cross the road. Wait there for me and I will come get you. I should be there in about fifteen minutes okay?"

Just like that, there was no rejection. He was coming for me and suddenly I released the air trapped in my lungs. All my fears had been for nothing.

I left the station and found the coffee shop just beside a subway shop. This was a busy part of the town; across the street were quite a number of pubs, Italian and Chinese restaurants and many estate agencies with pictures of Victorian and modern apartments on display. I noticed two destitutes sitting underneath a lamp post on torn pieces of cardboard begging for money. I dropped two 50p coins in front of each of them as I passed.

The coffee shop had chimes on the door that jingled as I entered. There were about a dozen other people already inside and they all looked up at me as soon as I entered. Some stared longer than the others and I imagined those who kept their eyes locked on me were wondering about the bruises on my face. I had almost forgotten that they were there. I wondered what Providence would think when he saw me this way.

It was warm inside. I made my way to the counter and ordered a large coffee. The lady behind the counter smiled warmly at me before handing me my order. I smiled back. There was nothing else to do. The crowded room seemed to clear for me as I looked for a spot to settle. I noticed a young woman with a man, probably her lover; she looked at me and then clutched her man's hand tightly as she whispered something into his ears. He raised his head then and lazily stared at me. I immediately saw the metal stud that pierced his bottom lip and the other by the corner of his left eyebrow. I waited by a corner not far from the door with my coffee and my luggage, waiting.

Waiting for Providence.

I saw him the instant he crossed the road. He was wearing a black leather jacket with a thick scarf round his neck, blue jeans and a pair of black trainers. His head was covered with a grey wool skullcap. He looked fuller than when I last saw him, but it was Providence with his springy walk and long legs.

I didn't wait for him to meet me in the shop, I couldn't. I grabbed the handle of my bags and stepped out of the shop into the cold and as soon as I did this, he looked up and saw me. He smiled and waved at me and I waved back. He quickened his pace and soon he was directly in front of me, almost too close for I noticed the instant transformation his face underwent as his eyes finally renewed their acquaintance with my face. I saw his surprise and then watched his eyes quiver slightly with anger or rage, I can't remember now.

"He did this to you." He said solemnly.

"I left him." I said.

He looked into my eyes deeply and I felt his hands touch my face carefully like a doctor would as he inspected a patient. His fingers were cold against my skin but they were soothing.

"He won't hurt you again." He said into my ears as he embraced me. "No one will ever hurt you again."

No one would ever hurt you again.

He took my bags and led me through the streets of Leicester—London Road, Victoria Park Road, Queens Road and Howard Street.

"It was hard leaving you behind in that house." He said, once we were off the busy street. "I didn't know if it was the right thing and I wasn't sure of Leicester either."

"You look happy and well." I said, reassuringly.

"Oh, I've managed pretty well." He said, smiling. "It was rough at first, you know, learning the trade and trying to get new clients and all, but Kelechi—the guy I told you about who has a business here, was very good to me. In no time I was making money too, clean money."

He looked happy as he spoke and I was glad for him. I smiled at him, showing him I was proud of him.

"Did you marry him?" He asked finally.

"Yes." I said. I waited for him to ask me if I was happy or if marrying James was what I wanted, but he didn't, instead he nodded slowly.

"I have my own place." He said suddenly. "It's wonderful not having roommates. God knows I can not take any more Thomases."

He laughed. I laughed with him. There was no weirdness between us. We would not be strangers to each other.

He once told me that he had found Jesus in the streets of London and it occurred to me as I followed him and listened to his voice, which jumped from a typical British accent to a more Nigerian drawl intermittently, that I too had found something in these very streets. I had found providence.

We arrived at his apartment on the corner of Montague Road just off Queens Road and from the distance I could see Clarendon Park. This was a much nicer neighbourhood than Belham Close. The street was neater and there was some smartness to it as well—the picket fences, the lawns, the identical structures.

"Don't mind the mess." Providence said, as he unlocked the door to his apartment. "I didn't have enough time to clean up after your call."

"It's okay." I said, following him inside.

His apartment was small, but very well put together. There was nothing out of place. The living room looked clean, almost sterile. There was the three-seater leather sofa and huge screen television and in one corner a small work area with a computer and printer. I turned to look at him and caught the smile he was trying to conceal. Modesty didn't wear well on him.

"You can sleep here." He said, leading me to a small

bedroom. "It's the spare bedroom. It's small I know but…"

"Thank you." I said, quickly. "It's okay."

"My room is this one." He said pointing to the door opposite. "If you need anything…"

I nodded and smiled.

"Okay," he said and dropped my suitcases, "I have to go out now and I will see you later."

When he left, I sat on the bed for a long while. The strangeness of the house and the thought of James and what he would do when he realized I was gone kept my mind occupied. I left the room after a while and explored Providence's home. Aesthetically, it was beautiful but there was something lacking. The house was so impersonal; he had no pictures on the wall or on the mantelpiece, nothing to show that it was his home. Then I ventured into his bedroom. As I shut the door behind me, memories of the last time I snuck into his bedroom in our London flat flooded my head. A slight dizziness swept over me and for a moment I panicked. I wanted to turn round and run from his room and yet I strongly wanted to stay.

His bed was made. There were no ruffles in the corners; the sheet was well tucked in. The dresser by his bed was bare, except for some files that were neatly arranged in one corner and beside them was a Bible. I walked to his wardrobe and opened it. As I now expected, everything in there was well organized—ironed shirts in one corner, in order of ascending hues, from whites and creams to greys and blacks, and in the other corner he hung his trousers. I pulled out one of the drawers and in it were neat rows of folded vests and underwear. I touched one of the vests, imagining it was his chest I stroked and I grabbed a pair of his boxer shorts and pressed it against my nose. It smelt of detergent, but I closed my eyes and sniffed harder, wanting to smell his intimacy.

When I opened my eyes, I noticed something hidden behind his clothes. It was tucked into one corner, but placed carefully so that nothing disturbed it. I reached in and pulled out an old photograph. It was in black and white. In it was a very young Providence, smiling and hugging a much older woman. He had her eyes and mouth. I turned to the back of the picture and read the inscription there: "Mama and Me". I flipped back to the picture and stared hard at it, every detail of it, as if searching for answers. He must have been at least seven when this picture was taken; even then he had a head full of hair. His mother was pretty but quite lean. I could not tell her age, she could have been thirty or even fifty and it wouldn't have made a difference. Worry lines marked her face, but even that could not disguise her beauty. She was smiling in the picture and I noticed she had perfect white teeth. She also had a gap in her front teeth. Her right hand that rested on Providence's back clutched a string of beads. I looked closer and realized it was a rosary. Providence too was wearing one round his neck.

I began to feel guilt. I felt I had violated something sacred. I had no business searching through his private things. I replaced the picture and made sure that everything else was at it was before I got there and then I left the room.

I sat alone in the darkness of the living room with the curtains drawn and I thought about that picture with his mother. It made me think of my mother as well and of home, Nigeria. I once again felt alone and cold and I cradled myself in a foetal position on the leather couch, resting my head on the armrest. I was this way when the door opened hours later.

"What are you doing in the dark?" Providence asked as he stepped in.

I sat up.

"I was resting." I said.

"What's the matter?" He asked. He sat beside me on the sofa.

"I was in your room." I said. "I saw the picture of you and your mother."

I looked down at my fingers. I wanted to tell him I

was sorry for searching through his things but the words wouldn't come out.

"It's alright." He said, "I did say you were welcome to go into my room."

"Is she in Nigeria?" I asked.

"She's dead." He said. "She died a long time ago."

"I'm sorry." I was.

There was a long silent.

"She was a remarkable woman." He said. "She was so strong and she loved me so much. She denied me nothing and I lacked nothing as a child because of her. I was her only son."

He stopped momentarily and his face seemed to morph into a sculpted mask, frozen in thought. His eyes were fastened to memories. I continued to watch him, unable to tear my eyes away from him. Then he laughed. This startled me. It was a muffled giggle.

"Do you want to hear an interesting story?" He asked.

I nodded. I wanted to know the source of his amusement.

"Well, it's about my family." He said. "How I was born."

"Tell me." I said. I wanted to know.

"My mother," he said, "was married to the father of my four elder sisters. The first year of their marriage had been very good despite her worry of not being able to conceive within the first few months. Eventually, she became pregnant and, like many first-time fathers, the man who would have been my father had hoped for a male child. But my mother gave birth to Ada, a girl. Months after Ada's birth, my mother became pregnant again and nine months later, Anuli was born. It was after Anuli's birth that the first signs of friction appeared in their marriage."

"How did she know?" I asked.

"My mother told me that after her second failure her husband began talking down at her, accusing her of making him a laughing stock among his kinsmen. He wanted a son, a male heir to ensure his family's name continued. And my mother had been willing to give him a son by all means. She even made promises to God", he said, "promising that her first male child would be dedicated to Him." When I was young, my mother would tell me that I would become a priest, because she had promised God. Can you imagine me, a priest?

In a strange way I could, I wanted to tell him, but I didn't.

"My mother was pregnant again only months after Anuli's birth. Again she prayed fervently for a male child. Nine months later, Ogechi was born, yet another female child. My mother was crushed when her husband informed her that he was taking another wife. She knew it was because she was unable to give him the much sought-after male child. She watched as her place as first wife was rapidly taken over by the new woman. My mother had to clear her things from the room she had shared with her husband and moved to the much smaller servant room, which could barely contain all her things as well as three babies. She felt her place in the house was finally threatened when the second wife became pregnant. "The woman was an arrogant whore." Providence said of the second wife. "She used to flaunt her swollen belly in front of my mother, singing songs of breeding fierce soldiers for her husband in a mocking and insulting way. And in retaliation my mother secretly prayed to God to punish her with a female child in order to shut her up. Yet, she bore a male child and it seemed at the time that my mother's humiliation had been final. And then it seemed that God had been listening and sought to exact a severe punishment."

I watched as the expression on his face changed again as he narrated the strange tale of his birth.

"The child, Chukwuemeka—even his name was chosen tauntingly to spite my mother for it meant *God has done well*—became very sickly and died only after a few months. Strangely, my mother cried for this child. No matter how great her resentment for the other wife, she did not have that kind of wickedness inside of her. She felt as a mother for another mother's loss. The second wife's arrogance was humbled by this incident and by her grief and their halved husband became isolated through his anguish, spending less time at home with them and when he was there, confining himself to his private room."

He paused for breath.

"Goodness!" He said. "Look at me just jabbering away. I'm sure you are hungry…"

"I want to know the rest of the story." I insisted.

"Are you sure you don't want me to make you dinner first and then maybe you can rest…?"

"Please," I begged, "finish your story."

"Okay." He said with a smile. "Shortly after Chukwuemeka's death, my mother was pregnant again and momentarily her husband focused all his affection on her. He hoped that this would be the son he had waited for, but alas! she gave birth to yet another girl, Ifeanyi. This was the limit for him; he returned my mother's bride price to her family signifying an end to their marriage and she left with her four daughters. My mother was quickly married off as a third wife to the man who would eventually father me. A single mother with four daughters would have had a very difficult life alone."

I detected a certain pain in his words when he spoke of how his mother was chased out of her home with his sisters.

"For a while she had no husband to care for her and my sisters had no father to protect them… they had no father… God sure listened this time when she cried for a male child… That's how I came along. Somebody had to protect them." He added the last parts with a cynical smile but even I saw through that facade. His mother's tales must have affected him more deeply. Like many mothers, she had been meticulously moulding him to be the direct opposite of the man she had earlier married. There is no doubt that his mother knew exactly what she was doing when she decided to feed her young son with these stories. She wanted him to be caring and protective towards women, especially towards her and his sisters. I wondered why his mother thought it wise to tell him so much especially as she had a husband who now cared and protected her and her children.

"My father was quite old when I was born. He was in his sixties." Providence said. "My half sisters, the later ones, used to tell me that I was a spitting image of our father—tall, dark and handsome." He said with a cocky smile. "He died when I was eight years old and I no longer have a mental picture of him."

"Don't you have a photograph of him?" I asked.

He shook his head.

"What do you remember then of him?"

"I know that he loved me and my sisters." He said. "And you know what's funny? Ironically, my mother's ex-husband came begging for her back as soon as he heard she had given birth to me. Apparently his second wife continued a losing streak of bearing him two daughters after my mother was kicked out unceremoniously. Of course my mother never returned to him and she made sure he never saw any of his daughters."

He smiled and shook his head solemnly. I watched his every gesture, totally fascinated by his tale.

"My mother named me Providence for she had promised me to God and from the day of my birth, she lived for me."

I had always wondered why Providence was named so. Providence. Why Providence? As far as definition went, it meant an event or circumstance ascribable to divine interposition. It also meant God, the Deity. I had wondered which one of these was more apt in understanding who he was and why he was named thus. Was he my divine interposition from the very minute I stepped into that house in Belham Close? Was our meeting some twisted act of fate? Or was he a God-man, with his occasional chanting and his moments of intimate prayers? I had always believed that there was a deeper meaning to his bearing that name. I was convinced that there must be something almost sacred about it all. But more so, I believed now that in that name his mother had hoped that he would become her provider as well. Providence. Provider.

He laughed when he said his mother would not allow anyone to carry him when he was a baby. She would spend hours just staring at him and telling him that he was God's gift, God's last laugh.

"When I fell sick as a child, my mother would never sleep. She would cry herself to sickness until I was well again. She made sure that I went to school and got an education. And I never let her down; I was always the best student."

He was proud of this fact; I could see the swell of his chest, a subconscious movement on his part, as he spoke to me.

"I got a scholarship to attend King's College in Lagos." He said.

"So you are a product of financial aid?" I said. "Some of us weren't lucky, you know!"

"I was just lucky." He said. "The truth is, maybe I shouldn't have gone."

"Why not?"

"It was at that time that my mother took ill." He said. "She got better the week I left for Lagos, but I always worried about her."

"Do you think you were responsible for her illness?" I asked.

He shrugged.

"She was just so attached to me." He said. "The shock of letting me go could have added to her stress."

"Maybe it was you who was so attached to her." I said.

"I wrote her letters every weekend." He said. "I knew she would always look forward to hearing from me."

"I'm sure she did." I said.

"It was dreadful at King's College." He sighed. "I had never seen so many boys or men before in my life in one space."

"What do you mean?"

"Look at it from my angle," he said gesturing with his hands, "I have my mother and two other mothers, four blood sisters and seven stepsisters and lots of aunts who were ceaselessly around… I was simply comfortable around women."

"I see what you mean." I said, smiling. "No wonder you are smooth with women." We both laughed at that.

"Seriously," he said, "it was rather intimidating at first for me. I found it hard to take a bath in the communal shower the first week. I was mocked endlessly."

"Surely, there must have been female teachers at King's College?"

"Well, there was Mrs. Welbeck, the music teacher and Ms. Tope Olagun who taught French and a few others." He said. "But it was a man's domain."

"Were you intimidated by that?" I asked.

"A little." He admitted. "But I had to deal with this new experience and come up with a way to remain the top of the class."

"So what did you do?" I asked.

"I overcame my fears." He said. "I started behaving like the other boys, but I read and read to be the best."

"To be the best?"

"I learnt that from my uncle." He said. "Uncle Sunny, my mother's much older cousin, who lived in Lagos. I used to stay at his house in Lagos when the school shut down for public holidays. He was my guardian."

Providence got up and stretched out a hand to me. I took it and he pulled me up. We stood facing each other. Providence clasped my face gently with his hands and then smiled.

"We should go and make dinner." He said. "I will tell you the rest of it while we cook, okay?"

"Okay." I said and let him lead me to the kitchen.

I had never seen Providence this way before. He was natural around the kitchen and knew exactly what to do. There was nothing effeminate about how he carried himself—he exuded manly confidence. He brought out a packet of chicken from the fridge, placed the chicken in an oven pan and dressed it with herbs, red peppers and a sprinkle of seasoning salt. He heated up the oven and then put the chicken inside. His movements were deft and I was impressed.

"You'll find some rice in the cupboard above the sink." He said to me, pointing to the cupboard. "Use the medium pot to cook some, okay?"

"Okay." I said. I was glad he was letting me help with the cooking. I felt so at home and welcome, but still I wanted to know the rest of his story. "So, your uncle inspired you to be the best?"

"He was a very unusual man." Providence said. "He was quite wealthy. He had this huge mansion in Ikoyi and so many cars. He was not married, so I could not understand why he needed to have so much around him."

"You mean he never married?" I asked.

"Never." He said.

"Then maybe he was overcompensating for something," I added.

"Oh, I believe he was." Providence laughed. "His servants were all foreigners."

"You are lying." I said.

"No." He said. "The cook was Indian. His driver was a mix of Greek and Nigerian, the gardener was Lebanese. My uncle was pretty determined to have only foreigners serve him."

"Was there a reason for this?"

Providence came over to where I was by the stove. He grabbed my hands and led me to the small kitchen counter. We both sat down.

"Well," I said, "why was your uncle so particular about the race of the servants he had?"

"His father had served an expatriate Brit in the 60's and 70's. My uncle would never forget the humiliation his father suffered on countless occasions. Uncle Sunny used to tell me to aspire to be better than the white man and to aim for the ultimate goal—conquering the white man in his own ground, in his own country and then make them my slaves."

"Is this what you believe?" I asked, a little shocked by this disclosure.

"It's what he believed." Providence said.

"But isn't that why you came to London?" I asked. "To conquer the white man in his own land?"

"Maybe." He admitted. "I wanted to travel like my uncle did, to Europe and Asia for business. And one day settle in England and then invite my mother over. My childhood dreams."

"But you came to England." I said.

"Yes, but my mother died in my third year at King's College." He said. "I was raised by my uncle until I finished university. I got used to his way of life."

"You got used to having foreigners serve you." I said. "Did that make you feel superior or accomplished?"

"My uncle felt accomplished." He said. "I don't know how I felt. I looked up to him like a father."

"Did he maltreat his servants?"

"No." Providence answered. "He treated them well, just like my mother used to tell me to always respect women." Providence said. "No matter what situation I find myself with women, I should respect them."

All these were the early influences in Providence's life. Every single episode moulding him and shaping him to be the man he had now become. And his very kindness to me was no coincidence after all. He could not have been any other way. He was my providence.

18

Serendipity

Two days passed before the thought of James crossed my mind. It was a blissful two days of waking up late into the morning to the sweet smell of fried bacon and eggs and coffee. Two days of waking up to the beautiful intense brown eyes of Providence, nearly not long enough before I settled with the reality of confronting James.

There was also the other issue that troubled me. Her name was Clarissa. She was Ethiopian and her stunning beauty left a sore ache in the eye. Providence had explained her off as one of the people he worked with, but I was not stupid, I knew by the way she looked at him and then at me that they both shared more than a passing fancy. She was in the house that first morning and left with him on his rounds. She was in the kitchen again that morning, with her delicately manicured fingers wrapped round a steaming mug of coffee and a toast held elegantly, like an accessory in her other hand. She beamed when I stepped into the kitchen.

"You are up." She said. "How are you today?"

"I'm fine." I said, attempting to sound as cheerful as she did. "Where is Providence?"

"In his room." She took a sip from her mug. "Let me go fetch him."

"No—it's alright." I stopped her. "I'm sure he will be out soon."

"So tell me." She moved over to one of the high stools and sat down. She crossed her long stockinged legs, leaving me wondering how long they were. "How long do you intend to stay here? I hope I am not being forward or anything?"

"I don't know." I answered but I wanted to tell her that I thought she was being forward.

"Providence tells me that you left your husband in London."

"Yes, I did." I said. I hated the way she questioned me. Her words carried the weight of condescension.

"Aren't you worried he will come looking for you?" She asked.

Just then Providence entered the kitchen. The look on her face changed to a wide smile and she uncrossed her legs and stood up, straightening her skirt as she did so.

"Ah, Ngozi," he said, "you are up."

"Yes, I am."

"What are your plans for today?" He asked. "Do you want to go out and do some sightseeing?"

"I don't know yet." I said.

"Maybe you should call your husband." Clarissa suggested.

There was a quiet that took over the next few moments. A seething rage simmered within me. I hadn't felt this angry before with another woman and yet I understood why this particular woman ignited such rage within me. I felt slightly inferior in her presence, her beauty seemed to overshadow any trace of prettiness that I once thought I had and her sophistication thwarted my domestic naiveté. For this I hated her. I hated her also for I knew she had an eye on Providence and she was bent on winning him over with her charm and sophistication—and the obvious fact that she was available. I was still married. And in her presence I felt like damaged goods. But my irritation with her did not stop me from grasping the truth to what she had just said. I had to call James before he started looking for me.

"Clarissa is right, Ngozi." Providence said. "I think it's time you call him."

Hearing him agree with her suggestion was like allowing him to wrap his hands round my neck and then strangle me. I felt a dull ache at the pit of my stomach.

"Are you alright?" He asked.

"Can I speak with you alone?" I looked at him unwaveringly until he followed me to my bedroom.

"What is it?" He asked. "If you don't feel comfortable calling James…"

"It's not that." I said. "I'll call him, today."

"Then what is it then?"

"Are you sleeping with her?"

Silence.

"Is she your lover? Girlfriend?"

If he lied then, I would have known. I held on to his eyes and his every movement, watching his pupils shift from side to side, followed the movement of his Adam's apple as it juggled slightly up and down in a swallow of saliva.

"I told you yesterday that we work together." He said.

"I know what you told me." I said. "That isn't what I asked?"

"What will it matter, Ngozi?" He asked.

"It matters to me." I said.

"Why?" He asked. "Remember that it was you who turned me away. I asked you to come with me and you refused. I am not a saint and I have been with other women… and Clarissa."

"Are you in love with her?"

"Why do you ask me these questions?" He asked. I could hear the discomfort in his words.

"Because I need to know what it is I am doing here." I replied. "Do you love her?"

"No." He answered. "I love you. It is you I want, but not like this, not when you are still committed to another man."

If he had lied, I would have known it. But he wasn't

lying. I knew because as he said he loved me, his eyes softened and I could sense his vulnerability. I took him in my arms and hugged him tightly. I felt his arm wrap round my waist and the imprint of his fingers hold me.

"Call him." He said into my ears. "Tell him it's over."

"Yes." I said.

When he finally left for work, accompanied by a pair of very long stocking-clad legs, I was not worried or suspicious, but instead overwhelmed by the knowledge that it was me he wanted. The only thing I had to do now was cut myself loose from James.

When I picked up the phone in the living room, a moment of paralysis overtook me. Playing right before my eyes was my life with James. I watched as he led me to his house. I watched how he made love to me. I watched how he would turn his back on me in bed once he was done. I watched his hands strike me. I watched because I could not recognize that woman from the one that stared at me from the mirror.

"Yeah, who is this?" His voice rang out from the other end. It sounded irritated, as if he had been disturbed from something important. "Hello?"

"James, it's Erika." I said.

I heard his sharp intake of breath. Was that relief or shock?

"Where the hell are you?" He shouted. "And what stupid game are you playing?"

For a moment I let myself believe that the reason he reacted that way initially was that he cared for me enough to worry about where I was and what may have happened to me. But just for a moment. The space around me seemed to shrink and my heart was beating fiercely.

"I'm not coming back, James." I said, and I listened to his stunned silence. "It's over between us."

"You'll be back." He said in a quiet measured tone, showing no sign of conciliation but only of his conviction. I heard the click of the telephone and the repeated echo of a dead tone.

The next time I tried contacting him was after a divorce petition was sent to him. He hung up on me repeatedly. When we eventually spoke he told me that he would not acknowledge the petition. He went as far as saying he wanted me back and that we could work out our differences. His voice sounded like the James I once knew when we were still courting over the Internet. With my heart closed to any form of manipulation I begged him firmly to let me go. I wanted nothing from him, not money, no settlements; I just wanted to be free of him. He said nothing. It took weeks before the lawyer friend of Providence informed me that James had acknowledged the divorce petition. With his help I applied for a decree nisi and by the fall of 1999 I was single again.

I was determined that I would not resign myself to sitting in Providence's flat like I did in James', doing nothing. When Providence was out showing houses to buyers, I would take long solitary walks round my new neighbourhood—from Montague Road with its quaint blocks of identical flats to the small African shop in St. Peters lane, Evington, where, to my surprise, I found things like crayfish, *garri* and *maggi* seasoning cubes. I discovered a new world as I trekked past Queens Road with the popular pub, Olives, the equally popular supermarket, Jacksons, and the £1 shop that sold off expired biscuits and evaporated milk to unsuspecting bargain shoppers. On my walks, I discovered Victoria Park was probably the nicest park in Leicester. Entering the park from Queens Road, you are immediately surrounded by the tall trees that lined the stone pavement. On one side was the bicycle path and on the other side the path made for pedestrians. In the middle of this all was the very large field where different teams played football during the summer. There was also a tennis court attached to the park and wooden benches scattered round. In summer, lots of whites would lie down in the lush field but more excitingly the Afro-Caribbean festival was held in the park every summer. I imagined Bessie here. She would have loved Leicester.

I also discovered the Seventh Day Adventist Church in London Road on one of my walks; it was an all black church now. Providence told me that all the whites left the church as soon as the population of the African and Caribbean Indian brethrens increased.

It was during one of my walks through Victoria Park, while I took in the scenic beauty of the fields and the colours from the flowers and butterfly that I was wrenched out of my reverie.

"Is that you, Ngozi?"

Even if a million years passed and I was partially deaf, I would still recognize that voice. The first time I heard that voice, it was singing of raindrops on roses. I could not forget how awed I felt by the girlish richness of that voice, a voice buttered by wealth and smothered with privilege.

"Oh my God, I can't believe it." Tiffany said. "I can't believe you of all people found your way to England!"

She was as thin as a rake and her cheek bones could cut ice. She stood poised like a dress-shop mannequin, clutching a snake skin purse in one hand and a shopping bag in another. Her eyes scared me, they looked hollow and heavily made-up. Her face was a pale grey due to the foundation applied to it, which made her shocking red lipstick stand out ghastly like a fresh wound. I always knew she was not born to be beautiful.

"Hello Tiffany!" I said, putting on my best British accent. "How do you do?"

"Oh, cut out all that sophisticated nonsense and give me a hug."

I felt her bones through her clothing and realized that the only emotion I could have for her was pity. She looked hungry and unwell in spite of the choking essence of the expensive perfume she was doused in and the haute couture gown she was wearing.

"Goodness," she pulled back to look at me, "it's always so good to see somebody from home. How long have you been in England?"

"Almost three years now." I said.

"My goodness, the High Commission would give any one a visa these days, don't you agree?" She started laughing.

I didn't join her. I didn't find anything she had just said funny but rather an attempt to ridicule me. To her, I would never be good enough.

"Three years you say?" She said. "So how did you get here? Why did you come?"

"I bought a ticket and got on a plane..."

"My God, you look fat." She said, feigning no interest in what I was saying. "If you want to be noticed by men you should learn to eat less. I knew I didn't finish teaching you how to become a lady—if you had only stayed a bit longer before running away."

I was not shocked by her words or her action. She hadn't changed much from that self-absorbed girl who jumped from one topic of discussion to another with a blink of an eye. I only wondered why I was standing out on the street listening to her.

"I really have to go, Tiffany." I said.

"You did run away." She continued, as if I hadn't spoken. "You ran away because you were fucking my brother."

"What?"

Her cackling laughter was as disturbing as her revelation. How could she have known that? No one else knew for sure what her brother and I did together except the two of us. Could he have told her? Could he? Could he have told her from the very beginning? And what was I to him, to them? Nothing. I was the stupid servant girl that lived across the road from their home and they could use me whatever way they liked. She wanted to dress me up like a doll and he wanted me to satisfy his racing hormones. Was that what it all was? Could it be?

"Oh, but it is true." She said. "You were fucking my brother. Don't act surprised. I didn't know at first but I had my suspicion after I was told that you were sneaking up to his room by one of our servants. And when I asked you, you lied to me."

She was still laughing and her eyes didn't move from my face. There seemed to be a determination on her part to capture whatever expression my face gave out. She was deriving pleasure from this, as if she had waited and plotted for this moment for years.

"And so that day you ran away from your home, I knew you were first with my brother. I saw you enter his room and I was so mad at you then that I went over to your house and told your aunty what you had been doing."

The smile on her face was so wide now that it seemed her face would crack with the effort. I didn't care if it did; I was still trying to absorb the truth of what this creature was telling me. She was the reason my aunt had tortured me that day, the reason I was thrown out of my home. It all made sense now, the certainty of Aunt Rosa that I had been with a man, I had always wondered, but now it all made sense. She knew because she had been told.

"Your aunt was so ready to believe me that I had no problem telling her how sad I was about what you were doing and how I didn't want my mother to find out or else it would have been trouble for your aunt and uncle." She laughed. "I got home in time, before you left Gerald's room. I saw you from the living room window as you snuck off, I thought you saw me. I knew your aunty would discipline you, but I didn't expect you to run away…I still had things to show you and teach you."

"I did not run away." I said, finally. "I was thrown out. Because of you. Because of what you did. How could you?"

"Stop this." She laughed. "I didn't do anything. Blame yourself. Think of what you did to me."

"What did I do to you?"

"You were sleeping with my brother." She said. "You were supposed to be my friend. I made you beautiful and gave you things. You were supposed to be my friend, not his."

"I was never your friend." I said, stepping away from her. "I was just a thing to you. I was nothing to you."

"Ngozi, let's not dwell on the past." She said. "Come, let me take you to my house…"

"Goodbye, Tiffany." I said.

It was like watching milk curdle the way her face changed. Gone was the ceramic smile and in its place was a scowl so intense that even crows would have been frightened.

"What? Are you too good to come to my house now?" Her voice was forced out of clenched teeth. "You should be thankful to me you know."

"For what?"

"You said so yourself, it is because of me that you are who you are. It is because of me that you had the guts to leave that wretched aunt of yours. I gave you a reason. I gave you more than a reason… You had always depended on people; I saw that even when we were young. You always lived off the scraps of others. So I made you up, did your hair, showed you how to use make-up and even gave you my clothes…"

"You gave me the things you didn't want—old worthless things." I said. "Don't lie to yourself that you were doing me any favours."

"Those worthless things were better off than anything you had." She said. "And you certainly had no problems receiving them. I saw the greed in your eyes. I knew you wanted to have what I had. You wanted to be me. And so I played along and let you. But that was not enough, you wanted more… you wanted my brother too. So I let you fuck him. But I knew that soon you would want more. You would maybe want my father and I would not let that happen."

"You are sick, if you believe anything you said." I turned my back to her and slowly began walking away.

"You know it's true." Her fading voice said. "People like you are all the same—always depending on others. Always taking, taking and taking. Good for nothing…"

Her bitter words dissolved with the rustle of the autumn leaves but not its harshness, not its sting, those would remain, etched deep within the crevices of my heart like an old recurrent backache that simply won't go away.

★

Providence always left money for me on the kitchen counter. He would tell me to call him if I needed anything. And on weekends he would take me shopping and to the movies because he believed this was what young women liked and this was the decent way men should treat women.

When he bought his car that August, he insisted that he take me on a long drive through the countryside one Sunday. When I got to the car, he rushed to open the door for me, like a gentleman. He took me for a picnic in the deserted woods and we made love by the flowing stream. He told me he loved me and asked me to marry him. With tears of joy in my eyes I refused him.

"Why?" He propped himself up on his elbows to stare at my face. "Don't you love me?"

"I love you." I said.

"Then why won't you marry me?" He asked. "Don't I give you everything you want? Is there anything I haven't given you—tell me?"

People like you are all the same—always depending on others. Always taking, taking and taking. Tiffany's words rang in my head.

"You've given me everything." I said.

"And?"

"It's time for me to start giving something back." I said.

"I don't want you to give me anything more than your love and for you to be my wife." He said.

"I want to be your wife." I said. "But I don't always want to feel that without you, there's no me. I want to be able to give something more back—something tangible. I want to be able to stand on my own as well. Can you understand this?"

The look in his eyes told me he didn't, but that he was

willing to try. What I found very hard to accept was his need to prove to me that I needed to be protected and cared for by him. I had become his responsibility. It was his duty to take care of me. I didn't have to worry about anything as long as I was with him. He told me this often in a playful manner and when he wasn't telling me this, he showed me in all his actions. And then there were Tiffany's scornful words that played in my head repeatedly like a broken record.

If I hadn't lived the life I had lived so far, I might have simply accepted this and been grateful to him for caring so much, but the truth was that accepting the role he invariably assigned to me with the freedom and security it promised only made me feel caged. Why is it that men believe it is their God-given right to dictate the role a woman should play within an environment, whether the abused victim or the well-kept mistress? Accepting that role would mean giving up my rights to be truly independent, it would take away the significance of my packing my bags and walking away from James. Accepting his innocent generosity was a price much too high for me to pay.

"Will you marry me someday?" He asked, finally.

"Yes, Providence." I said. "I will, but not today."

Epilogue

Dear Ngozi,

How are you? And how are your husband and London?

My dear friend, it has been a very long time since we spoke to each other or even communicated. I quite understand that we are all quite busy and this life we live, it just runs so fast that before you know it, a week is gone, then a month and then a year is over before you can sigh!

I am compelled to write you this letter because I have just got some grave news regarding your family. Two days ago, I got a visit from a young lady who claims to be your sister. Her name is Ofunne. She told me she was staying with your uncle, Kachi. I believed her because she looks just like you, only darker. She told me that your mother wanted you to know that your father is dead. He died almost a week ago now and based on your custom, he can only be buried after the new yam festival period is over. She said his people had picked October for him to be buried.

Her message for you is for you to come back home. Your mother wishes this. She wants you to be there to bury your father. This is what she wants me to pass on to you.

I am sorry for your loss Ngozi. I truly am sorry.

After meeting your sister, I am convinced that you have a wonderful family, one who misses you and loves you. I really can't understand why you never wanted to talk about them or why you never could tell me the truth about why you never wanted to see them again. I can understand why you may not like your brother after witnessing his arrogance the first time he came for you, but you must understand also that he is a man and men like him are very proud. I suppose your father was very much like him and this is maybe why you have resisted them, but behind their show of masculinity they may love you and want to protect you. I only hazard a guess of course; I really can't say what it is you have kept hidden for all this while.

I also do not understand why you have not bothered to respond to the emails I have sent to you previously. Uloma has complained also that she didn't get any response from you after all the emails she has sent to you. And no one answers your telephone anymore. I tried several times and for a long time now that number is no longer valid.

I worry for you at times Ngozi. Are you really okay? From the pictures you have painted in the past about your life there and how James treats you, I am sure you are doing fine. But my dear, don't be like those other Nigerians who after they travel abroad and make it big, they forget about everyone who helped them along the way as well as their family. Please, I beg you not to become one of them. Remember the story I told you of my cousin, Ese? The one who travelled to Italy and ignored her family? The same one who took me to Italy? Do not become like her. Your family and your true friends are the most important people in your life.

Enough from me, I have spoken too much already. Again, I am indeed sorry for your loss and I hope you would read this email and respond to it. It would be nice to hear from you again. Be well, my sister. Remember, some people here still love you.

Princess.

Providence had stumbled on me crying in a corner that evening. He came up to me and held me close.

"Shhhhhhh!" He whispered into my ears, "Bad day in

the office? You don't have to cry."

"No." I said. "That's not it."

"What's the matter?"

"I have to go away" I said. "I have to go back home—to Nigeria."

I felt his muscle tighten and his sharp intake of breath.

"Hey, you don't have to go nowhere." He said comfortingly. "You are a British citizen now."

"No, I have to go." I cried. "You don't understand, my father just died."

"Oh baby, I'm so sorry." Providence said.

"I'm not." I said. "I'm happy he is dead."

Providence pushed me back so he could look at my face. Yes, I saw the questions in his eyes as well as the concern. I turned away from him, wanting to tell him what my father did to me and at the same time being aware that I had never told anyone before. I had never told anyone because telling it would make it too real for me, no more a dream, no more a nightmare. But the weight of knowing it happened and not being able to discuss it with anyone was slowly becoming too much for me alone.

"He raped me when I was a child, repeatedly." I said, quietly. "I have never told anyone. I've been so ashamed."

I felt his arms around me again and his warm breath on my nape.

"It's okay." He said. "It was not your fault."

It was not my fault. It was not my fault. It was not my fault.

Finally I could see that and I knew, as he said, that it was going to be okay.

That email was the reason I came back. I needed to see for myself that he was really dead.

We were on our way to my village, Ezi. The day before, the three of us, Princess, Uloma and I had chartered a car to take us the seven hours from Lagos to my village. I was not surprised that after all those years, life in Ezi remained almost the same as it was in my childhood—static, resisting ferociously any outside influence of modernity. From the little I had heard, the roads there were still the very same red earth that marked my feet as a child, families who could not afford to dig a well in their compounds still sent their children and women to the stream to fetch water and the many villagers still depended on their farms as the number one means of their livelihood. But one thing had changed though; electricity had finally come to the village. Not all villagers had this, but the houses of those who had children living in the big cities like Lagos, Abuja, Port Harcourt and other thriving cities all had electricity. It was a mark of their respectability and these houses would be lit up during the festive periods. Even when there was no power from the electric company, the ever-noisy generators would further reinforce their respectability in cases of doubt.

I marvelled as Uloma recounted all this news to me. She had appointed herself my official updater, and over the previous three days since I had returned, she had filled my ears with the changes that had taken place since I left the country. Nothing escaped her tongue or criticism, from the open celebrations that greeted the death of General Abacha to the news of how Madam Goodwill's beer parlour was burnt down following the Yoruba-Hausa riots of 1999. I took in everything she told me, even the gossip I suspected Princess disapproved of, known only when Princess managed to catch my eyes discreetly and shake her head.

But that morning as I sat in front of the rented car, all I could really think of was that letter from Princess and how it had led to my eventually returning home. Yes, it was that email that set in motion my resolve to come back and speak my truths with everyone. I had to tell mother about what father did to me. I needed to speak my truths and tell Princess and Uloma how it really was with James in London.

I felt a tap on my shoulder and when I turned round I noticed Uloma had inched her face close to mine.

"What will you do when we get there?" She asked.

"I don't know." I answered. "I guess we would go to my compound and meet my mother."

"Will you remember how to get there?" She asked.

"There are some things you never forget, Uloma."

"And when last did you see your mother?" Princess asked.

Her question felt like a brutal ripping away of a scab from a wound that had not yet healed. Painfully, it reminded me that I had not seen my mother since I was sent away from home. More questions flooded my head; what did she look like now? Would she remember me? Would I still feel the love that used to flow from her?

"I was still a child when I saw her last." I said.

It was dusk already when the car drove into the compound. A lot had changed here and yet a lot had remained the same. The huge guava tree still stood in all its majesty at the corner of the house. At once, the equally regal and beautiful fading image of the woman I knew as mother flickered in my head; even if her face was slowly becoming a blur.

I looked at the tree and my eyes were drawn to the crude-looking well that was now situated near where mother used to plait my hair. I noticed also a small group of women sitting underneath the tree. They all wore the traditional black mourning garb, their hair wrapped in scarves and their eyes cast permanently to the earth. I found myself shivering slightly at their posture—legs clasped together and stretched out in front of them, arms stretched and crossed on their lap. They hummed silently but distinctly a native dirge. These women were very old and I imagined that they too were widows. For a frightening moment, I pictured my mother like this, sitting on the bare ground like these women, dressed in black with her naked skull covered with a black scarf and I shivered.

"Are you okay?" Princess whispered into my ear. I nodded.

The driver parked the car at the clearing beside the house. By now we had attracted the attention of the neighbours. I noticed through the rear-view mirror that a small crowd had gathered at the entrance of the compound. They were mostly little children and some teenagers along with some mature-looking girls. They had all come to see who it was who had come with the fancy car. I looked away, distracted by the movement at the front door. Two little children had come out from the house; they looked like twins and were wearing matching outfits. One of them walked directly to the car and caressed the mudguard by the driver's side.

"What do you want to do now?" Uloma asked quietly.

I said nothing. My eyes were drawn back to the entrance of the house where a young beautiful woman stood. She had an almond-shaped face with bright brown eyes that stared straight into the depth of me. Her nose was small like mine and her lips were full and slightly pouted. Sadness clouded her eyes and yet I sensed that there was more trapped within them. Her hair was tied up like the women who sat by the well, but unlike them, she wasn't dressed up in black. She wore an old green-patterned dress that lacked any lustre or shine and made her look deceptively older than her age. It was my kid sister, Ofunne.

I opened the door of the car and got out. I tried shutting the door but my hands were shaking so badly. I left it open and walked slowly round the rear of the car to the front of the house where she stood. I couldn't quite believe how much she had grown. The last time I saw her she was still quite little but now she looked like a full-grown adult.

"Sister," she said as soon as I stood before her.

"Ofunne," I said, wanting to call her sister also but giving in instead to feeling her name on my tongue once again, as if calling her that would in a way make her more solid before me, more real and less of a dream or distant recollection.

"Mama is inside the house." She said. "She really wants

to see you. Come, I'll take you to her."

She stretched out her right hand to me and for a moment I just stared.

"Come." She insisted and I took hold of her outstretched hand.

Her hand was soft, so soft and it felt strange in mine. This touch seemed to have pulled me into her, sending shockwaves through my entire body. It was a pleasant shock, not hostile but loving. Her palm seemed a little moist and cold, almost papery and yet I knew somehow that if that hand had touched me in the dark, I would have recognized it and known it belonged to me, like I belonged to her. I would have known it was my sister.

I looked back briefly and nodded at both Princess and Uloma who were still sitting in the car. They both nodded back.

Inside the house, there were more people seated at various corners. They all looked at me curiously as my sister led me through the living room. I was surprised that I still recognized quite a few of them and by the look in their eyes, it was apparent that I was no stranger to them either. Each of them had known me as a child and each of them must have at one point or the other wondered about my connection to the rain that fell at my birth and the fact that I was quite different from other members of my family.

I spotted Nnamdi at a corner with one of my uncles. They were speaking quietly to each other, each leaning to the other's ear to whisper. Just as I got to the door of my mother's room, Nnamdi raised his head and our eyes met. I looked intently at him for a long time, inwardly demanding that he confirm to me what I knew he most certainly was hiding. It struck me then that the look in his eyes was exactly the same as it was that night many years earlier when I had stumbled out of the house to wash away the filth of my father and noticed him at the entrance to the compound. He had looked away from me that day, but I had caught the apprehension and fear in his eyes, just like

I could now sense clearly his dread and uneasiness.

"She's in there." Ofunne said tilting her head towards the door of the bedroom. "She would see you now."

I dragged my eyes away from Nnamdi and again I was looking into the face of my sister. Her lips parted in a half smile that was obviously meant to encourage me. We were still holding hands and I felt a reassuring squeeze from her.

I let go of her hand and slowly pushed the door open. I was confronted by a darkness that seemed to crowd and envelope the single kerosene lamp that was placed on the floor, at the centre of the room. Gradually my eyes began to register the sparse furniture in the room; the tiny wooden bed, which had now been stripped of any bedding, a clay water pot that stood at the foot of the bed, a metal portmanteau that I remember clearly from my childhood—mother used to keep all her fine things in there. I noticed also the raffia mat on the floor in front of the bed as well as the frail woman who sat on it. She looked gaunt and aged and the black dress she wore hung loosely on her skinny frame. Her head had been scraped bald. It did not hit me immediately that this was my mother until she raised her head up to look at me.

"Ngozi, my child," she said in a very low voice.

"Mama," I replied.

She lifted one of her hands weakly to beckon to me and I rushed to her, crouching down to join her on the mat and placing my head on her chest. I heard the constant beat of her heart in my ear as the tears flowed freely from my eyes.

"Ngozi," she said. "It took you so long to come and visit me."

"I'm sorry, Mama." I cried.

"It's so good that you have come back." She said. "It's so good."

I let her hold on to me for a while, selfishly wanting to be smothered by her love and cowardly holding off my confessions. I had made up my mind before I got there that I must tell her everything. I knew she was grieving and must be allowed to mourn but I felt she had a right to know what father did to me. I had been silent for too long and now my truth must be told. I was even prepared for a denial or rejection. This was why I needed to feel her love selfishly, if for the last time.

"After the burial," she said, "you must tell me all that you have been doing with yourself, I am dying to know."

"Yes, Mama." I said. "But there's something I must tell you first."

"Yes, my child."

I took a deep breath and began to speak. As I spoke, I watched her eyes fill up with the weight of my words and slowly two lines of tears crawled down each of her cheeks like two translucent snails. Though she cried, I searched her eyes for bewilderment and surprise but instead I was confronted by knowledge. She knew. She had known all this while and yet like Nnamdi, she had said nothing. Done nothing. Was this also a betrayal? Or had she been powerless?

My whispered confessions continued deep into the night. I hid nothing. I spoke my truths, holding nothing back. For once unafraid.

For once, *unbridled.*

The end

The Author

Jude Dibia was born in Lagos, Nigeria.

His short stories have appeared on blackbiro.com and africanwriter.com and in some print journals in Nigeria.

He is the author of *Walking With Shadows*, a novel that has been praised for tackling, with some insights, the homosexual theme.

Unbridled won the Ken Saro-Wiwa prize for prose administered by the Association of Nigerian Authors and NDDC on its release in Nigeria in 2007.

Jude Dibia lives and works in Lagos and is currently working on a third novel.

Other titles by Jacana

A Basket of Leaves:
99 Books that Capture the Spirit of Africa
by Geoff Wisner

Beginnings of a Dream
by Zachariah Rapola

Coconut
by Kopano Matlwa

How We Buried Puso
by Morabo Morejele

O'Mandingo!
The Only Black at a Dinner Party
by Eric Miyeni

O'Mandingo!
Before Mandela was Mandela
by Eric Miyeni

Six Fang Marks and a Tetanus Shot
by Richard de Nooy

African Psycho
by Alain Mabanckou

The Uncertainty of Hope
by Valerie Tagwira

Bitches' Brew
by Fred Khumalo

Seven Steps to Heaven
by Fred Khumalo